"You ... her face agai... Then she pu... turned to face Nick. "You saved my life and I thank you for it."

The raw emotion was gone, and as her chin came up and she looked at him she was every inch a princess for all the dust and her travel-stained clothing.

Her courage doused the fierceness of his anger and the heat in his blood, but Nick could not find it in himself to be gracious. "That is my job," he said, his voice cool. "To deliver you back alive and in one piece to your father."

"You will not let me thank you?" She took a step that brought her toe to toe with him. "They kiss to say thank-you, the English, do they not?"

With Pavan solid at his back he could not retreat. Anusha put her hands on his shoulders and stood on tiptoe, her body pressed against his. For an endless moment her mouth touched his, warm and soft.

Her lips parted slightly—an invitation he knew she did not understand. Time stood still while he fought the temptation to snatch her to him, plunder that beautiful mouth, lose himself in an innocence that wanted him. *Him.*

* * *

Forbidden Jewel of India
Harlequin® Historical #1121—January 2013

LOUISE ALLEN

FORBIDDEN JEWEL OF INDIA

HARLEQUIN®
entertain, enrich, inspire™

Recycling programs
for this product may
not exist in your area.

ISBN-13: 978-0-373-29721-4

FORBIDDEN JEWEL OF INDIA

Copyright © 2013 by Melanie Hilton

www.Harlequin.com

Printed in U.S.A.

**Did you know that these novels are also
available as ebooks? Visit www.Harlequin.com.**

Chapter One

The palace of Kalatwah, Rajasthan, India—
March 1788

Patterns of sunlight and shade fell through the pierced stone panels on to the white marble floor, soothing to the eye after miles of dusty roads. Major Nicholas Herriard rolled his shoulders to loosen them as he walked. The physical stresses of the long journey began to fade. A bath, a massage, a change of clothes and he would feel human again.

Running feet, the faint, sharp scratch of claws on marble. The hilt of the knife in his boot came to hand with the familiarity of long practice as he twisted to face the side passage, crouched to meet an attack.

A mongoose shot out of the opening, skidded to a halt and chittered at him, every hair on its body fluffed up with aggravation, its tail stuck out behind like a bottle-brush.

'Idiot animal,' Nick said in Hindi as the patter of running feet became louder and a girl followed the mongoose, her wide crimson skirts swirling around her as she caught her balance and stopped. Not a girl, a woman, unveiled and unescorted. The part of his brain that was still dealing with an attack analysed the sound of her footsteps: she had changed direction twice just before she emerged, which meant this was one of the off-set entrances to the *zanana*.

She should not be here, outside the women's quarters. *He* should not be here, staring at her with all the blood in his brain heading south, his body poised for violence and a weapon in his hand.

'You may put away your dagger,' she said and it took him a moment to adjust and realise she was speaking in lightly accented English. 'Tavi and I are unarmed. Except for teeth,' she added, showing hers, white and regular between lips that curved into a smile of faint mockery. It masked, he was certain, shock. The mongoose twined between her bare, hennaed feet, still grumbling to itself. It wore a gem-studded collar.

Nick got a grip on himself, pushed the knife back into its sheath as he straightened and brought his hands together. *'Namaste.'*

'Namaste.' Over her own joined hands dark grey eyes studied him. The shock seemed to have turned to suspicion edged with hostility and she was making no effort to disguise either emotion.

Grey eyes? And skin like golden honey and hair that showed streaks of mahogany and deep brown as it fell down her back in a thick plait. His quarry, it seemed, had found him.

She did not appear disconcerted to be alone, unveiled, with a strange man, but stood there and contemplated him. Her full red skirts, weighted with heavy silver embroidery, hung just above her ankles, giving a glimpse of close-fitting trousers. Her tight *choli* revealed not only delightful curves and elegantly rounded arms decked in silver bangles, but also an unsettling band of smooth golden midriff.

'I should go. Excuse me for disturbing you,' Nick said in English and wondered if he was perhaps the more unsettled of the two of them.

'You have not,' she replied with crushing simplicity in the same language. She turned and walked through the opening she had appeared from. '*Mere pichhe aye,* Tavi,' she called as the skirts of her *lehenga* whisked out of sight. The mongoose followed obediently, the faint click of its claws fading along with her light footsteps.

'Hell,' Nick said to the empty passageway. 'That is quite definitely her father's daughter.' Suddenly a simple duty had become something else entirely. He squared his shoulders and strode off in the direction that led to his rooms. A man did not become a major with the British East India Company by being disconcerted by acid-tongued young women, however beautiful. He needed to clean himself up and seek an audience with the raja, her uncle. And after that, all he had to do was to transport Miss Anusha Laurens safely halfway across India, back to her father.

'Paravi! Quickly!'

'Speak Hindi,' Paravi reproved as Anusha entered her room in a flurry of skirts and trailing scarf.

'*Maf kijiye,*' Anusha apologised. 'I have just this moment been speaking to an Englishman and my head is still translating.'

'*Angrezi?* How can you be speaking to any man, let alone an *angrezi?*' Paravi, plump and indolent and her uncle's third wife, raised one exquisitely plucked eyebrow, but she pushed aside the chessboard she had been studying and sat upright.

'He was in the corridor when I chased Tavi just now. Very big with hair of pale gilt and in the red uniform of the Company's soldiers. An officer, I think—he had much gold on his coat. Come and see him.'

'Why so curious? Is he so handsome, this big *angrezi*?'

'I do not know what he is,' Anusha confessed. 'I have not seen one so close since I left my father's house.' But she was curious. And there was something else, a tug of yearning, deep inside, at the memory of another male voice speaking English, of another big man, scooping her up in his arms, laughing with her, playing with her. The man who had rejected her and her mother, she reminded herself as the memory turned sour.

'He is different from the men I am used to, so I cannot decide if he is handsome or not. His hair is so pale and tied back tightly and his eyes are green and he is tall.' She waved her hands to illustrate. 'He is big all over—broad shoulders, long legs.'

'Is he very white? I have never seen an *angrezi* before except from a long way away.' Paravi was becoming interested.

'His face and his hands are golden.' *Like my father's*

were. 'But the skin of all the Europeans goes brown in the sun, you know. Perhaps the rest of him is white.'

Imagining *all* of the big Englishman produced a not-unpleasurable shiver which he did not merit. But any novelty was welcome in the restricted world of the *zanana,* even if this novelty brought with him unsettling reminders of the world outside the fort. The faint sensual tingle was lost in a wave of something close to apprehension. This man made her uneasy.

'Where has he gone now?' Paravi uncoiled herself from the heap of cushions she had been occupying. The mongoose immediately dived into the warm spot she had created and curled up. 'I would like to look on a man who makes all those expressions chase across your face.'

'To the visitors' wing—where else should he go?' Anusha tried not to snap. It was not flattering to be told her face betrayed her. 'He was very dusty from the road, he will not be seeking audience with my uncle like that.' She gave herself a little shake to chase away the foolish fancies. 'Come with me to the Sunset Terrace.'

Anusha led the way through the familiar maze of passages, rooms and galleries that filled the western wing of the palace.

'Your *dupatta,*' her friend hissed as they left the women's quarters to cross the wide terrace where the raja would sometimes sit to watch the sun sink over his kingdom. 'There are no grilles here.'

Anusha clicked her tongue in irritation, but unwound the neglected length of cerise gauze from her neck and draped it so it covered her face to the chin. She leaned on the inner balustrade of the terrace and looked down into the courtyard below. 'There he is,' she whispered.

Below, on the edge of a garden threaded with rills of water in the Persian manner, the big *angrezi* was talking to a slender Indian she did not recognise. His body servant, no doubt. The man gestured towards a door.

'He is telling him where the bath house is,' Paravi whispered from behind her own *dupatta* of golden gauze. 'There is your chance to see whether Englishmen are white all over.'

'That is ridiculous. And immodest.' She heard Paravi laugh softly and bristled. 'Besides, I am not in the slightest bit interested.' Just burningly, and inexplicably, curious. The two men had vanished into the guest rooms overlooking the garden. 'But I suppose I had better see whether the water has been heated and someone is in attendance.'

Paravi leaned one rounded hip against the parapet and glanced up as a flock of green parakeets screeched overhead. 'This man must be important, do you not think? He is from the East India Company and they are all-powerful in the whole land now, my lord says. Far more important than the Emperor in Delhi, even if they do put the Emperor's head on their coins. I wonder if he is to be the Resident here. My lord said nothing about that last night.'

Anusha rested her elbows on the parapet and noted that her friend seemed to be in favour with her husband. 'Why would we need a Resident? We do not do so very much trade with them.' The intriguingly pale head appeared below as the man re-emerged from the door to the guest rooms. 'I suppose we might be in a useful position for their expansion—that is what *Mata* used to say. Strategic.' Her mother had much to say on most subjects, being both well read and greatly indulged by her brother the raja.

'Your father is still a friend to my lord, even though he never comes here. They exchange letters. He is a great man in the Company: perhaps he thinks we are more important these days and deserving of a Resident.'

'It must be a matter of great importance for him to bestir himself to think of us,' Anusha said. Her father had not visited the state of Kalatwah since the day, twelve years ago, when he had sent his twelve-year-old daughter and her mother back, displaced from his home and his heart by the arrival of his English wife.

He sent money, but that was all. Her uncle added it to her dowry chest when she refused to spend it. He told her that she was foolish, that her father had no choice but to send her and her mother home and that Sir George was an honourable man and a good ally of Kalatwah. But that was the talk of men, of politics, not of the love that broke her mother's heart, even while she agreed with her brother that there had been no other option.

Her father wrote to her uncle, she knew that, for he would tell her there were messages. There had been a note a year ago when her mother had died. She had not read it any more than she had read the others. The moment she saw her father's name she had thrown it on the brazier and watched it burn to ash.

From the flash of dark eyes behind the veil Paravi was sending her sympathetic glances, which is not what she wanted. No one had any right to be sorry for her. Was she not, at twenty-two, the pampered niece of the Raja of Kalatwah? Was she not indulged with the right to turn down every approach that had been made for her hand in marriage? Was she not supplied lavishly with clothes and jewels and servants and all the luxury she wished for? Did she not possess everything that she could possibly want?

Except knowing where I belong, the nagging little voice in her head said, the voice that, for some reason, always spoke English. *Except knowing who I am and why I am and what I am going to do with the rest of my life. Except for freedom.*

'The *angrezi* is going to the bath.' Paravi drew back a pace from the parapet even as she craned to see. 'That is a fine robe. His hair is long now it is loose,' she added. 'What a colour! It is like that stallion my lord sent to the Maharaja of Altaphur as a gift when the monsoon ended, the horse they called the Gilded One.'

'He has probably got as high an opinion of himself as that animal had,' Anusha said. 'But at least he bathes. Do you know, many of them do not? They think it unhealthy! My father said that they do not have *champo* in Europe—they powder their hair instead. And just wash their hands and faces. They think hot water is bad for them.'

'Ugh! Go and see and tell me about him.' Paravi gave her a little push. 'I am curious, but my lord would not be pleased if he thought I was looking upon an *angrezi* without his clothes.'

He would also have much to say if his niece was

discovered doing just that, Anusha reflected as she ran down the narrow stairway and along the passage. She was not at all sure why she wanted to get closer to this stranger. It was not any desire to attract his attention, despite the shiver which was, of course, simply a normal female reaction to a man in his prime—far from it. She did not want those green eyes studying her—they seemed to see too much. There had been a flash of recognition in them when they had met. Recognition and something far more basic and male.

She left her sandals in the doorway and peeped around the corner of the bathhouse. The Englishman was already naked and face down on a linen sheet draped over the marble slab, his body gleaming with water. He rested his forehead on his linked hands as one of the girls, Maya, worked the mixture of *basun* powder, lime juice and egg yolks into his hair. Savita was bent over his feet, oiling and massaging. Between head and heels there was a great deal of man to be seen in an interesting shading of colours.

Anusha walked in with a warning nod to the two girls to stay silent and keep working. His neck was the colour that his face and hands, both hidden by his wet hair, had been. His shoulders, back and arms were a paler gold. His legs were lighter still and the skin behind his knees was almost white, a pinkish shade. The line where his belt must habitually lie was very clear, for his buttocks were as pale as the backs of his knees.

His legs and arms were dusted with brown hair, she noticed. It was wiry and much darker than his flaxen head. Was his chest like that, too? She had heard that some Englishmen were so hairy that their backs were covered with a pelt of it. They must be like bears. She wrinkled her nose in disgust at the thought, then found she was standing right next to the slab. How did his skin feel?

Anusha reached for the jar of oil, poured a little into her palms and placed them flat, one on each shoulder blade. Under her hands she felt his muscles tighten, the skin twitch with the contact of the cool liquid. Then he relaxed again and she brought her hands sliding down slowly until they rested at his waist.

The pale skin felt just like any other skin, she decided. The muscles though, those were…shocking. Not that she had any basis for comparison, of course. She had never touched a man's naked flesh in her life.

Maya began to rinse his hair, pouring water from a brass ewer and catching it in a bowl. Savita had moved up to his calves and was kneading the long muscles. Anusha found she was stuck, unwilling, for some mysterious reason, to lift her hands, too disconcerted by the feel of a man's body to venture any further.

Then he spoke, the vibration of his deep voice reaching her through her palms. 'Am I to hope that you will *all* be joining me in my room after this?'

Nick felt the stir in the air, the faint pad of bare feet on the marble. Another girl—he was being treated as an honoured guest, which boded well for his mission. The strong, skilled fingers massaging his scalp made him want to purr, the muscles of his feet and ankles were relaxing into something approaching bliss. The new arrival brought with her a faint suggestion of jasmine to mingle with the sandalwood of the oil and the lime in the *champo*. He had smelt that earlier, somewhere.

Hands, coated with oil that had not been allowed to warm, settled on his back and hesitated. In comparison to the other two, this attendant was either unskilled or nervous. Then his brain placed the scent as the hands slid downwards to his waist and stopped again.

'Am I to hope that you will *all* be joining me in my room after this?' Nick said, in English. As he expected the sure hands at his head and on his calves did not pause in their smooth rhythm, but the fingers at his waist tightened into claws. 'All three of you at once should be most pleasurable,' he added with deliberate provocation, his voice sultry with suggestion as he teased her. 'I shall ask for the bed chains to be fixed to the ceiling hooks to make a swing.'

There was a sharp indrawn breath and the claws tightened in a fleeting pain before she lifted her hands away. 'How interesting that even the bathhouse attendants here speak good English,' he added. It was only sporting to let her know he had realised she was there and had spoken deliberately. The faintest hiss of indrawn breath, the silken whisper of her clothing, the brush of air on his skin and she was gone.

Nick found he was breathing hard and made himself relax. If he was feeling aroused it was because he was stark naked while his body was massaged by highly skilled hands. George's daughter had nothing to do with it. The little witch had doubtless thought it would be amusing to play a trick on him—she would not make the same mistake again. He made his mind blank and gave himself up to the sensations surrounding him.

'Well?' Paravi clapped her hands for the maids. 'We will drink pomegranate juice while you tell me all about him.' She cocked her head on one side and her nose ring swung with the movement, its tiny gold discs jingling.

'He is a pig.' Anusha plumped down on the pile of cushions opposite and disentangled her scarf with an impatient tug. 'He knew it was me, even though he had his eyes closed, and he deliberately provoked me with indecent suggestions. The man must have eyes in the back of his head, or he uses witchcraft.'

'So he had his back to you?' Paravi appeared to find this disappointing.

'He was lying face down on the slab being massaged and having his hair washed.'

'So how did he know it was you?'

'I have no idea. But he spoke in English to trap me.' Paravi clicked her tongue. Anusha took a deep breath and attempted to report dispassionately. 'He is not *white*, but the parts of him that have not been in the sun are pinkish. Like the muzzle of a grey cow is. Only paler.'

'So.' Paravi stretched. 'He uses witchcraft, he is the colour of a cow's nose and he is not a fool. Is he a good lover, I wonder?'

'He is too big,' Anusha said with the absolute confidence of a woman who had studied all the texts on the subject and had looked at a very wide range of detailed pictures while she was at it.

A wife was expected to have considerable theoretical

knowledge of how to please her husband and *Mata* had made sure that her education in that area had not been neglected. Anusha sometimes wondered if knowing so much was not responsible for her reluctance to agree to any of the marriages that had been proposed for her.

If one had the luxury of choice it did make you look at the man concerned very carefully while you considered the matter. And then you tried to imagine doing those things with him and…and, so far, those mental pictures had been quite enough to make her reject every one of the suitors offered to her.

'Too big?' Paravi was still dwelling on her description of the scene in the bathhouse. Her eyes were wide with an amused surprise that Anusha was not certain she quite understood.

'How could someone so large be supple and sensual?' she added in explanation, with what she felt was crushing logic. 'He would be a lump. A log of wood.' He had certainly felt like teak under her hands. A contrary memory flickered through her mind of him twisting, fast as a snake, the knife in his hand. But that had simply been trained violence, not the subtle magic of the sensual arts.

'A lump,' her uncle's wife echoed, her lips curling into a wicked smile. 'I must see this human log more closely.' She gestured to the maid. 'Find out at what hour my lord holds audience with the *angrezi* and in which *diwan*.' Paravi turned to Anusha, suddenly every inch a rani. 'You will join me in my gallery.'

Chapter Two

Nick changed, choosing his clothing with some care—the message from the raja had stipulated no uniform. When the escort came he walked, relaxed, between the four heavily armed members of the royal bodyguard. He had not expected to be received with anything but warmth, but it was good to have that confirmed. If Kirat Jaswan had decided his interests lay elsewhere than with the East India Company now that his sister was dead, then Nick's mission would have become both dangerous and exceedingly difficult.

He supposed, if diplomacy failed, it was possible to remove an unwilling, intelligent and able-bodied princess from a heavily fortified palace in the middle of her uncle's kingdom and get her back across hundreds of miles to Delhi with an angry raja's troops at his heels, but he would prefer not to have to try. Or to start a small war in the process.

As it was, he felt good. He was clean, he was relaxed by the bath and the massage and the amusement of teasing the infuriating female he had to escort out of here.

Now, with her mother dead, and her father's own wife gone, there was no one to hurt by George removing his daughter from the raja's court and turning her into an English lady. And there were a number of very good political reasons for bringing her to Calcutta into the bargain.

Nick strode into the *Diwan-i-Khas*, the Hall of Private Audience. In his peripheral vision he was aware of marble pillars, the men in the robes and the ornate *safa* turbans of the elite on either side, of guards, their weapons drawn in ceremonial salute.

He kept his eyes on the slight figure in a gold embroidered *chauga* seated amidst piled cushions on the silver-embossed throne on the dais before him. As he reached two sword-lengths from the steps he made the first obeisance, aware of the flutter of silks, the drift of perfume, from behind the stone grillework of the gallery. The ladies of the court were there, watching and listening. Those in favour would have access to the raja, would give him their opinion of his guest. Was Miss Laurens there? He was certain that curiosity would have brought her.

'Your Highness,' he said in English. 'Major Nicholas Herriard, at your service. I bring salutations from the Governor of the Calcutta Presidency with most grateful thanks for the honour of my reception.'

The white-clad *munshi* looked up from his writing desk at the raja's feet and spoke in rapid Hindi. Raja Kirat Jaswan replied in the same language while Nick kept his face studiously blank.

'His Highness, Lord of Kalatwah, Defender of the

Sacred Places, Prince of the Emerald Lake, Favoured of the Lord Shiva…' Nick stood frozen in place while the *munshi* reeled off the titles in English. '…commands you to approach.'

He stepped forwards and met the shrewd dark brown eyes that were regarding him from beneath the jewelled and plumed brocade of the turban. Overhead the ropes of the *punkah* fan creaked faintly.

The raja spoke. 'It gives me pleasure to welcome the friend of my friend, Laurens,' the secretary translated. 'You left him in good health?'

'I did, your Highness, although low in spirits from the death of his wife. And…another loss. He sends letters and gifts by my hand as does the Governor.'

The secretary translated. 'I was sorry to hear of his wife and that his heart is still in grief, as mine is for the death of my sister last year. I know he will have shared my feelings. There is much to discuss.' He waved a hand at the *munshi*. 'We have no need of a translator, I think,' the raja added in perfect English. 'You will join me and we will relax, Major Herriard.'

It was a command, a great favour and exactly what Nick was hoping for. 'My lord, you do me honour.'

The rani's position in the women's gallery around the audience hall was the very best position for observing and listening. Anusha had settled comfortably against the piled pillows next to Paravi as maids placed low tables covered in little dishes around them.

'We should hear well,' said the rani as they waited for the raja to arrive. The acoustics had been carefully designed in all the rooms: in some to baffle sound, in others to enable eavesdropping with ease. Here, in circumstances where the raja would consult with his favourite after a meeting, a conversation in a normal tone would reach easily to the pierced screens.

'Savita tells me that your log of wood is as supple as a young sapling,' Paravi added mischievously. 'Such muscles…'

Anusha dropped the almonds she had just picked up. Rummaging in the cushions to retrieve them at least gave her the chance to compose her face and suppress her unruly imagination. 'Truly? You amaze me.'

'I wonder if he has read all the classical texts,' Paravi continued. 'He would be so strong, and most vigorous.'

Anusha took an incautious mouthful of nuts and coughed. *Vigorous*…

'And he has very large…feet.'

There was no answer to that, especially as she was not sure what Paravi meant and suspected she was being teased. Anusha feigned interest in the arrival below of the male courtiers as they poured in to fill up the hall in a noisy, jostling, colourful mass. As the servants went from niche to niche, lighting the *ghee* lamps, the mirror fragments and gems in the walls and ceilings began to reflect back the light in scintillating patterns like constellations in the darker sky of shadows.

Faintly, there was the sound of the musicians tuning their instruments in the courtyard. It was beautiful and familiar and yet Anusha felt an ache of something she was beginning to recognise as loneliness.

How was it possible to feel lonely when she was

never alone? To feel she was not part of this world when it had been her life for ten years, when she was surrounded by her mother's family?

Her uncle walked through the crowd and took his place, gestured for the courtiers to be seated, then beckoned.

A tall figure in a *sherwani* of gold-and-green brocade over green *pajama* trousers walked through the seated men to the steps of the throne. For a moment Anusha could not place him until the pale gold of his hair, falling on his shoulders, caught the light. He bowed his head, his cupped right hand lifting to his heart in the graceful gesture of obeisance. As he straightened she saw the green fire of an emerald in his earlobe.

'Look,' she whispered to Paravi. 'Just look at him!' In the costume of the court the major should have looked more ordinary, but he did not. The brocade and the silks, the severe lines of the long coat and the glitter of gems, made the pale hair and the broad shoulders and the golden skin seem more exotic, more strange.

'I am doing so!'

The raja motioned impatiently to the servants and they lifted the cushions from the foot of the dais and arranged them on the right side of the throne where the *munshi*'s desk had stood. 'You will join me,' Kirat Jaswan said.

'My lord. You do me honour.' The Hindi was accurate, perfectly accented. The big Englishman sank down and crossed his legs beneath him with the ease of an Indian. The raja dropped his hand to his shoulder and leaned over to speak.

'I cannot hear,' Paravi complained. 'But here is the food, they cannot both whisper and eat.'

Indeed, as a succession of small dishes were presented to the raja, and he offered them in turn to the *angrezi*, the two men straightened up and most of what they said could be heard. But, to Anusha's frustration, it was all the most innocuous conversation.

She ate absently, her eyes on the fair hair beneath, the glimpses of the Englishman's profile as he turned his head to answer her uncle. His voice held the easy rhythms of a man who had not only been taught Hindi well, but who used it, day in, day out. What had he said his name was? Herriard? A strange name—she tried it out silently.

Then the food was finally cleared away, the scented water and cloths presented for the washing of hands and the great silver *hookah* was brought, with an extra mouthpiece for the guest. Both men appeared to relax as the music began.

'They are discussing something of importance now,' Paravi said. 'See how they use the mouthpieces to shield their lips so that no one can read them.'

'Why should they be so concerned? It is only the court around us.'

'There are spies,' the rani said after a swift glance. She lifted her hand with apparent casualness to shield her own mouth. 'The Maharaja of Altaphur will have men in the court and agents here amongst the servants.'

'Altaphur is an enemy?' Surprised, Anusha twisted to face her. 'But my uncle considered his request to wed me and sent him a fine horse when I refused. He said nothing then about any enmity.'

'It is safer to pretend to be friends with the tiger who lives at the bottom of one's garden than to let him see you know about his teeth. My lord would not have allowed the match even if you had agreed, but he made it seem the refusal was a woman's whim, not a ruler's snub.'

'But why is he an enemy?'

'This is a small but rich state—there is much to covet here. And, as you said earlier, we are in a position that interests the East India Company so they will make concessions to whoever rules, perhaps.' Paravi spoke as though she was just working this out, but Anusha sensed a deeper knowledge behind the words. She caught an edge of fear in the other woman's voice. Much had been hidden from her, she realised. Even her friend had been wearing a mask. No one had trusted her with the truth. Or perhaps they just thought her not important enough: the niece with the English blood in her veins.

'There will be war?' The state had been at peace for almost seventy years. But the court poets and musicians told the stories of past battles and of terrible defeats as well as glorious victories, of the men riding out, dressed in their ochre funerary robes, knowing they were going to their deaths, and the women filing down to the great burning pyres to commit *jauhar,* ritual suicide, rather than fall into the hands of the conqueror. Anusha shuddered. She would choose to ride out to die in battle, not go to the pyre.

'No, of course not,' the rani said with a confidence

that Anusha did not believe. 'The Company will protect us if we are their allies.'

'Yes.' It was best to agree. Anusha looked down at
the golden head, bent listening. Then the Englishman
looked up to meet the raja's eyes and she caught the in-
tensity in his face as he spoke with sudden passion, his
hand slashing out in a gesture she could not interpret.

The court was moving back to clear space for a
nautch. The dancers entered amidst the music of the
bells on the silver chains around their ankles. Then
they began to move, perfectly together, their wide, vivid
skirts swinging out like exploding fireworks. But the
two men did not spare them a glance and Anusha felt a
cold finger of apprehension trail down her spine.

She went to her bedchamber unsettled and restless,
her mind churning with her anxieties over the threat
from across the border and the humiliation of the bathhouse.

'Anusha.' Paravi came in, her face serious.

'What is it?' Anusha dropped the book she was
thumbing through and pushed back the loose hair that
spilled over her shoulders.

'My lord wishes to speak with you privately, without
his councillors. Come to my chamber.'

Anusha realised that there were no maids present—
neither her own, nor any with the rani. She stood up
from the low couch, slid her feet into sandals and followed Paravi while her mind whirled with speculation.

Her uncle was unattended, his face starkly under-lit
by the little lamps flickering on a low table by his side.

Anusha made her reverence and waited, wondering why Paravi had pulled her veil over her face.

'Major Herriard here has come from your father,' Kirat Jaswan said without preamble. 'He is concerned for you.'

Her father? Her pulse jolted with something close to fear. What could he want with her? Then the raja's wording struck her. 'Here?'

The big man stepped out of the shadows and bowed, unsmiling. He was still in Indian dress. The lamplight caught the gleam of the emeralds in his ear lobes, the silver embroidery and buttons of his coat. He looked both exotic and utterly comfortable, as at home in this guise as he seemed in the scarlet uniform.

'I thought you were from the Company,' Anusha challenged him in Hindi. 'Not my father's servant.'

The raja hissed a word of reproof, but the Englishman answered her in the same language, his green eyes meeting hers with a bold, assessing stare. No man should look at an unveiled woman not of his family like that. 'I come from both. The Company is concerned about the intentions of the Maharaja of Altaphur towards this state. And so is your father.'

'I understand why they should be concerned about a threat to Kalatwah. But why is my father thinking about me after all these years?' Her uncle did not reprove her for not veiling herself. It was as though he was suddenly treating her as an Englishwoman, she thought with a shiver of alarm. The rani had slipped back into the shadows.

'Your father has never ceased to concern himself

with your welfare,' the man Herriard said. He sounded irritated with her and when she shook her head in instinctive denial he frowned. 'He saw the offer of marriage from Altaphur as a threat, a way of pressuring the Company through you.'

Her father knew about that? Kept such a close watch over her? It took her a moment for the meaning to force its way through resentment and the unsettling atmosphere of conspiracy. 'I would have been a hostage?'

'Exactly.'

'How dreadful, that I might inconvenience the Company and my father in that way.'

'Anusha!' The raja slapped his palm down on the table.

'Miss Laurens—'

'Do not call me that.' Her knees were shaking, but no one could see beneath the long skirts of her robe.

'It is your name.' Presumably the man spoke to his troops in this manner. She was not one of his troops. Anusha's chin went up—that stopped it trembling as well.

'Your father and I agree it would be better for you to return to his house,' her uncle said. His quiet voice with its expectation of instant obedience cut across their hostility.

'Go back to Calcutta? Go back to my father after he threw us out? He does not want me, only to stop me interfering with his political schemes. I hate him. And I cannot leave you and Kalatwah when there is danger, my lord. I will not run away—never!' In her mind the crackle of flames and the clash of steel mingled with the sound of a big man's belly-laugh and her mother's stifled sobs.

'Such drama,' Herriard drawled, blowing the swirling images away like a draught of cold air. She itched to slap his well-defined jaw. 'Ten years ago your father was in an impossible position and did the only honourable thing open to him to ensure the well-being of yourself and your mother.'

'Honour! Pah!'

Herriard went very still. 'You never, in my hearing, defame the honour of Sir George Laurens, do you understand?'

'Or?' Her neck muscles were so tense it was painful.

'Or you will find it a matter for regret. If you will not leave because your father commands it, then do it for his Highness, your uncle. Or are your grudges so deep that you would hamper the defence of his state, the safety of the family, to indulge them?'

Grudges? He can calmly dismiss feelings about the betrayal of love, the rejection of a family, as a grudge? The marble floor seemed to quiver like sand beneath her feet. Anusha choked back the furious retort and looked at her uncle. 'Do you want me to go, my lord?'

'It is best,' Kirat Jaswan said. He was everything to her: ruler, uncle, surrogate father. She owed him her total obedience. 'You…complicate matters, Anusha. I would have you safe where you belong.'

So I do not belong here? No matter how she had been feeling these past months, this was too sudden, too abrupt. Her uncle had cast her out too, as her father had. Now she truly was adrift with nowhere to call home. To protest, would be futile, and beneath her. She was a Rajput princess by training, even if her blood was mixed. 'I do not belong with my father. I never did, he made that clear as crystal. But because you, my lord and uncle, ask it, I shall go.'

And she would not weep, not in front of that arrogant *angrezi* who had got what he came for, it seemed: her surrender. She was of a princely house and she had her pride and she would do what her ruler commanded and not show fear. If he had commanded her to ride into battle to her death with his troops she would have done. Somehow that felt less frightening than this. 'When must I go?'

The Englishman Herriard answered. It was as though her uncle had already washed his hands of her and had given her over to the other man. 'You leave as soon as the vehicles and animals can be gathered and the journey provisioned. It is a long way and will take us many weeks.'

'I remember,' Anusha said. Weeks of blank discomfort and misery, clinging to her mother who was too proud to weep. Sent away because the big, loving, bear of a man who had hugged her and spoiled her, who had been the centre of her world and her mother's universe, had cast them out. Because love, it seemed, was not for ever. Expediency conquered love. It was a lesson that had been well learned.

Then what Herriard had said penetrated. 'Us? *You* will take me?'

'Of course. I am your escort, Miss Laurens.'

'I am so *very* sorry,' she said, baring her teeth in a

false smile. She would make every league a misery for him, if she could, the insensitive brute. 'You obviously do not wish for this duty.'

'I would walk the entire way in my bare feet if Sir George asked it,' Major Herriard said. The cold green eyes looked back at her without liking or anger, as hard as the emeralds in his ears. 'He is as a father to me and what he wants, Miss Laurens, I will ensure that he gets.'

A father? Just who was this man whose devotion went so far beyond a soldier's obedience? 'Fine words,' Anusha said as she turned to leave. 'I do hope you will not have cause to eat them.'

Chapter Three

'If that man sends one more message about what I must and must not take I will scream.' Anusha stood in the midst of harried, scurrying maids and searched for a word to describe Nicholas Herriard. With a phrase quivering on her tongue she caught Paravi's amused gaze and compromised. *'Budmash.'*

'Major Herriard is not a villain or a knave,' the rani said, her tone of reproof in conflict with the curve of her lips. 'And he will hear you—he is only on the other side of the *jali*. It is a long journey. He is right to make certain you will have everything you need, yet not too much.'

'What is he doing there?' Anusha demanded, raising her voice. If the wretched man was listening behind the pierced screen wall then he deserved to hear her opinion. The men who ruled her life had left her two choices: she could weep and give up or she could lose her temper. Her pride would not allow the first, so the major must bear the brunt of the other. 'This is the women's *mahal.*'

'There is a eunuch with him and curtains have been hung around the room,' Paravi hissed. 'He is checking everything as it is packed.'

'Hah! My uncle says I may have twenty elephants, forty camels, forty bullock carts, horses...'

'And I say it is too much,' said a deep voice from behind the far wall of pierced stone. Anusha jumped and stubbed her toe on a studded chest. 'Anyone would think you are going to marry the Emperor, Miss Laurens. And besides, your father will want you to wear Western clothes and jewels in Calcutta.'

'*Mata* told me about those clothes.' Anusha marched across a stack of carpets until she was next to the *jali*. A large shadow on the silk hangings was all she could see of him through the screen. 'Corsets! Stockings! Garters! She said they were instruments of torture.'

There was a snort from the other side. 'They are not things a lady mentions in the presence of a man,' Herriard said, laughter quivering in his voice.

'Then go away. I do not require your presence here. I do not require your presence at all, anywhere, gloating because you are getting your way. If you listen from hiding like a spy, then you must endure whatever I say.' There was a faint moan from the rani behind her. 'Go away, Major Herriard. Twenty elephants are no slower than ten.'

'Twenty elephants eat twice as much as ten,' he retorted. 'We leave the day after tomorrow. Anything that is not ready, or will not go on half the transport you have listed, will be left behind. And whilst I feel the greatest satisfaction in following your father's wishes, I am not gloating.'

Anusha opened her mouth to retort, but the sound of footsteps leaving the other room silenced her. It was intolerable to be prevented from arguing because the man had the ill manners to remove himself.

'Find me a dagger,' she said, narrowing her eyes at the nearest maid, who was apparently rooted to the spot. 'That at least I will take—I can imagine a nice broad target for it.' And she would take all her jewels because when she was in Calcutta and Major Herriard was no longer her jailer she would need them to pay for her escape from her prison. From her father's house.

Her dagger was in her hand and she would use it because the wretched *angrezi* was shouting at her and shaking her and drums were beating the alarm and there was danger all around.

'Ah! *Ra*—' Anusha's shriek of *rape* was choked in her throat as a large hand clamped over her mouth. She had been asleep, dreaming, but now—

'Quiet,' Nicholas Herriard hissed in her ear. 'We must leave, at once, in secret. When I take my hand away you will whisper or I'll clip you on the jaw and carry you out. Do you understand?'

Furious, frightened—*do not let him see that*—Anusha nodded and he removed his hand. 'Where are my maids?' He jerked his head towards the corner and she opened her mouth to scream as she saw the two crumpled bodies lit by the flickering light of one *ghee* lamp. The hand came back, none too gently. The skin bore the calluses of a rider and chafed her lips. He tasted of leather.

'Drugged,' he murmured in her ear, pressing his palm tight over her mouth to foil her attempt to bite. 'There are spies, I cannot risk it. Listen.' He freed her mouth again.

Now she was awake she realised that the drums that had been echoing through her dream were real, their sound vibrating through the palace. She had never heard them like this, at night, so urgent. 'An attack?'

'The Maharaja of Altaphur has moved fast. There are war elephants and cavalry not four hours distant.'

'He discovered you are here? That you had come for me?' Anusha sat up, dragged the covers around her as Herriard sank back on his heels beside the low bed. He was wearing Indian dress again, but now it was plain riding gear with boots and a tight, dark turban to cover the betraying shimmer of pale hair.

'He was already mobilising his troops—he must have been to get so close so fast. Then his spies told him that someone from the Company was here, perhaps that I intended to take you away, perhaps that I was negotiating. My guess is that he decided on a pre-emptive strike to seize the state before your uncle made an alliance with the Company.'

'My uncle will not surrender to him!' The floor was cold under her bare feet as she scrambled out of bed, the night air chill through the thin cotton of her shift.

'No, he will stand firm. The raja has already despatched riders to his allies in Agra and Gwalior and to Delhi. The Company will send troops as soon as it receives the news and then I suspect Altaphur will back down without further fighting. Your uncle only has to withstand a siege for a matter of weeks.'

Was he attempting to soothe her with easy lies? Anusha tried to read his face in the gloom and control her churning stomach. 'You will stay here and fight?' Why one more soldier would make any difference, she did not know, but somehow the thought of this man at her uncle's right shoulder made her feel better. He was arrogant, aggravating and foreign, but she had no doubt that Major Herriard was a warrior.

'No. You and I are leaving. Now.'

'I am not going to leave my uncle and run away! What do you take me for? A coward?' His eyes flickered over her and she was suddenly aware of how thin her garment was, of how her nipples had peaked in the cool air. Anusha swept the bedcovers around her like a robe and glared at him as he got to his feet. 'Lecher!'

'I rather hoped I could take you for a sensible woman,' he said with a sigh. He added something under his breath in English and she pounced on it.

'What is this? A *tutty-hooded female*?'

'Totty-headed. Foolish,' he translated. 'No, clawing my eyes out is not going to help.' He caught her wrists with contemptuous ease. 'Listen to me. Do you think it will help your uncle to have to worry about you on top of everything else? And if the worst happens, what are you going to do? Lead the women to the pyres or become a hostage?'

Anusha drew in a deep breath. *He is right, may all the demons take him.* She knew where her duty lay and she was not a child to refuse out of spite. She would go, not because this man told her to, but because her raja willed it. And because this was no longer her home. 'No, if my uncle tells me to go, then I will go. How?'

'You can ride a horse?'

'Of course I can ride a horse! I am a Rajput.'

'Then dress for riding—hard riding. Dress as a man and wear tough cloth and good boots, wrap your hair in a turban. Bring a roll of blankets, the nights are cold outside, but only pack what you must have. Can you do that? I will meet you in the court below. *Jaldi.*'

'I may be *totty-headed*, Major Herriard, but I am not a fool. And, yes, I understand the need to hurry.'

'Can you dress without help?' He paused on the threshold, a broad shadow against the pale marble.

Beyond words, Anusha threw a sandal at him and its ivory toe-post broke against the door jamb. He melted away into the darkness, leaving her shivering, the drumbeats vibrating through her very bones. For a moment she stood there, forcing herself to think clearly of what she must do, then she ran to the two maids. Under her groping fingers the blood beat strongly below their jawbones. Spies or not, they were alive.

She lifted the nightlight and took it round the room, touching it to the wicks of the lamps in every niche until there was enough light to see by. The mirrored fragments in the walls reflected her image in a myriad of jagged shards as she pulled out the last of the trunks, the one containing clothes for use on the journey. She dressed in plain trousers, tight in the calf, wide at the thigh, then layers above, topped by a long, dark brown split-sided coat. Her soft riding boots were there and she pulled them on, slid a dagger into the top of the right one and another, a tiny curved knife, into her belt.

It was quick to twist her hair into a tight plait to pile on the crown of her head and she wrapped and tied a turban out of dark brown cloth, fumbling as she did so. Sometimes she secured her hair like this when riding, but her maids had always tied it.

Money. How much money did Herriard have? Anusha pulled the long cloth free, rummaged in the trunk again and found the jewels she had intended to wear as they arrived in Calcutta, chosen to emphasise her status and her independence. She stuffed the finest into a bag, coiled her hair around it and rewrapped the turban.

Two blankets rolled around a change of linen, toilet articles, a bag containing hairpins and comb, tinder box. What else? She rubbed her temples—the drums stopped her thinking properly, invaded her head. Soon someone would come to check on her, fuss over her, shepherd her to the inner fastness of the palace where she really wanted to be. Where it was her duty not to go.

Anusha found her little box of medicines, added that, rolled up the blankets, tied them with leather straps and caught up the bundle in her arms. The walls were honeycombed with passages and stairs and she took one of the narrowest and least-used ways down, tiptoeing as she reached the doorway.

But Herriard had seen her. He stepped away from the wall, his eyes glinting in the reflected torchlight, and reached for the bundle.

'I can manage. No, not that way, I must say goodbye to my uncle, to the Lady Paravi—'

'And risk being seen? They know what we are doing and they have other things to think about just now. Come *on*.' He pushed her in front of him through the door, back into the palace. He seemed to know the way as well as she, pulled her into alcoves as servants ran past, knew when to stop and slide into the shadows to avoid a distracted sentry, his attention on someone shouting on the battlements.

A slender figure stepped out right in front of them and she stopped so abruptly that Herriard ran into her and gripped both her arms above the elbow to steady himself. His body was hard and immovable against her back and his voice was a soft rumble. Suddenly she was glad of his size. When he released her it was as though a bulwark had been removed.

'Ajit, are the horses ready?'

'Yes, *sahib*,' the man said and she recognised the major's servant. He must have run up the steep road from the base court for he was panting. 'Pavan and Rajat and a good mare for the lady. The lower gate is still open for soldiers taking up positions outside the walls, but we must hurry or we will be noticed.'

They ran, skidding on the black stones worn smooth by the passage of elephants and horses and men over hundreds of years, hugged the walls that loomed over them, slowed at every one of the gates where the road changed direction, all the better to confuse attackers if they got within the outer defences.

One more gate, Anusha thought, as she bounced

painfully off a ring set in the wall. There was a cry
ahead, a thud and Herriard stopped, bent over Ajit's
sprawled figure.

'Collarbone, *sahib*,' the man gasped. 'Broken. I am
sorry.' He sat up and she saw his right shoulder sloped
down at an unnatural angle. In the torchlight his face
was grey.

'You must stay.' Herriard helped him to his feet and
propped him up against the wall. 'Go back up and see
the court physician. He is to be trusted. Tell him to let
his Highness know we are safe away.'

'*Sahib*, take my bundle, too—there are weapons.'

'I will. You take care, Ajit, my friend, I will see you
in Calcutta.'

Herriard picked up the fallen bundle, took Anusha's
arm and dragged her on. 'How good a rider are you?'
he demanded as they slowed for the final gate before
the lower court. He stopped, watchful, the shadows of
the vicious spikes set at the height of an elephant's forehead lying in bars across his face.

'Excellent. Of course.' She looked up at the rows of
handprints at the side of the gate, left by the women who
had gone through it to become *sati* on their husbands'
funeral pyres. She shuddered and the Englishman felt
it and followed her gaze.

'Another good reason for not marrying a maharaja
twice your age,' he observed as he took her elbow and
steered her into the courtyard.

'Do not touch me!'

He ignored her until they were past the bustle of the
elephant lines and into the straw-strewn stables, vir-

tually empty now the cavalry had ridden out. Then he stopped, jerking her against him. He would say it was so he could keep his voice low, but she knew it was a show of dominance.

'Listen to me, Miss Laurens. Hard as it may be for you to believe, your beauty does not inflame me with lust and, even if it did, I am not fool enough to waste time dallying with you when a small war is about to break out around our heads.'

He released her and began to strap the blanket rolls behind the saddles of the three horses that still stood in the stalls: a handsome, raking grey, a smaller, well-muscled black and a bay with the brand of her uncle's stud. 'Take this.' He thrust the bay's reins into her hand. 'When I need to touch you, I will touch you, and when I do you had better be prepared to obey me because it will be an emergency. I promised your father I would get you back to him, but I did not promise him not to tan your backside in the process.'

'You…*swine*,' Anusha hissed.

Herriard shrugged. 'If I am, then I am the swine who is going to keep you alive. And, while we are on the subject of touching, I should point out that you are the one who sneaked into the bathhouse and touched me when I was naked. Your hands were cold and your technique could do with some work.' He led out the other two horses and tied the black's reins on its neck—the blanket rolls were strapped to its back. 'Here, I'll give you a leg up.'

'I do not need your help.' Anusha jammed her foot in the stirrup and swung into the saddle. 'And I only wanted to see—' She shut her mouth in confusion at where her temper had led her.

'See what?' He was up on the grey now. In the torch-light his lean features showed nothing but amused curiosity.

'What colour you were,' Anusha snapped.

'And your curiosity was satisfied?' Herriard clicked his tongue and the grey and the black moved out into the yard. Anusha dug in her heels and sent her horse after them.

'Yes. Where you are not touched by the sun you are pink. Not white at all.' She would not be shamed or embarrassed by him.

'I suspect that after many days with you I will be turning white on a regular basis,' he said. 'Now, be quiet and cover yourself.' He pulled the tail of his turban round and tucked it in to veil the lower part of his face. Seething, Anusha followed his example and the three horses passed out of the main gate and down the road towards the town without challenge.

She twisted in the saddle for a last look at the great walls towering above her, the fort that contained a palace, the palace that had been her home. Now she was simply a fugitive, neither Anusha, the raja's pampered niece, nor Miss Laurens, the rejected daughter of an Englishman. The thought was frightening and strangely liberating. She did not have to think about where she was going or how she would get there—for days she would be floating on the stream of fate.

At the pressure of her heels the bay drew alongside

Herriard's big grey. 'Where do we go?' she asked in English. She had best practise it, she supposed.

'Allahabad to start with. Speak Hindi.'

'So we do not attract attention?' Anusha tucked the end of the cloth more snugly into the turban as he nodded. 'You do that without a word spoken. You are too big and too pale.' She would die rather than admit that she found the sheer size of him comforting.

'With my hair covered I can be taken for a Pathan,' Herriard said.

'They are tall and light-skinned and they have grey eyes, some of the men from the north, I have seen them,' she agreed. 'But your eyes are green.'

The town was seething like a disturbed ant heap with the news of the maharaja's approaching army. The bay snorted and sidled at the press of bullock carts, the running figures and the trains of camels. Herriard reached for her rein, then withdrew his hand when she hissed at him. She had her mount back under control within seconds.

'I am flattered that you noticed my eyes.' He skirted round a cow that lay in the middle of the road chewing the cud as it ignored all around it with complete indifference.

'You should not be. Of course I noticed—you are different. Strange,' she added to make certain he did not think it a compliment. 'It is a long time since I saw someone like you.'

He did not answer her, but guided his horse around a spitting, grumbling knot of camels and out over the rickety bridge that spanned the river. So, he was either not easy to goad or he simply dismissed her as unimportant. The moon was up, noticeable now they were away from the torches and the fires, and the *angrezi* stood in his stirrups to survey the road in front of them.

'We can take that track there.' Anusha pointed. 'It cuts through the fields and it will be deserted now. We will make better time and no one will see us.'

'And we will leave the tracks of three horses plain on soil that is trodden only by bare feet and oxen. Here, on the road, we will be less easy to track.'

At least he explains, Anusha conceded, then the implication hit home. 'We will be followed?'

'Of course. Once it is realised that you are no longer in the palace the maharaja's spies will pass the word out. I am counting on half a day's start, that is all.'

Anusha's stomach tightened. Suddenly the Englishman's frankness was no longer so welcome. 'It is more dangerous out here than in the fort. Why did we not stay there until help came?'

He shot her a glance, the silvery light catching his eyes, making them unreal, like the greenish pearl of the inside of a shell. 'Because your uncle could not be certain that he could protect you within the palace. Your father makes you a very tempting prize for a man who wishes for nothing but his own power and to keep the Company at bay.'

'I was in danger *within* the palace?'

'I think so. I removed you easily enough, did I not?'

'Yes.' She took a deep breath. Treachery, spies, danger, lies. And she had thought her life had been so tranquil, so…boring. *I could have been kidnapped at any time.*

'Frightened?'

'Of what?' she demanded. 'There is much to choose from.'

That surprised a laugh from him. 'Of the pursuers, of the journey, of where you are going. Of me.'

'No,' Anusha lied. She was afraid of all of those things, but she was not going to admit it. His faint snort of derision showed what he thought of that.

'You appear to be competent, so I imagine you will evade pursuit,' she said. It seemed important to convince him of her courage, her ability to undertake this journey. 'I look forward to being able to look around me, to see things openly and not through the screens of a travelling palanquin. I will deal with my destination when I get there. And as for you, Major Herriard, you are a—' She searched for the equivalent in Hindi and resorted to English. '*Gentleman*, are you not, if you are an officer? And my mother said that *English gentlemen* must behave honourably to ladies.'

'That is the theory,' he agreed, his voice dry. And then he laughed and spurred his horse into a canter, leaving her to follow, her body tight with apprehension.

Chapter Four

'**W**hy are we stopping?' Anusha demanded. The horses had dropped into a trot and then a walk as Major Herriard turned off the road. Beneath their hooves the ground was stony and uneven. 'This is a terrible surface, we cannot canter on this.'

'Are you going to question every decision I make?' he asked without turning his head.

'Yes.' Now she did not have to concentrate on keeping her aching body in the saddle the desire to slide off and simply go to sleep was overwhelming. Perhaps when she woke it would all have been a bad dream.

'The moon will be down very soon and then it will be hard to see where we are going. There are trees over there, cover. We will make a temporary camp and sleep until sunrise. I turned off here because the ground will not show tracks.'

'Very well,' Anusha agreed.

'That is very gracious of you, Miss Laurens, but your approval is not required, merely your obedience.' Herriard was a dark shape now as he sat motionless on the horse and studied the small group of trees and thorn bushes in what was left of the moonlight. He spoke absently, as though she was peripheral to his interest.

'Major Herriard!'

'Call me Nick. Stay here. Your voice has probably scared off anything dangerous lurking in there, but I will check first.'

Nick. What sort of name was that? She translated to take her mind off the fact that she was suddenly alone and things were rustling in the bushes. Quite large things. Was *nick* not something to do with a small cut? Well, that hardly suited him—the man had the subtlety and brutal force of a sabre slash.

'There is a small shrine in there, a stone platform we can sleep on and some firewood. We can light a fire and it will be shielded by the walls,' he said as he rode back to her side. 'There are water jars for the horses, which is good fortune.'

'You would plunder a shrine?' Anusha demanded, more out of antagonism than outrage as she guided her horse after him. Taking water was hardly plunder.

'We will do no damage. We can leave an offering if you wish.' He swung down as he spoke and came to hold up a hand to her.

'I can manage. And what is a Christian doing leaving an offering at a Hindu shrine?' Her feet hit the ground rather harder than she had been expecting and her knees buckled. Nick's hand under her elbow was infuriatingly necessary. 'I said I can manage.'

He ignored her and held on until she had her balance. It felt very strange to be touched by a man, a virtual stranger. It felt safe and dangerous all at the same time. 'It would cause no offence, I imagine. And after twelve years in this country I am not at all sure what I am. A pragmatist, perhaps. What are you?'

It was a good question. She supposed she had better decide before she reached Calcutta. Her mother had converted to Christianity after she had lived with Sir George for five years. For ten years Anusha had gone with her to church. And in Kalatwah she had lived as a Hindu. 'What am I? I do not know. Does it matter, so long as one lives a good life?'

'A sound philosophy. At least that is something we do not have to fight over.' He did not unsaddle the horses but loosened the girths and then dumped their kit on the stone platform.

'We do not have to fight at all, provided you treat me with respect,' Anusha retorted. *And stop watching me like a hawk.* She found a twiggy branch and began to sweep an area clear of the leaf litter that might harbour insects or a small snake.

'I will treat you with the respect that you earn, Miss Laurens.' Herriard…*Nick*…hefted an urn over to the stone trough by the horses and poured out water. 'You are a woman and your father's daughter, which means I do not deal with you as I would a man. After that—' he shrugged '—it is up to you.'

'I do not wish to go to my father. I hate my father.'

'You may wish what you will and you may think what you wish, but you will not abuse Sir George in my hearing. And you will obey me. Stay there.' In the semi-darkness she could not read his face, but Anusha heard the anger. Again he showed that fierce, puzzling, loyalty to her father. He turned and walked away.

'Wait! Where are you going?' Surely he was not going to punish her by leaving her here in the dark?

Nick vanished into the scrub and she heard what sounded like boots kicking at the low branches. When he walked back he was doing something to the front of his trousers and she blushed in the gloom. 'There is a nice thick bush there,' he said, gesturing. 'With no snakes.'

'Thank you.' With as much dignity as she could muster Anusha stalked down the three steps to the ground and over to the bush. The mundane implications of being alone like this with a man were beginning to dawn on her. There might be vast areas with hardly a bush. How was she supposed to manage then? The wretch seemed to have no shyness, no modesty about mentioning these things at all. Never, in the ten years until she had chased Tavi and found herself in that corridor with Nick, had she been all alone with a man, even her uncle or one of the eunuchs.

When she emerged his attention was, mercifully, on lighting a small fire in an angle of the wall. The flames made a pool of light on the platform, but would be hidden from anyone approaching from the direction they had come. A bed of blankets had been made up close to the fire.

In the shadows she could see the stumpy pillar of the Shiva *lingam* and the firelight glinted for a moment on something that trickled down its side. 'People have been here recently.' She went and looked at the pool of fresh oil on the head of the ancient stone phallus, the spray of flowering shrub that had been laid on the curve of the stylised female organ that it rose from.

'I have,' Herriard said as she joined her hands together in a brief reverence. It seemed that, whatever his beliefs, he knew how to show respect to the gods, if not to her. More in charity with him, she turned back and he gestured to food laid out on a large leaf beside the blankets. 'Here. Eat and drink and then rest. Do not take anything off, not even your boots.'

'I have no intention of removing anything!'

'Then you are going to have a very uncomfortable few weeks, Miss Laurens. Oh, sit down, I am far too weary to ravish you tonight!'

That was a jest. She hoped. Warily Anusha sank down on to the blankets. 'Eat and keep your strength up. Now we can only rest for a short while. Tomorrow night I hope we may take longer.'

'Where are you going to sleep?' She took a piece of *naan*, folded it around what looked like goat's cheese and ate, surprised at how hungry she was.

'I will not sleep. I will keep watch.'

'You cannot do that every night,' she pointed out.

'No,' Nick agreed. 'I will rest when it is safer and where you can keep watch.' He tore off a piece of the flat bread and ate it. She caught a glimpse of strong white teeth.

'Me?'

'Look around you, Miss Laurens. Who else is there? Sooner or later I must sleep. Or are you not capable of acting as a look-out?'

'Of course. I am capable of anything. I am a—'

'Rajput, I know. You are also your father's daughter, which should mean that there is a brain in there some-where, despite all evidence to the contrary.'

Anusha choked on a mouthful of water from the flask. 'How dare you! You are used to this sort of thing, I am not. I have been dragged from my bed, forced to ride through the night with a man—I have never been alone with a man for ten years—I am worried about Kalatwah…'

'True,' Nick conceded. It was not much of an apol-ogy. 'I will do my best to preserve your privacy and your modesty, but you must behave as much like a man as you can, for your own safety. Do you understand that?'

'As you guessed, I do have a brain,' she retorted. 'Now I am going to sleep.'

'Namaste,' he said, so politely that he must be mock-ing her.

'Namaste,' she returned as she rolled herself into the blankets. She would just close her eyes, rest her aching body. But she would not sleep—she did not trust him.

Anusha woke, suddenly and completely alert, with that thought still in her mind. She had been foolish to fear, it seemed. Her rest had been undisturbed, her blan-kets were still tight around her. Herriard was moving about, attending to the horses.

From the light it was just past dawn and she must have slept for at least two hours. And he had slept not at all. Anusha watched from beneath half-closed lids as he checked the horses, led them to a patch of longer grass where they might snatch a few mouthfuls. Lack of sleep seemed to have simply made him more alert, the lines of his face tauter.

He was not at all like the men she had lived among for so many years, Anusha decided. Most of the Indian men were slender, lithe. There was an English word and she searched for it. Yes, *sleek*, that was it. Nick Herriard was not sleek, he was too big, too overtly physical. The high cheekbones, the big nose, the strong chin—all asserted power and will. Anusha remembered the feel of his muscles under her hands and shivered, just as he turned and found her watching him.

She thought that colour came up under the golden tan, then he gestured towards the fire. 'There is water heating if you want to wash. I will go and scout the road.'

Anusha waited until he had walked out of sight, his musket in one hand, then disentangled herself from the blankets. She used the convenient bush, then washed as best she could. He came back, whistling tactfully, as she was rolling up the blankets.

'All right?' He did not wait for her answer, but squatted by the fire and began to make tea, throwing leaves into the boiling water from a pouch that lay amongst the food he had set out. It was the same as last night and the bread would be dry. And she supposed from the brisk manner with which he was preparing it that she should have done this while he was away. She had never been without servants before, either.

'Eat,' Nick said, pushing the food towards her and

pouring tea into a horn beaker. 'There is no one in sight, we should get on.'

'When will we be able to get more food?' Anusha chewed on the dry bread and wondered if the cheese had been this pungent the night before.

'When we come across someone who can sell us some.'

'The next big village is—'

'We are not going through villages, big or small. Do you want to leave flags to mark our route?'

'But surely they will give up? We could be anywhere by now.'

Nick washed the stale *naan* down with tea that was too hot and contemplated the haughty, exquisite face of the young woman opposite him. It was a reasonable question and she was sorely in need of reassurance and comfort, despite the mask she was putting on.

But what Anusha was going to get was a bracing dose of reality and he was going to allow his irritation with this entire situation to ride him. It was the only way he was going to be able to ignore the tension in his groin and the heat that seemed to wash through him whenever he looked at her. Or when she looked at him. He was still recovering from the impact of those grey eyes studying him as he dealt with the horses. It was odd that she should affect him so—Miss Lauren's spiky personality was hardly alluring.

'How many armed men do you think it would need to take me?' he asked. When she just shook her head, he answered himself. 'Eight, ten perhaps. I have three muskets, but we have lost our other marksman and be-sides, muskets take time to load. I am good, Miss Lau-rens, and lucky—I would not be alive today if I was not—but I am just one man. And the maharaja's spies will have told him that. It will be a blow to his pride that you have escaped him, so he can easily spare a dozen riders to come after us. And they'll know we'll be heading east, that is the logical direction to go in.'

He expected fear, possibly tears. Instead she looked at him down the straight little nose that she had defi-nitely not inherited from her father and said, 'Then teach me to load a musket and go somewhere that is not logical.'

So, he had not been wrong—she had her father's in-telligence after all and her late mother had the reputa-tion for both learning and political cunning. He could have his hands full with her. Even as he thought it he winced at his choice of words—he wanted very much to have his hands full of Anusha Laurens.

'All right, I'll teach you to load, that makes sense.' At least, it would if she could manage it. He had short India Pattern muskets with him, not the British army Land Pattern version, but even so she would be wres-tling with a weapon almost forty inches long. 'And I can aim directly at the Jumna River to find a boat and not head further south-east to Allahabad. But I must do it by the sun and stars—there were no detailed maps of this area and any deviation will add time.'

'I do not wish to be with you, Major Herriard, but I would like even less to be with that man. Take however long is necessary.'

'Then we will go more to the east than the road to Allahabad,' Nick said, getting to his feet and recalculating. The map that he had studied before he had set out was fixed in his memory, but it was sketchy to put it mildly.

'The muskets?' she demanded, rising from the dusty stone with the trained grace of a court lady.

The wish that he could see her dance came into his head, irrelevant and unwelcome. A well-bred lady would only dance with her female friends, or for her husband. To do otherwise was to lower herself to the level of a courtesan. Nick found himself pursuing the thought and frowned at her, earning a frigid stare in response. She was not used to being alone with men, and it was a long time since he had been alone with a respectable young woman for any length of time. How the devil was he supposed to treat her? What did he talk to her about?

'Muskets?' Anusha repeated, impatience etched in every line of her figure. She was slender, small—the top of her head came up to his ear. He would have to stoop to kiss her... Nick caught himself, appalled, and slammed the door on his thoughts, remembering another slender woman in his arms, of how fragile she had been, how clumsy she had made him feel. But Miranda had been frail as well as fragile—this girl had steel at her core.

'When we stop to rest at noon.' He was equally impatient now. The more distance they had between themselves and the fort, the happier he would be. He strapped the blanket rolls on the bay horse and led Rajat, Ajit's black gelding, forwards for her. In a crisis he could let the bay go and leave her with a horse as highly trained as his own Pavan.

'Why this one?'

Must she question everything? But he almost welcomed the irritation, it distracted him from fantasies and memories. 'He knows what to do. His name is Rajat; let him have his head.'

Anusha shrugged and mounted. Nick tied the end of the bay's long leading rein around his pommel and led them away from the shrine, not back to the track but out across the undulating grasslands, following the line he had mentally drawn on the map in his head.

'This is deserted,' Anusha observed after half a league.

'Yes. Except for the tigers.'

'We will starve or be eaten. You are supposed to be looking after me.' She did not sound petulant, merely critical of an inefficient servant.

Nick breathed in hard through his nose and controlled his temper. 'We have plenty of water. The streams are still running. The horses will sense tigers.' *I hope.* 'Food we can do without for a day or two if necessary. I am, as I promised your father and your uncle, keeping you safe. I never made any promises about comfort.'

She was silent. Then, 'Why do you dislike me, Major Herriard?'

Pavan pecked, unused to a jerk on his rein. 'What? I do not know you. And I am not used to young ladies.'

There was a snort and he glanced across at her. The little witch was grinning. 'That is not what I heard.'

'Respectable young ladies,' he said repressively.

'No?' She was still laughing, he could hear it, although she was managing to keep her face straight. 'Is your wife not respectable?'

'I do not have a wife.' *Not any longer.* Nick gritted his teeth and concentrated on scanning the undulating plain before them, plotting a route away from the stands of trees that might harbour a striped death.

'But why do you not have a wife? You are very old not to have a wife.'

'I am twenty-nine,' he snapped. 'I had a wife. Miranda. She died.'

'I am sorry.' She sounded it; the mocking edge had gone from her voice. 'How many children do you have? Will you marry again soon?'

'I have no children and, no, I have no intention of marrying again.' He tried to remind himself that this intense curiosity about family was simply the normal Indian polite interest in a stranger. He was inured to it, surely, by now?

'Oh, so you were very much in love with her, like Shah Jehan and Mumtaz Mahal. How sad.' When she was not being imperious or snappy her voice was lovely, soft and melodious with something deeply female in it that went straight to the base of his spine.

'No, I was not—' Nick snapped off the sentence. 'I married too young. I thought it was expected of me as a career officer. I married a girl I thought was suitable, a sweet little dab of a thing with no more strength to cope with India than a new-born lamb.'

'What was she doing here, then?' Anusha brought her horse alongside.

'She was newly arrived in India as part of the Fishing Fleet.' She murmured a query and he explained. 'The shiploads of young ladies that come out from England. They are supposed to be visiting relatives, but actually they are on the catch for a husband.

'I should have taken one look at Miranda Knight and realised that the country would ruin her health within the year. And it did. If I had not married her she would have gone back to England, wed a stout country squire and be the mother of a happy family by now.'

'She must have loved you to marry you and risk staying here,' Anusha suggested.

'Do not turn this into a love story. She wanted a *suitable* husband and what did I know about marriage and how to make a wife happy with my background?'

'What background?'

He glanced at Anusha, saw her read his mood in his face and close her lips tightly. After a moment she said, 'I beg your pardon,' in careful English. 'I forgot that the Europeans do not like personal questions.'

He was going to be alone with her for days, weeks probably. It was foolish to make a mystery out of himself. Best to get the questions over and done with now. 'My parents made a suitable, loveless match. It turned very rapidly into boredom on my father's part, then anger when my mother persisted in wanting…more. I am not certain I would know what a happy marriage looks like.'

How simple it sounded put like that. All those years

of distress and unhappiness, not just for his mother but for the little boy in the middle, aching for the love that both parents were too busy tearing each other apart to give. He was not a little boy now, and he knew better than to expect love. Or to need it.

'Oh.' She rode in silence for a while. Then, 'So you have many mistresses now? Until you marry again?'

'Anusha, you should not be discussing such things.' She regarded him quizzically. Of course, she was used to an entirely different model of marriage and sexual relationships. 'There is no reason for me to marry again. I do not live like a holy man—a *sadhu*. But neither do I have more than one mistress at a time, and none at the moment.'

'And did you have a mistress while you were married? No, do not say *Anusha* like that. I want to understand.'

'No, I did not. Some men do. I do not think it right.' And his resolve had been sorely tried after a few weeks of Miranda's vapours. However careful he was, however gentle, she had decided that sex was crude, unpleasant and for one purpose only. Her relief at becoming pregnant and having a good reason to bar him from her bed had been all too obvious. The familiar guilt came back like an aching bruise: he should have had the self-control to stay out of her bed until she had grown acclimatised to India, talked to her. Not got her with child.

Women before and since had assured him they found bliss in his arms. It seemed he was an acceptable lover and a failure as a husband.

'I am sorry if I should not have asked these things.

Thank you for explaining,' Anusha said in English, sounding not at all contrite.

'Don't mention it,' he replied in the same language. She was demanding, both emotionally at some level he was not used to, as well as practically. And she was distracting him, taking him away from the present and into the past, and that was dangerous.

The hairs were prickling on the back of his neck—he had learned to listen to his instincts. Nick wheeled Pavan. The grass was still long and lush although the ground was dry. The light wind was already blurring the marks of their passage so it would be hard to see how many horses had just passed.

Anusha had turned with him. 'There is no one behind us,' she said. 'Is there?'

The prickling unease was still under his skin. Nick stood in his stirrups and shaded his eyes. There, in the distance, was a small puff of dust kicked up by a group of riders coming at the gallop. 'There is. See?'

Chapter Five

'There is no cover, not for three horses.' Anusha was proud of how calm she sounded. She could not see the pursuers, but if Nick said they were coming, then she believed him. She loosened the little dagger in her sash.

'Follow me, exactly,' he said and turned to ride over a hard-pan of dry baked mud where the rains had once made a large pool. At the middle he swung down from the grey, took the bundles from the back of the bay horse and flung them over Pavan's saddle. 'Stay here.' He swung up on the bay and left the hard ground. As soon as he was on the softer earth he kicked it into a gallop, then lashed it across the flanks, swung down and rolled clear as it careered off into the distance.

'Take Pavan.' He tossed her the reins when he got back to her. 'Walk slowly towards that bush.'

Puzzled, but obedient, her heart thudding uncomfortably high in her throat, Anusha did as she was told. Behind her Nick walked backwards, sweeping a branch over their tracks. She realised as she reached the bush that it was on a very slight swell in the ground, but even so, it was too thin and too low to hide a donkey behind, let alone two horses.

'Are you going to shoot the horses?' She slid to the ground as he backed behind the thorn bush next to her.

'No need.' He removed both saddles, then whistled, two clear notes, and the horses folded their legs, sank to the ground and rolled on to their sides, necks stretched out. 'Get down.'

Anusha lay behind the swell of Pavan's belly as Nick spread the dun-coloured blankets over both animals, then propped the two muskets up on Rajat's flank and began to check over his hand guns. He laid everything out in order—ammunition, guns, sabre—loosened the knife in his boot and then glanced across at her. 'Army horses, both of them,' he explained, then glanced down at her hand. 'What the devil have you got there?'

'A knife, of course.' She would keep the one in her boot hidden until it was absolutely necessary and she had to kill someone. Or herself. A dark excitement was surging through her, as strong as the fear. She wanted to hurt the people who were attacking Kalatwah, her family, her kingdom. For the first time she understood what had taken those warriors out to fight to certain death, understood the spirit of the women who had gone to the flames rather than face slavery and shame.

'You are not going to need it.'

'But there will be a fight, a battle.' She could hear them coming now, the faint drum of hoofbeats. The maharaja's men had picked up their tracks.

'Not unless I have made a mistake.' Nick was rubbing handfuls of dust over the musket barrels to mask their shine. 'They should ride past, find the bay, conclude it was a ruse to send them off the road.'

'But we must kill them!'

'Bloodthirsty little wild cat,' Nick said, low-voiced. She sensed amusement in him. He had a strange sense of humour if he found this funny. 'If they do not come back, then the maharaja knows they have found us and will send more men. If they go back without seeing us, he will conclude we have gone another way.'

'Oh. Strategy.'

'Tactics, to be exact. Now, be quiet.'

There were eight riders. They passed at the gallop, vanished. Anusha released her pent-up breath and slid a little closer to Nick.

Time stretched on. Her left leg was becoming numb. *'They have gone.'*

'Wait.'

As Nick spoke she heard them returning more slowly, scanning the ground as they came, the bay on a leading rein. They rode past, then the only sound was the buzz of insects, the rumbling of Rajat's stomach under her ear, the mew of a hawk high overhead.

'Stay here.' Nick began to ease away. 'You can let go of my coat.'

'Oh!' Anusha's fingers cramped as she released her death-grip. 'I didn't realise I was holding it.' But Nick was already moving, a musket in each hand, pistol in his sash, keeping low over the ground as he dodged from bush to bush.

It was like trying to see a ghost—if she took her eyes from him he would vanish. She blinked and he was gone into the long grass. Even behind the bulk of the horses she felt incredibly exposed, utterly alone. She had not realised what a large emotional space he filled. An infuriating, man-shaped, protective space.

What would she do if she heard shooting? Anusha studied the weapons he had left behind. One musket, one pistol, the bag that contained the ammunition, his sabre. Now was not the time to learn how to reload, but she could take it all to him. She worked out the best way to carry the weapons, wondering if the horses would obey her and get to their feet.

A hand closed around her ankle.

Anusha twisted, her knife in her hand, her other lashing out, fingers bent, nails raking down.

Nick laughed and rolled to one side, releasing her foot. It was the laugh that made her temper snap, that and the long-held tension. Anusha dropped the knife and launched herself at him, intent on hurting his male pride, if nothing else.

The next moment she was flat on her back with her hands pinned above her head and the weight of one very large man on top of her. And he was still laughing. 'Wild cat. I was right.'

'You—' Words, and breath, failed her. 'Get off me.'

For a long unfathomable moment he stared down into her eyes and his own seemed to darken. Nick stopped laughing. For an instant she thought he had stopped breathing.

'It is not seemly,' she managed to say as her mind tried to assimilate all the new sensations of a hard male body pressed against her own softness. She liked them. All of them.

'No, it is not.' Nick rolled off her and got to his feet in one fluid movement. *He is as supple as a young sapling,* Paravi had said. Heat washed through her. 'I am sorry, I could not resist it. You were quivering like a hound wanting to be let off the leash.'

'I was listening for shots,' Anusha said with as much dignity as she could muster, flat on her back and filled with what she was horribly afraid was sexual desire. 'Have they gone?'

'They have, no doubt thinking that only a fool would head into the wilds with only two horses and a princess.'

He meant to mock her when he called her *princess,* she knew that. 'And *are* you a fool?'

Nick reached down a hand and hauled her to her feet. 'No, but I am going to do it anyway.' He pulled the blankets off the horses and brought them to their feet with a whistle, shaking like dogs to get rid of the dust. 'We will ride on a league or so and when we are out of earshot I will bring down some game for dinner. Then the muskets will be empty. We will rest a while, drink and I will show you how to load.' He picked up one of the guns and looked from it to her with a grin. 'Although I think you will have to stand on a rock to do it, Miss Laurens.'

'Do not call me that.' It was intolerable that he should treat her so casually and yet address her with *angrezi* formality by the name she rejected.

'Anusha, then?'

'Anusha,' she agreed warily. 'Nick.'

They remounted and rode on in a silence that seemed somehow more companionable than it had yet done.

After two leagues Nick halted and left her with the horses while he took the guns and padded off into the scrub. 'Drink,' he said, 'and get into the shade.'

'Yes, Major,' she muttered, but did as she was told, not that there was much shade to be had.

Anusha heard four gunshots and when he returned Nick had a sand grouse and a hare dangling from his hand. That was good shooting with a musket, she knew.

He hunkered down in the small patch of shade beside her and reached for the canteen of water. It spilled from the sides of his mouth and she watched it run through the stubble on his cheeks, saw his Adam's apple bob as he swallowed.

'You are a soldier, so this is taking you from the army,' she said when he put down the water and ran the back of his hand across his mouth. 'Why did they not send a diplomat for me?'

'Because there was always the chance that something like this might happen. And I am a diplomat, of sorts. I move between the army and the princely courts as the Company requires.' It explained why his Hindi was so good.

'But this is not for the Company, this is for my father.'

'His interests and those of the Company coincide when it comes to removing you from this situation,' Nick said drily. 'But he is so senior that if he wished me to go on his personal business there would be no objection.'

Sir George is like a father to me, he had said with the force of deeply held feeling. At the time the words had been a puzzle. Now, watching the relaxed, broad-shouldered figure, a startling idea struck her, and with it a stab of something that was disconcertingly like jealousy.

'Are you my father's son?' she demanded.

'No!' Nick frowned at her. 'Whatever made you think that?'

'You look like him, you said he was a father to you.' Now she felt a fool. But a suspicious fool, even so.

'I do *not* look like him. I am the same height, the same build. But my eyes are green, his are grey—like yours. His nose is hooked, mine is straighter, my hair is lighter.'

Why was that a relief? If he was her half-brother, then she would have nothing to fear from him as a man, or from her own unruly desires. 'But if you feel so much for him, then I suppose your real father is dead.'

'No, he is in England. I have not seen him for twelve years, when he sent me out to join the Company as a writer at the age of seventeen.'

'A clerk? That is very humble for a gentleman.' Her mind kept worrying at that flash of relief. Surely she would not be jealous if Nick was her brother? That was very petty, for she did not love her father, after all. He could have fathered half-siblings all over Calcutta for all she cared—he would treat them and their mothers as badly as he had her, she was sure. She did not want to think about him—he did not want her and she did not want him. She should forget him, but the pain would not let her, like an old wound around her heart, forever nagging and weakening.

'A writer's post is the first rung on the ladder,' Nick said. He seemed to be looking inwards, not at her, and whatever foolish emotions were plain on her face. 'With luck and hard work—and provided one stays alive—it is very difficult for a writer not to become wealthy.'

'So you must have been pleased at the opportunity.'

He was frowning, as though the memory was not a pleasant one. 'Pleased? No, I was appalled. So I refused. I had no ambition to be a writer, no desire to go into trade, no wish to leave England. It did not help that I had no idea what I *did* want to do.

'So then he beat me, cut my allowance and, when that did not work, had me forcibly delivered to the ship. Halfway out I contracted some kind of fever and I would have died if it were not for Mary—Lady Laurens. She deposited me, like a half-dead rat, on her husband's front porch and he took me in.'

Anusha stiffened at the name. Lady Laurens, her father's wife, the woman he had married before he came to India and who had refused to come with him. And then, fifteen years after they had parted, she decided it was her duty to be with her husband. Instead of ordering her to stay away as any wronged husband should have done, her father had allowed his wife to come out to India, had dismissed Sarasa, Anusha's mother, and sent them back to her brother.

The disobedient, wilful wife, the one who had not

borne him any children, was rewarded and the faithful mistress and companion, the mother of his daughter, discarded.

The memories of that day were still vivid. Despite the tears and the preparations she had not believed her mother when she said they must go. And then the ship from England arrived early and they were still in the house and there was Lady Laurens and all her baggage in the front yard and Sir George's other family at the back. Sarasa had shut herself into the women's quarters and ordered her servants to load their baggage animals immediately. She would not wait to be ordered out of her own home by this interloper.

But Anusha, not understanding, had run out to look for her father and wriggled through the bearers and the carts and the chaos. She had slipped up the steps on to the veranda and heard her father's voice inside and a strange woman, speaking English, and she knew her mother was right: his wife who was a stranger to him had come and he did not want them any more.

She had turned around, swallowing the tears and the awful hurt, and bumped into a stretcher that had been laid out across chairs in the shade. On it there was a still figure.

Now she stared at Nick. 'But I saw you! I saw you lying on the veranda. You were skinny and white and I thought you were dead. You were white and your hair was like straw.'

'I thought I was dead, too,' Nick said with a twist of his mouth that might have been dark humour or might have been remembered pain. 'Between them George and Mary saved my life and my future.'

'You were a boy, so more interesting than a mere girl, no doubt, even if you were not their blood,' Anusha said, then bit her lip as she heard her own betraying bitterness. For her pride's sake he must not think she cared.

'You think I was a substitute for you?' Nick got up and began to tie the legs of the game securely together. 'No. I was a distraction at first, I think, something for them to worry about together as they rediscovered each other. And then, when I confounded all the doctors and did not die, George grew to like me and to take an interest in my career. But you have always come first in his heart.'

He tightened the knots and hooked the limp bodies over the pommel of his horse, not seeming to hear her snort of derision. Did he think her a fool to believe that? If she had any value to her father, he would not have sent her away. He only wanted her now because she had become a political pawn in some violent game of chess.

'For Mary, I was almost a son, that is true. She had lost a child at birth and then was unable to have any more.'

'Is that why my father left her for all those years in England? Why did he not get another wife if she could not give him sons?'

'Because that is not legal in England. You must get a divorce and that is a ghastly process.'

'Then why did he not bring her to India?' Anusha demanded, determined to get to the bottom of this.

'They became…estranged after the child's death.

The doctors said there would be no more children. She would not come to India with him, so he provided for her financially and left her in England.' Nick swung up into the saddle and waited while she stood where she was, frowning up at him. 'They corresponded and somehow things healed with the years. Then she received a letter from his secretary when Sir George was very ill with fever and decided it was her duty to be with him.'

'My mother nursed him when he was ill,' Anusha flared. 'He was better before the letter could have reached her. That woman had no need to come and because she did, he sent us away.'

'She was his legal wife,' Nick said with what sounded like strained patience. 'Things are different in English society, the laws are different. If you want to know any more, you must ask him—I have no right to discuss it.'

Anusha mounted Rajat and sent him after Pavan with an impatience that made the black break into a canter. She reined him back, fuming. 'So you are not his son, you are his obedient servant?'

'Indeed,' Nick said, so placidly she could have slapped him. He was humouring her. She wanted to fight, to argue, to shout at him and she did not understand why. Her fight was with her father—if she did not manage to escape before he had her in his clutches again. She fell in behind the grey and glared at Nick's back. His very upright back.

He was good to look at, she admitted. His broad shoulders tapered to a narrow waist cinched by a dark blue sash; the skirts of his coat fell over the saddle, but she had seen his naked body and knew his buttocks were firm and shapely, his thighs long-muscled. He rode as though he and his horse were one, easy in the saddle and yet as focused as an archer before he loosed the bowstring.

'Stop sulking,' he said without looking back.

'I am not sulking,' Anusha retorted, startled to realise that she was not. *I am looking at your body and thinking that I desire you, that I would like to put into practice all those things that the texts show a woman and a man can do together...* Aghast, she blinked, as though that would turn him into a short fat clerk or a skinny youth or... No, Nick Herriard was still just as he had been when she closed her eyes and so was the hot, tight feeling low in her belly. She had to do something.

'*Ma ub gayi hu,*' she said and dug her heels into Rajat's flanks.

'Bored? You are *bored?*' she heard Nick say as she passed him. 'Hell, woman, what do you get up to in Kalatwah every day if you find this boring?'

'I find *you* boring,' she tossed back and slapped the reins on her mount's neck. For a moment she thought he would let her go, then the hoofbeats behind her speeded up, began to gain. Anusha glanced back over her shoulder—Nick had taken up the challenge and was racing.

'Little witch,' Nick muttered under his breath. He was tempted to let her go, gallop off her sulks and bad temper. If she had been a youth, he would have done just that, but, he thought with resignation, she was George's daughter and they were in tiger country and so—

'*Chalo chale,* Pavan!' The big grey needed no urging. He gathered his hocks under him and surged after his stable-mate. Damn it, but the girl could ride, she had not exaggerated. *I am Rajput, indeed,* he thought as he let her keep the lead for the moment. *She's going to be a handful to turn into a little English lady.*

He eased the reins and Pavan responded, up to the black's flank now, then his nose was level with the girth. Anusha looked across and grinned and kicked for more speed.

Nick looked at the strong, slim legs gripping the horse, remembered the feel of her hands, cool and hesitant on his bare skin, and shuddered as the wave of desire went through him. *No.*

His hands must have jerked. Pavan pecked, recovered and, with a triumphant little crow of laughter, Anusha urged Rajat ahead again. Then there was a sinuous movement in the dust before them, the black horse swerved violently and jumped clear over the lethal creature beneath its hooves.

Anusha was thrown sideways, landed out of the saddle, high on Rajat's neck, then fell, tumbling in the sand towards the king cobra that had reared up, hood spread, furious and lethal.

Chapter Six

Nick swung out of the saddle as Pavan reared to avoid the other horse. He rolled as he landed, his hand drawing the dagger from his boot even as he came to his feet. The reptile swayed, hissing, its hood spread wide, its head darting from side to side, undecided whether to strike at the nearer danger—Anusha sprawled motionless—or himself, moving, but further away.

'Lie still!' He waved his hand and the glittering eyes followed the movement, the coils shifting to balance the swaying, deadly head. Anusha was either unconscious or frozen in obedience, he could not tell. Nick edged further to the side, still gesturing with his hand, drawing the creature's attention from her body.

Then Anusha moaned and stirred, her fingers clenching into the sand. She must have been stunned, he realized, as the snake swayed back, raising itself to strike the closer figure. There was no time for subtlety or calculation. Nick launched himself into the narrow space between her body and the cobra, his left arm coming up to take the strike, his right swinging round to plunge the knife into the body below the hood as its fangs fastened on his wrist.

As it bit he slammed his left fist down on to the ground, taking the snake with it, pulled out the knife, struck again and ducked back instinctively as another knife flashed down past his shoulder to slash into the thick, writhing body. Nick wrenched his arm free from the fangs and fell back, pulling Anusha with him away from the creature's thrashing death throes.

'It bit you.' She twisted in his arms, tore at his sleeve. 'A tourniquet, hurry. Then we must cut the wound, squeeze—'

'It did not bite me.' Nick tried to get a grip on her, steady her so he could check her for injuries, but she pulled free and caught at his clothing, as intent on his wounds as he was on hers.

'Do not be a fool, of course it bit you. We have minutes at most. Less, if it caught a vein.' There was a thready note of panic beneath her sharp orders. Nick ripped back the sleeve so she could see his arm and the leather wrist band he wore to support an old injury when he was riding for long distances. 'Oh.' She touched the two deep indentations in the leather with a shaking finger. 'Did it go right through?'

Had it? With a sick twist in his gut Nick unlaced the strap. The skin beneath was marked by the pressure of the bite and she caught at it, stretched it smooth with both hands to check for punctures, then snatched up the leather and held it to the light.

'*Oh,*' she said again and swayed where she huddled

in the dust. 'But it might have missed the strap. It might have killed you.'

'And you might have broken your foolish little neck,' he snapped, his fear for her mixing with his body's re-action to the struggle with the cobra, that sickening re-alisation that it might have left its venom in his body. He hated snakes, would sooner face a tiger than a big king cobra, and his stomach was churning now. What if he had hesitated, had let that fear master him? Anusha would be dying in his arms now.

Stop it, he snarled inwardly. Imagining death slowed you down, got you killed. *You did not hesitate, you are both alive.*

The snake had ceased to twitch. Anusha was the only target for his feelings. 'What the devil were you playing at? Are you hurt? Have you broken anything?'

'No, I am not hurt. Why are you angry? I helped you, I had my knife—' Her turban had come off, her hair lay in a coil as thick as the great snake across her heaving breast and her face was paler than he had yet seen it. She still clasped his left forearm with both hands, then released it with a sob and burrowed into his lap as he sat on the crushed grass.

Instinctively his arms closed, cuddling her close. Against his body he could feel her, rounded and slen-der and trembling, and he smoothed his hand down her back, the fine hairs escaping from her plait catching on the roughed skin of his palms. Could she feel his heart pound, his pulse race? Was it the aftermath of the en-counter with the snake or something far more danger-ous, a response equally as primitive?

Lust burned through his veins, the desire to possess, to celebrate being alive, to bury the memory of that second when the flat black eyes had locked with his and he looked at his death. And he wanted her, wanted this woman who was an innocent and who must stay that way.

Anger was the only way to deal with it, anger at himself, anger at the woman in his embrace. 'What the hell are you doing with a knife? You are not safe out with a weapon.'

Anusha recoiled against the cage of his arms, the pressure of her squirming backside on his groin only inflaming both desire and temper even more. 'Of course I have a knife! You saw it when the maharaja's men came. And I can use it.' She was shaking still, but with shocked anger, not with fear now. 'They will not take me alive. I—'

'If they take you alive, someone can rescue you. If you are dead, you are dead and a lot of use that will be, except to start a war,' Nick snarled as he opened his arms and she fell with an undignified thump from his lap to the ground.

He got to his feet and pulled the knives from the limp body of the cobra. Hers was an expensive, deadly little gem with a damascene blade and a jeweled-ivory handle. He wiped it and stuck it in his boot next to his own. 'If you have lamed Rajat...'

'You cannot beat me. I am a princess,' she flashed at him, scrambling to her feet. Apparently his exasperation was all too clear on his face and she had remembered his empty threat to tan her backside.

'Then behave like one,' Nick said and bent to check the black's legs.

'Is he all right?' Anusha asked after a minute's crackling silence.

'Yes,' Nick conceded and made himself look at her. The turban was back in place, but she was still ashen and her lips were compressed tightly as though to hold back a sob or to stop herself shouting at him.

'You were afraid,' she said, a statement not a question. 'That is why you are angry with me.'

'Only a fool is not afraid of a king cobra,' he said flatly. If a man had accused him of fear, he would have struck him.

'I was not…I did not mean—' She broke off and shook her head, impatient with both of them. 'You did not hesitate for one second. *That* is what I meant. You were right to be afraid and yet you risked your life and killed it. My father sent a brave man for me.'

The wide grey eyes fixed on him and Nick felt the colour rise over his cheekbones as he fought the need to look away from the painful honesty in her gaze. If he walked across and took her in his arms, she would yield to him, he realised. Not out of wantonness or admiration for his actions, but because something had happened just now that stripped feelings bare and left only what was elemental and basic. Anusha was too brave and too honest to hide those feelings. And too innocent to know what they were, he told himself.

'Are you certain you are not hurt?' he asked as though nothing had been said since she asked him about the horse. Anusha nodded, her expression once more veiled and wary, that moment of burning clarity gone. She turned and he watched her closely as she walked across to take Rajat's reins and stroke his sweaty neck. She moved stiffly, but that was all.

'You...' she began, her face against the horse's shoulder. Then she pushed herself upright and turned to face Nick. 'You saved my life and I thank you for it.' The raw emotion was gone, and, as her chin came up and she looked at him, she was every inch a princess for all the dust and her travel-stained clothing.

Her courage doused the fierceness of his anger and the heat in his blood, but Nick could not find it in himself to be gracious. 'That is my job,' he said, his voice cool. 'To deliver you back alive and in one piece to your father.'

'You will not let me thank you?' She took the step that brought her toe to toe with him. 'They kiss to say *thank you*, the English, do you not?' With Pavan solid at his back he could not retreat. Anusha put her hands on his shoulders and stood on tiptoe, her body pressed against his. For an endless moment her mouth touched his, warm and soft.

Her lips parted slightly, an invitation he knew she did not understand. Time stood still while he fought the temptation to snatch her to him, plunder that beautiful mouth, lose himself in an innocence that wanted him. *Him.*

Instinct told him not to hurt her pride or give her a challenge. Hands at his side, he returned the pressure of her mouth, then raised his head. 'Unmarried young ladies of good family do not kiss men, I fear,' he said with a smile to take any sting from the words. His body tightened painfully, but he thought he had kept the desire from his face.

'No?' Her eyes were wide and very dark and the colour was up under the fine skin of her cheeks and temples. 'Then I will not do it again.'

'Good.' She was destined for marriage, this girl, not a dalliance. While he was briefing Nick for this mission Sir George had confided that he intended to make a good match for his daughter with an eligible Englishman. And he, Nick Herriard, soldier, adventurer, failure as a husband, was most definitely *not* eligible, even if he would ever be rash enough to give up his heart for another pounding.

He kept his voice light and amused as he turned to his horse. 'All I can say is that I have the deepest sympathy for the poor man who has to turn you into a young lady.'

'I am a young lady already.' Anusha pushed her foot into the stirrup and mounted, although not after a moment or two of undignified hopping about. She was more shaken than she let on. Behind that sharp tongue and fierce courage there was a vulnerability that made him want to protect her from whatever threatened—the maharaja, snakes… Men like himself.

Nick swung into the saddle. 'You are not an *English* young lady and that is what he will want you to be.'

'Hah! Corsets,' Anusha muttered.

'And curtsies and learning to dance and to converse with men at parties.' Nick had his temper under control again. He seemed positively amused, describing such indecent things as dancing with men, talking to them.

It was very dangerous to mix the sexes like that. She was discovering it only too vividly herself and this was just one man. Anusha gave herself a little shake. It was incredible how danger and a shock made one feel. For a moment back there every inhibition had vanished, leaving only a primitive urge to lie with this man, to roll naked in the dust with him. She could only hope he had not realised.

How did Englishwomen cope with this constant nearness to the opposite sex? But perhaps they were not really alone with them as she was with Nick, perhaps there were rules and older married women to stop things becoming…elemental.

But English women were allowed to fall in love, so Mama had told her. Even in Altaphur, for a lady of the court, one with influence, there was the possibility of choice. *Is that why I kept turning down those marriage offers? Did I think it would happen for me as it did for her?*

Apparently her mother had taken one look at her father and then acted in the most scandalous manner to make sure she met him. Anusha could not understand it. Her own first sight of an *angrezi* as an adult woman most certainly did not provoke any desire to place her entire future in his hands, whatever alarmingly lustful feelings he provoked. And her mother had done that foolish thing—she had fallen in love and thought George Laurens had too. Obviously he had not. Or he had fallen out of love, which proved how fickle men were. How cruel.

She urged Rajat up alongside the big grey so she did not have to look at Nick riding in front of her. That had been what had led to all this in the first place.

'I do not want to be an English lady,' Anusha stated.

'What do you want, then?' he asked, still tolerant. Anusha shot him a sideways glance, but his face was unsmiling.

'To travel.' It had never occurred to her before, but now, experiencing the freedom and the dangerous excitements of being free, it was as though she could see the entire world unrolling before her.

'Rich unmarried European ladies of rank travel alone, often in disguise, I have read of them. A Lady Montague, I think, and others. I will go to Europe and North Africa and the lands of the Middle Sea.' Moving on, not settling, meant she would never have to decide who she was, would never have to face not belonging anywhere.

'Eccentric spinsters,' Nick said with distaste. 'Rich ones with a bee in their bonnet. They end up sick and old, dying in some ramshackle castle, miles from family and friends, preyed upon by unscrupulous dragomen and fortune hunters.'

'Spinsters? That is an English word I do not know. Do ladies spin, then? And why would they have bees in their hats?' Bonnets she did understand. Mama had told her about ludicrous *angrezi* hats. And piles of false hair even when one had perfectly good hair of one's own and corsets to pinch you in and push you out and padding.

'Unmarried women who are on the shelf—beyond marriageable age—are called spinsters. And having a bee in your bonnet is to have a foolish obsession with something.'

'Hah! Well, I am not on a ledge, it is only that I do not choose to surrender myself to some man. And I have no bees in my hair. But when I have my money—'

'What money?' Nick enquired and this time when she glanced across at him she saw he was smiling, a quizzical smile that made her want to hit him.

'My father is a rich man, is he not? So I am rich. I am his only child.'

'He will make you an allowance, of course. When you marry a man he approves of, then he will settle money on you for your children.'

He was telling the truth. She had learned to believe what Nick said in that calm way he used when he was explaining things. So, she would have money, although there would be more when she married. And she had her jewels. There were not many, but they were very fine. And perhaps her father would feel guilty about the way he had treated her and her mother and she could persuade him to give her more money, more gems, enough to run away with.

It had been foolish to give Nick some hint of her plans, even if he mocked them and did not believe she could do it. 'Is it acceptable for a lady to be alone with a man as I am with you?' she asked after a few moments, the continuation of her earlier thoughts presenting a possible escape. Surely not, not when there was the possibility of a kiss like the one they had just shared.

He had hardly touched her and yet her heart was still beating too fast as she thought of it

'It is not. It is scandalous, but there is no need for anyone to know how you reached Calcutta,' Nick said. There was something in his voice, or perhaps the sudden tension in the long body, that warned her that she was on dangerous ground, but she did not understand why.

'Yes, but if they *did* know,' Anusha pressed, 'will they not think I am no longer a virgin and refuse to receive me?'

'Are you suggesting that it would be assumed that I would have ravished you?' Nick enquired, his tone so even that for a moment she missed the fury beneath it.

That was a way out of having to be turned into an English lady. 'Well, there might be suspicions…' Carelessly she had let the thought colour her voice and he picked up on it at once.

'And you would blacken my name, impugn my honour so that you could wriggle out of whatever plans your father has for you?'

There was no mistaking it now—he might as well have hit her over the head with a brass cooking pot to express his anger. 'I am sorry,' she stammered. 'It would be thought so very bad of you, then?'

'It would bar me from decent society and jeopardise my position in the army, besides causing me deep personal shame,' Nick said tightly. He was staring straight ahead between Pavan's ears but the colour slashed across his cheekbones like a warning flag. He was looking, sounding, very angry, almost as if she had pricked his conscience. Which was absurd because he was behaving just as he ought.

'Then I would never say anything about it,' Anusha hastened to assure him. This *angrezi* honour was a very different thing. Any Indian nobleman who had such an opportunity would snatch at it without hesitation, use her as a bargaining counter to secure concessions and riches from her uncle in return for marrying her once she had been compromised and shamed. They would think Nick a fool. He, it seemed, would consider them wicked and unprincipled. 'Only…someone must know we are together.'

'There will be a handful of people who will know that this journey did not take place with a full escort from your uncle. They will be left under the impression that I had my groom with me and you had a palace eunuch and a maid with you.' He appeared to be relaxing again a little.

'Then perhaps it would be better if we pretend that I am your brother,' she suggested. 'I am dressed like a youth. If we practise that, then we can enter Calcutta unobtrusively.' And it would make life much more comfortable. Nick made a sound that was halfway between a laugh and a snort. 'You do not think you can think of me that way?' True, she could not imagine him as a brother, either. 'Your sister, then?'

'I have no sister, so I do not know how to behave to one, but I can assure you, I find it hard to think of you in that role.' This time it was definitely a laugh, but one with an edge to it.

'No sisters? Brothers?'

'I am an only child, unless my father has remarried, although I doubt he would find anyone who would have him.'

'So your mother is dead?'

'Yes.' From the set of his jaw he did not appear to want her sympathy on that. She could understand it—when people sympathised with her about *Mata* she was hard pressed not to cry, even now.

'But then your father sent his only child away. Did he not desire to keep his heir by his side?' Nick had said his father had bullied and beaten him to make him come to India and had then forced him on to the ship.

'There was little to be heir to,' Nick said. 'My father is a second son so it was up to him to make his own way in the world. He could have gone into the army or the navy, the church or have made the small estate he inherited from an uncle into a larger one. He chose to marry a woman for her money and then to spend it on drink and gaming. She made the mistake of falling in love with him and spent the rest of her life breaking her heart over him.'

'His father must have been angry,' she ventured. It must have been dreadful growing up in such a household. It had been bad enough for *Mata*, but at least the break was final and she did not have to live with a man who abused her.

'My grandfather disowned him.'

Nick said it lightly as though it were no great matter, but Anusha sensed that it was, that it was like a black cloud somewhere in Nick's consciousness. 'Then why did your father not want to keep you with him? I would have thought—'

'I was no use to him and I criticised him,' Nick said. 'When my mother died I—' He broke off as though he realised he was betraying more of his secrets than he had intended. 'We quarrelled badly. I seem to have been a reproach to him whenever he looked at me. I took after my mother in looks, a little, and I was probably a sanctimonious brat.'

She still felt the pain of her father's rejection twelve years ago very deeply—how must it feel to have a father who spurned you, a grandfather who had cast his son, and therefore his grandson, away?

'Your grandfather is still alive? Is he an important man?'

'I suspect he will live for ever. He is sixty-eight now and, reports say, as tough as a whip. As for importance, he is a marquis. Like a maharaja, I suppose. A duke would be a very senior maharaja. A marquis comes next. Then an earl is a third-ranking nobleman—a raja.'

'So you are a milord?' *Mata* had tried to explain the English nobles to her, but it was very complicated and strange.

'No. I do not have a title. My father is styled the Honourable Francis Herriard. His elder brother uses my grandfather's second title, Viscount Clere—he is called Lord Clere. My grandfather is the Marquis of Eldonstone.' He glanced across at her and the expression on her face seemed to lift his mood, for he grinned at her. 'Confused?'

'Completely. Why are you not a prince?'

'Because only the sons of the king are princes and they are usually dukes as well.'

'But—' She broke off as Nick reined in and sniffed the air.

'I smell smoke.'

People, danger? Her dagger, the one in her boot that Nick had not found, was still there when she reached down and trailed her fingers unobtrusively over it, bracing herself for whatever was going to be thrown at them this time.

Chapter Seven

Nick inhaled deeply. 'There is a village ahead. I can smell cow dung burning.'

'Will it be safe?'

Please let him say it will be, pleaded the tired, frightened part of her mind, the part she was trying so hard to ignore. The thought of the company of other women, of being able to wash, to sleep on a bed, even if was only a crude *charpoy* with ropes threaded on a wooden frame, made her ache with longing. And this was only the second day.

Anusha stiffened her spine. She had boasted that she was *Rajput* and she would not show weakness even if Nick said this was not safe and they must spend the night in the open again with no food.

He sent her a flickering look. Reassurance or assessment? 'Let us hope so. This has been an eventful day and, speaking for myself, I have had about enough of it. We are a long way from any source of news here, they cannot have heard about us,' he added.

They saw the goats first, then the white humped

cattle. Small boys, sticks in hand, leapt up from where they crouched guarding the animals and dogs came skirmishing out, barking.

'*Are*!' Nick called. 'Where is your home?'

They crowded round, skinny in their skimpy loin cloths, all dark eyes and eager tongues, chattering in excitement and vying to point out their village to this man on horseback who towered above them. He was surely a raja, Anusha heard them say, a great warrior with his firearms.

'Do many men on horseback come this way?' she asked, leaning down to speak to the tallest lad.

'*Nahi.* Not for many months, not since the tax collectors came before the rains.'

Nick caught her eye and nodded approval of the question. Their pursuers had not visited here—they were safe for a night at least.

'We are travellers,' he said. 'Will you take us to your headman?'

The boys broke into a run, streaming ahead of them, the dogs yapping. The village appeared behind a low bluff of land: a dozen or so round huts of mud brick, their roofs thatched with thin branches and straw, the whole surrounded by a mud-brick wall, mended here and there with bundles of thorn.

Women were gathered round a well and they turned, pulling their veils across their faces with one hand as they balanced the big copper water vessels on their heads with the other. Their clothes were vivid crimson and orange and sharp, acid green. The men clustered in the gateway, the boys falling silent as the headman walked forwards to deal with this unexpected visitation.

He was bent, thin-shouldered, but had once been tall. His drooping white moustaches fell below his chin and his turban was huge, a construction of twisted white-cloth ropes coiled together.

Nick swung out of the saddle, dropped the reins and put his hands together. *'Namaste.'* Anusha followed his example, waiting behind him as the greeting was returned.

'We come from the west,' Nick said in his clear, idiomatic Hindi. 'We travel to the Jumna to sail down to meet the Mother Ganga and we seek shelter for the night.'

There were murmurings and much gesticulating at the mention of the sacred River Ganges. The villagers would feel they had gained merit by helping pilgrims.

'Welcome.' The headman's rheumy eyes studied Nick and then turned to her as she stepped to his side, pulling the tail of her turban across her nose and mouth—she had no wish to offend.

'This lady is under my protection. I take her to her father,' Nick said.

They were too polite to stare or to speculate. The group parted, ushering them into the compound, and the headman called to the women, 'Wife! Daughters! Make our guests welcome.'

Anusha expected to be hurried off out of sight, but the headman was speaking to Nick as he led him towards the largest hut.

'You will drink opium?' Nick turned to her.

It was a traditional welcome in the villages, she knew that, although she had never been offered it. 'You use opium?' she asked.

'Smoke it, do you mean?' He looked at her and grimaced as though at an unpleasant memory. 'I have done. I think in my time I must have tried everything that this land offers that is supposed to lead to forgetfulness. But, no, I do not smoke it now—the dreams it gives lead nowhere. Like this it is harmless. The most it will do is ease your tiredness and your bruises a little.'

They sat down cross-legged on a straw mat opposite the headman, flanked by two men who looked enough like him to be his sons. With the studied care of a ritual he placed a dark-brown substance into a small cloth funnel on a stand, then poured in water. As it drained through into a boat-shaped wooden vessel below, one of the others poured it into the cloth funnel on the other side of the stand. It took some time, the careful pouring and collection, re-pouring... Anusha began to feel lightheaded. Perhaps that was part of it, part of the process to relax the weary guest.

Finally the old man seemed satisfied. He poured a little of the liquid over the little metal Shiva *lingam* in the centre of the stand, then cupped his right hand, filled it and extended it to Nick. Nick bent forwards and sucked the liquid directly from the side of the wrinkled palm.

The man gestured to him and Nick held out his own right hand, cupped to receive a trickle of the liquid, then turned to her. 'Drink.'

Anusha bent forwards as he had done and touched her mouth to the side of his palm below his little finger. Under her lips the flesh was warm, yielding; the touch seemed sensual and intimate. A gesture of trust.

'Suck,' he murmured, so she did, swallowing the bitter liquid, his hand tipping so that her lips moved against his palm. Her tongue came out, just the tip to catch the final drop, and she looked up and saw his eyes, dark and fixed on her face. Slowly, she leaned back, her gaze still locked with his.

The headman coughed. Nick turned, bowed his head. '*Dhanyvad.*' Anusha bowed too, echoing the thanks. 'Go now,' he murmured. 'The women are here for you.'

Anusha woke, disorientated and stiff, on a thin mattress of quilted cotton. Ropes creaked under her as she shifted and her nostrils were filled with the smells of cooking, of cattle, of dried-dung fires.

They were in a village, she recalled as she sat up and looked around her, squinting into the shadowy boundaries of the round hut.

'You are awake?' The soft voice behind sounded wary. Anusha twisted around and smiled at the elderly woman standing just inside the door. She must seem strange and shocking to her, a woman in youth's clothing.

'Yes. I slept well.' The woman came further in and, from the quantity of bangles and the size of her nose ring, Anusha realised she must be one of the headman's wives. 'Thank you for your hospitality, you are very kind.'

The woman made a gesture with her hands—hospitality to travellers was expected. 'Where are your woman's clothes?' she asked.

'I have none. I had to leave them behind.'

'This man, this *angrezi* who speaks like us, he is your lover?' The woman sat down on the end of the *charpoy*, wariness replaced by lively curiosity.

'No! I mean, he is my escort. My bodyguard to take me to my father. There is a man who would marry me by force and I...my father does not want him to wed me.' It hurt her pride to use her father as an excuse, but it was an explanation that would make sense to the other woman.

'Ah. My name is Vahini. What is yours?'

Anusha thought of lying. But what was the point? 'Anusha. And he is Herriard *sahib*.'

There was whispering outside. 'Come, then. Our visitor is awake,' Vahini called and the hut was filled with a dozen women of all ages, all staring. 'This is Anusha and she has no women's clothes and she flees from a bad man to her father.' There was much sympathetic muttering.

'I could not carry clothes, I had to run away very quickly,' Anusha explained.

That provoked tutting and shaking of heads. Then one of the younger women stood up. 'She is of my size. It is not right that she is with a man and has to dress as a youth.'

'I cannot ride as a woman,' Anusha protested as the speaker left the hut.

'But when you are not travelling, then he should look

on you as a woman,' one of the others said. 'If he looks at all. It is only fitting. Padma will have something.'

When Padma returned, her arms were full of cloth. 'You must wear this tonight,' she said, shaking out a deep-blue *kurta, lehenga* and red trousers. There were sandals as well, and a gauzy red veil and a long blue scarf.

Anusha looked at their faces. They were poor. These were probably Padma's best clothes out of very few, perhaps they were her wedding clothes. She had no gift to reciprocate with, only gem stones, and they were of no use to villagers miles from anywhere and who would probably be cheated if they tried to sell them.

'That is very kind and these are beautiful,' she said as she ran her hand over the intricate metallic embroidery around the hems. 'When I reach my father's house I will have them returned to you with a gift from my heart in thanks.'

'Then we will bring water and you may wash,' Vahini announced, her words sending some of the younger women scurrying out. 'And you can tell us all about yourself. How many years do you have?'

Washing and changing was obviously going to be a public performance. Anusha put a brave face on it—to be clean she was prepared to answer any number of questions.

The women gathered together around the cooking hearths, the firelight flickering across their faces, gleaming off nose rings, bangles and the flash of a smile. Behind, in one of the huts, a child whimpered in its sleep and someone got up to go to it. Others moved back and forth, bringing water, chopping vegetables, carrying food to the men who sat before the headman's hut.

She felt soothed and yet also emotional. The way these women lived was so distant from her own mother's privileged, cultured life, but they had gathered her to them like a long-lost daughter. It had been like talking to *Mata* again. They had asked about her suitors, told her about marriage settlements for the younger women, laughed about their husbands, teased her gently about Nick.

Paravi was a good friend and yet she could not talk to her as she had to her mother. And of course, these women, kind and motherly as they were, were not the same. *Mata* had died a year ago of a sudden fever. One day she had been there, strong, intelligent, passionate. The next, gone. In the last few hours before she had sunk into unconsciousness, she had held Anusha's hand, her speech rambling and faint.

'Love, Anusha,' she had muttered. 'It is life. It is the only thing. Even if it breaks your heart. Love…'

Sometimes love sounded wonderful, worth pain, worth loss. And sometimes it seemed too dangerous, too much of a risk. *Oh,* Mata, *I wish you were here to talk to.*

Anusha found her vision was blurred, blinked to clear it and realised she was looking at Nick, sitting cross-legged on a mat beside the headman at the centre of the male group. They were all smoking thin black cheroots that she suspected had come from his saddlebags and discussing something with much animation, but also careful attention so that each gave his opinion.

Nick said something, straight-faced, and there was a gale of laughter, echoed by the boys who were hiding behind the hut, watching their elders. Someone called out to them and they ran off.

At last the food was laid out, the cheroots stubbed into the dust and the men began to eat. Only then did the women gather round their own fire and begin their meal. Careful of her borrowed clothes, Anusha sat where she could watch Nick from beneath the hem of her veil as she lifted it to eat. He was so at ease, so relaxed, that it was hard to remember that he was one of the Company, a foreign soldier and the ally of the father who had rejected her.

'He is a fine man, that one,' someone said, low-voiced, and the women moved their heads in the sinuous shake of agreement that the *angrezi* never seemed to master. Except Nick—he could do it, she realised. 'He moves like one of us,' the woman added as if reading her mind. 'He is a warrior.'

'Yes,' Anusha agreed. 'He is a brave and skilful fighter.' And a wise one, she thought, recalling the way he had eluded the maharaja's troops.

'Perhaps your father would give you to him,' another voice suggested. 'He would make you fine sons.'

'No!'

Nick looked up, unerringly at her, even though she was veiled and he could not know what she was wearing. Shaken, Anusha dropped the hem of her veil, her breath suddenly tight in her chest.

A warrior, brave and skilful. A handsome man, despite his unfamiliar looks and those uncanny green eyes. A kind man, for all his imperious orders. A man who showed respect equally to a raja and a humble villager. It felt like the bars of a lock sliding into place, each with a click in her brain. You learned early to pick locks in the *zanana* to find treasures and secrets. Was Nick Herriard a treasure, one that she wanted to hold, to possess?

'He does not want a wife,' she replied. *It cannot be him.* Which was a good thing, for however much she might desire that man—and the ache low in her belly and the tingling that went through her when he touched her told her that she *did* desire him—she feared him also.

He would deliver her to her father and then he would watch her like her father's hunting hound, alert for any attempt to escape, for she had been foolish enough to let him glimpse her hopes and dreams. If she was foolish enough to fall in love with him, then she would make herself as vulnerable as her mother had done, for this man was so like her father: strong, independent, arrogant in his self-confidence. If he wanted something, he would go after it, if he no longer wanted it, then no sentiment would stop him rejecting it.

But even if he did desire her his duty to her father would keep him from acting on it. *It cannot be him*, she repeated to herself and shivered a little at the loneliness that crept upon her. She would be trapped in the alien world of the *angrezi,* amongst people who knew that her mother had not been married to her father and who would despise her for it, amongst people who expected her to wear those horrible clothes and follow their alien ways and she would never be free. Never belong.

The food was eaten, the dishes cleared. Anusha tried to help and was pressed back into her place, a guest. It would never have occurred to her to so much as hand a plate to a maid in the palace. Now she saw the thin, work-worn hands of the women who shared their food with her and felt ashamed to be waited on. 'Please, let me do something.'

The woman nearest her smiled and went into her hut, came out with the fretful baby in her arms and offered it to Anusha. She cradled it cautiously and clucked her tongue at it. The small face wrinkled up, prepared to wail, then the child thought better of it and stared instead. Anusha stared back, then stroked its cheek with one finger. It wriggled its hand free of the wrappings and curled minute fingers around hers.

She began to croon to it, rocking it back and forth, soothed by the warm weight in her arms. All too soon its mother returned, smiling, and took her sleeping baby back to lay it in the hut and a pang went through her. Freedom and no husband meant no children, no baby of her own to cradle, no tiny hand curling trustfully into hers. Heat pricked at the back of her eyes and Anusha took a deep, shuddering breath. Where had that come from, that fierce desire for a child? Honesty gave her the answer—it had come with her awareness of Nick, her desire for him. Their children would be tall, golden-skinned, pale-eyed, brown-haired. They would be hostages to fortune, she reminded herself. Just as she had been.

The rhythm of drumbeats had her starting up, tense and ready to run, before she realised that it was the patter of hand drums from amidst the circle of men. Anusha relaxed back and the drumbeats settled into a pattern, a *tala* of sixteen beats. The other men began to clap on the correct beats: one, five, thirteen with a wave of the hand on the empty beat, nine.

The women shifted round in their places to watch, clapping too, and one of the men got up and began to dance, his bare feet slapping on the hard earth, his body twisting and swaying. Another man stood, then two more and the drumming became stronger as another musician joined in. Anusha realised it was Nick, his hands moving over the taut skins of the *tabla* as though he had known this music from birth.

'Come,' Vahini said. The women rose and began to dance too, out of sight of the men, their skirts whirling out into multi-coloured bells as they spun round. Anusha did not need a second invitation. Her lingering aches and pains, the tinge of melancholy over the baby, the unsettling desire for Nick—all vanished in the familiar intoxication of dance.

She looked up as she joined crossed hands with the woman opposite her, whirling round in the centre of the circle of clapping dancers. She leaned back and the stars spun above her in the deep-blue velvet of the heavens and the smoke curled up and somewhere, out beyond the village, a jackal howled, infinitely lonely.

The beat of the drums became her pulse—the pulse

of desire and the need to dance for Nick, a thing she must not do, a thing only fit for a courtesan or a nautch-girl.

The laughter of the women was clear over the drum-beats. One of them was singing, a song without words, to mark the *raga*, the melody, of the music. Nick glanced across, careful not to stare or cause offence, but they were hidden behind the huts, only their shadows, thrown by the firelight, danced against the walls.

Anusha was dancing with them—he heard her laugh and take up a snatch of the song. How he knew it was her voice he could not have said. He had never heard her sing, or, he realised with a shock, laugh out loud. But she was there, happy for a short while. She had never known poverty or simplicity like this before and yet she was at home here. Would she ever laugh like that after George had her turned into an English lady?

He almost missed a beat and caught himself, focused on the taut skin under his fingertips. She was an un-married woman and her place was with her father, and then her husband. The Indian world she had known for twelve years was no longer safe for her.

Then why was there this nagging uncertainty at the back of his mind? He lost track and threw up a hand in apology as the dancer shot him a reproachful look. He was feeling sorry for the girl, that was all. She would settle soon enough with a husband and babies. Some-one began to sing, a love song, yearning and sensual. Nick let his hands follow the new, subtle, rhythm run-ning beneath the *tala*. The beat echoed his pulse, the pulse became a need, an uncomfortably insistent physical demand.

Damn the woman. She was doing nothing overt to tease him sexually—she was too inexperienced for that, whatever her theoretical knowledge, and yet he could feel her as though she sat next to him running those long cool fingers down his back, down his legs— With a cry from the singer the dance ended. Nick fought for control, thankful for the *tabla* in his lap, hiding his embarrassing state of arousal.

'Aye!' the man sitting next to him exclaimed. 'You will dance now?'

'No.' Nick shook his head. 'No, I cannot dance.' What he wanted now was his bed, a flask of *raki* and oblivion, but he was not going to get it, he knew. It would be poor return for the villagers' hospitality if he left now.

'Sing, then,' the man urged.

None of the songs he knew in Hindi were fit to be sung within women's hearing—they were camp songs, marching songs. 'Very well,' he said. 'I will sing in English for you.'

That provoked a buzz of interest. Nick tapped out the tune on the little drum then,

Our 'prentice Tom may now refuse
To wipe his scoundrel master's shoes,
For now he's free to sing and play
Over the hills and far away...

Chapter Eight

The queen commands and we'll obey,
Over the hills and far away.
We all shall lead more happy lives
By getting rid of brats and wives
That scold and bawl both night and day
—over the hills and far away.

At dawn the words of the song still ran around Anusha's head as she dressed in her riding gear and folded the borrowed clothes carefully into her pack.

So that was what Nick thought of wives and children, was it? She should have guessed, instead of feeling sorry for him that his wife was dead. Probably he had been grateful for the freedom, if he would but admit it.

As she came out of the hut he was whistling the same tune. Anusha marched over to the horses and dumped her pack at his feet. 'Is that what the *angrezi* call music?'

'Yes.' He had washed his hair and it was still wet, clinging to his head in the sunlight as it dried patchily into fairness again. 'What is the matter with you this morning? Did you get out of the wrong side of the bed or have you been drinking *raki* with your new friends all night and have a hangover?'

He was talking incomprehensible rubbish. What difference did it make what side of the bed she got out of? And what would she be hanging over?

'Neither. And that is not proper music.'

'It is soldiers' music.' Nick strapped the pack onto the saddle. 'Have you eaten?'

'I have.' She turned her back on him and frowned at the huts, the villagers going about their morning business. 'This is a poor village.'

'I am sorry I could not find you a better one, Princess.'

'I do not mean that!' Anusha swung round and stumbled over her own feet. Nick steadied her with a hand on each arm and raised an eyebrow in a particularly infuriating manner. 'I mean that we have taken food they can ill afford.'

He nodded. 'But we cannot refuse hospitality and I cannot give them the money I need to get you home.'

Home? Hardly, she thought. But there were aspects of it she could exploit. 'I will have my father send them a cow in calf.'

'A what? How the devil do you expect Sir George to transport a pregnant cow halfway across Rajasthan?'

She shrugged and his big hands slid up and down her arms, trailing shivers in their wake. 'Your wonderful East India Company can do anything. No doubt someone will work it out if the important Sir George Laurens commands it.'

His long fingers tightened, banding her upper arms. 'What has put the vinegar on your tongue this morning, Anusha? I had hoped that female company, food, a good night's sleep would put you in a better mood.'

'Nothing is wrong with my mood. You had best look to your hair—it is dry and the wind is tangling it.' As she spoke it blew across his face and he let go with one hand to swipe at it. 'Oh, leave it to me.' A strand had tangled in his eyelashes which were thick, and far too long, in her opinion. They hid his feelings all too well when he chose to lower them. 'Stand still.'

Nick did as she asked, uncharacteristically obliging, while she reached up and brushed the hair from his face, caught the final strands between finger and thumb, then pushed it back to the sides of his face with her palms. 'Where is the cord to tie it?'

'In my pocket.' He rummaged while she stood there and tried not to think about the strong bones of jaw and cheek, the way his hair felt like raw silk, the faint prickle of stubble on cheeks that had doubtless been shaved hurriedly in cold water. They were standing very close, her face tipped up to his so she could see what she was doing. If she slid her hands into his hair, took half a step closer and he bent his head…

'Got it. You can let go now.' There were traces of colour over his cheekbones when she lifted her hands and stepped back. Warmth from her skin—or was her closeness responsible for it? Surely not—Nick had managed to control any amorous instincts she might provoke with unflattering ease so far.

'Say your goodbyes, we are going now.' He turned

on his heel with the precision of a soldier and strode off to the headman's hut. Anusha glared after him, then caught Vahini's sympathetic gaze. The other woman rolled her eyes and lifted her hands, palms up. The gesture needed no words. *Men!*

By the time she had made her farewells Nick was mounted, his hair hidden beneath a turban again. 'Come on, we did not get up at dawn in order to linger here until the sun was hot.'

That was something she recalled from her days living in her father's house—the European obsession with punctuality and time. There was one clock in the palace in Kalatwah, and a man who carefully wound it, but no one looked at it for the time, only enjoyed the wonderful whirling works and the chimes. What did a minute, or thirty, matter? The sun was guide enough to the routines of the day.

The boys ran with them for half a mile, the dogs barking at their heels, jaunty tails curled over their backs. When their followers fell back Nick raised a hand in salute and kicked Pavan into a canter. Anusha looked back, but they had been swallowed up by the rolling landscape and she and Nick were alone again.

'You never showed me how to load a musket,' Anusha said when Nick brought down some hares for their supper the next day.

'No more I did. We got distracted talking of my coming to India, if I recall.'

And about my father rejecting Mata *and me and that woman he called his wife coming to take our place.*

Anusha schooled her face to show none of her thoughts. 'That is so. You will show me now?'

'Very well.' He tied the hares to the saddle bow and rested all three muskets against a tree. 'I will do this one, you follow what I am doing with one of the others. You take a cartridge, like so.' She fished one out of the pouch. 'And bite the end off.' Anusha grimaced at the bitter taste of the black powder. 'No, don't swallow it, spit if you have to. Tip a little into the pan, like this. Lower the hammer—don't bang it down!—then tip the rest down the barrel with the bullet and the wad and pull out the ramrod.'

He waited patiently while she struggled to pull out the long rod, her hands ending up over her head before she found she could stand on a rock for the extra height. 'And ram down the charge. Take out the ramrod—unless you have run out of bullets and want to spear the enemy—put it back. There, you have loaded a musket.'

'It was very slow,' she grumbled.

'Indeed, we would have been overrun by the enemy or eaten by the tiger by now. Try again.'

'I need more practice,' Anusha lamented when the second musket took almost as long as the first. 'You do it so fast.'

'I was drilled in it until I could load in the heat of battle or in total darkness. Even on an elephant.' Nick took the weapon back from her and ran his hand down over the barrel, down the polished stock, like a lover caressing a woman. 'Like all things, it needs practice.' He glanced up. 'Now what have I said to put you to the blush?'

Practice. 'Nothing!' Of course making love needed practice as well, not just the theory gained from looking at books and listening to the married women. She would be hopelessly clumsy at first—her foolish daydreams about Nick catching her in his arms and being enraptured by her sensual skills were just that, foolish. And, of course, if he did try such a thing, common sense would take over and she would push him away, slap his face, remind him of who he was and who she was. 'Nothing at all.'

And she did not want him to make love to her anyway, not really. He might be beautiful to look at, but he was her father's man and he had no sympathy for her at all. Perhaps Nick was jealous of her. She pondered the idea as he slid the muskets back into their sheaths on the saddles. He had been like a son to her father all these years and now a real child of Sir George would be in his home.

'Do you enjoy fighting?'

'Yes,' he said without hesitation.

'Killing?'

'Not for itself, no. If the enemy would all surrender or run away, I would be very happy, but if they want to kill me, then…' He shrugged. 'I find satisfaction in the politics of war, the use of strength to gain power and then build on it. But I enjoy doing that by talking and dealing just as much as by fighting.'

'You would have been a very poor clerk,' she observed as they moved off again.

'Indeed I would. Sir George saw that, too—you both know me better than my own father did.'

'Perhaps he did not realise when you were so young that you would want to be a warrior.'

'Perhaps. I certainly did not.' They fell silent as the horses began to pick their way down a slope towards what must be a stream, its water hidden by thick foliage and trees.

'Where are we?'

'About seventy-five miles west of Sikhandra. If we keep going in this direction, we will find the Jumna River just above or below that town, then we can take a boat down to the confluence with the Ganges and then down to Calcutta.' Nick spoke absently, his head moving as he scrutinised the land ahead and then the increasingly soft ground beneath their horses' hooves.

'What are you looking for?'

'Tiger.'

'Oh.' It came out as a squeak and Anusha turned it into a cough. She had seen many tiger hunts, but only with scores of armed men, beaters, elephants and stout stockades for the watchers. Out here she felt as though slitted amber eyes were already fixed on her unprotected back.

'I am comforting myself with the thought that a tiger is likely to be at least as scared of us as we are of it,' Nick remarked.

'*You* are scared?' That was no help at all. She did not want Nick to be capable of being scared of anything. He had admitted to being frightened of the cobra, she recalled. But he had killed it anyway, without hesitation. Soldiers must be afraid a lot of the time and have to learn to ignore it. She wished she could.

'Oh, yes,' he said with a cheerfulness that had her glaring at his back as her stomach swooped. They were in tall grass now, over the heads of the horses. 'There could be anything in here—rhino, buffalo, tiger, leopard. Keep talking nice and loudly.'

Her mouth felt as dry as dust. Anusha groped for something to say as Pavan plunged down the stream bank and up the other side. 'Look.' Nick pointed down at the mud. 'Tiger spoor.' The paw prints looked enormous.

'I wish I was on an elephant,' Anusha confessed as they rode up the other side.

'That,' Nick agreed drily, 'makes two of us. The grass is getting shorter though.'

'What do we do if one attacks us?' She tried to speak as lightly as he did.

'I kill it with great skill and bravery while you ride in the opposite direction as fast as you can.'

That was comforting. 'Have you killed many tigers?'

'This would be the first.'

Oh. 'Are you not supposed to be reassuring me by telling me there is no danger and you have it all under control?' she enquired, despising herself for the fact that her hand shook on the reins.

'If you were an empty-headed chit, I would, yes. As it is, you'd see right through that and, if you are on edge, then that's two of us watching like hawks. There,' he added as they came out of the tall grass on to the higher, drier ground, 'We can see for miles now.'

Anusha let out her breath in one *whoosh* of relief. 'Is an empty-headed chit like a totty-headed female?'

'More or less.' He was grinning, the wretch. 'I said you appeared to have your father's brains.'

'I have my mother's. She was an educated and intelligent woman!'

'Remind me to start you on the subject the next time we are in heavy cover,' Nick said, digging his heels into his horse's flanks. 'If you had made that much noise back there, every tiger for forty miles would have headed for the hills.'

'Oh! You…you…*man*!' But he was already almost out of earshot. Anusha gathered the reins and sent her mount after his. Insolent, scheming, manipulative man. He had deliberately played on her nerves back there. He should be cosseting her, soothing her fears, treating her like a lady. Seething, she rode on.

They had spent another night in the open on an island in a small river, another day untroubled by tigers or pursuing troops, then a night in an abandoned herder's hut. Anusha stretched as she rose at dawn, wanting warm water and hot food and a pile of soft cushions.

Nick was boiling water for the usual strong tea that she was learning to tolerate, if not like. He had been restless the night before and had left her to sleep alone in the hut. She heard him padding around outside every time she woke and there were faint blue shadows like thumbprints beneath his eyes.

'Did you not sleep last night?' she asked. She squatted down beside him and studied his face. 'You look tired.' She did not want to think of him having any vulnerabilities, it made him too real.

'I dozed.' Nick shifted and stood up as she lifted a hand to touch the lines of strain at the corner of his eye. He had become more taciturn over the past twenty-four hours, she realised. Anusha searched her memory for anything she had done to anger him, but could find nothing. Perhaps he was simply bored with her company, tired of this journey. He stopped kicking at the fire and glanced at her, frowning. 'We should be near the Jumna by now.'

'That is good, isn't it?' Anusha ventured.

'Yes,' he agreed. 'Of course. Never mind my mood, I am just…distracted.'

I am just bloody randy, Nick thought with deliberate crudity in an attempt to shock himself into focus. But it was more than that—he didn't want to have *a* woman, any woman. He wanted this one, and for more than a tumble. He wanted to make love to her, slowly. He wanted to uncover those long limbs, that honey-coloured skin, unbind the thick plait the colour of toffee and teak. He wanted to lose himself inside her slender, strong body. *That innocent body*, he reminded himself as he had throughout the long, restless night pacing around the hut while Anusha slept inside.

The urge to seduce her warred with the instinct to protect her. He had felt it with Miranda, although his wife, whom he failed, had simply expected it, whereas Anusha alternately spurned his offers of help or pretended to berate him for scaring her with tigers.

For some reason, while he had found it easy enough to lie beside her in the open, the enclosed hut felt dangerously intimate and, once the thought had got hold of his imagination, his body had done the rest to ensure a sleepless night. No amount of reminding himself what a wilful, haughty, unpredictable—and completely untouchable—female she was helped in the slightest.

And, worst of all, perhaps, in the small hours, came the suspicion that the ache he was feeling was not just desire, but loneliness. He wanted to reach out to something within her that she was not prepared to let him touch.

The landscape was every shade of grey and violet in the pre-dawn light. As they rode, it gradually brightened and the colours intensified until the river valley was plain before them. There were the craggy hills behind, still purple in the shadow of sunrise, the lush green fringing the watercourse, the short-cropped grass and scrub where village flocks had eaten their fill. In the distance, downriver, there was a haze of smoke marking a town or a big village.

A buffalo cart loaded with sugar cane creaked across the rough track ahead. '*Namaste!*' Nick called to the driver. 'What place is that, brother?' He pointed downriver. 'Is it a big town? Can we find a boat there?'

'It is Kalpi, brother, and only one or two *kos* away,' the man said and pondered the other questions. 'Yes, it is big, for they make sugar there and there is much trade. Assuredly you will find many boats.'

Nick waved his thanks and turned Pavan to take the track downstream. 'Almost there, then. Have you been on a river before?'

'No, only the lake. Is it pleasurable?'

'It can be,' Nick said with some caution. Goodness knows what they would find to hire or buy. Something with separate sleeping accommodation for Anusha, that was certain. He wasn't spending more than a week cooped up at night with this woman, her big, questioning grey eyes and soft, inquisitive hands and his own aching loins. Not if he could help it.

They were closer to the river now and it spread across perhaps half a league, its numerous channels braiding into loops and sandbanks. They would have the current to help them down, but he'd need someone who knew the river over a good distance, not simply a local boatman—

What is that? In front. Movement jerked him from a mental list of things to be done and back, with a jolt, to the present. Three men came out of the trees to the right, two on foot, one on a horse. Nick twisted in the saddle: two more men on foot behind them. The river cut sharply into the bank to their left, to the right the land rose to a heavily forested bluff. They had ridden right into an ambush.

'Dacoits.' He drew his sabre. 'Stay behind me and don't stop, whatever happens. I'm going to ride them down.'

One of the men on foot knelt, lifted something to his shoulder.

'And keep low—they have guns!' He sent Anusha a rapid glance, saw the dagger in her hand and then kicked Pavan straight at the man with the musket. It would spoil his aim, he would get up and run—

The blow, the pain, came before the sound of the

shot. Nick reeled in the saddle, grabbed for the pommel, his left shoulder on fire. He hung on grimly, locked his fingers and raised the sabre. Pavan, trained to battle, rode right into the gunman, lethal hooves slashing, then turned, answering the pressure of Nick's knees, to charge the horseman. A sweep of the sabre and the man was screaming, clutching his face where blood streamed down, before spurring for the forest.

There did not seem to be any sound. As if time had slowed, Nick hauled on Pavan's reins and the excited horse spun again. Anusha had ridden Rajat straight at the third man and the black was rearing, lashing out. Behind them the remaining dacoits were running for cover.

Rajat's front hooves hit the ground and the terrified man scrambled to his feet and dived into the brush. Anusha turned, her face white, the dagger clenched in her raised fist. There was blood on it. He saw her lips move, but he could not hear what she was saying. The pain in his shoulder was monstrous, a beast dragging at nerve and muscle with savage claws.

'Go!' he managed to shout. 'Ride for the town!' But she paid no heed. Perhaps he had made no sound, Nick thought as the forest tilted. Something was wrong, the ground shouldn't be…

Chapter Nine

We have done it! With a cry of triumph on her lips Anusha twisted in the saddle, brandishing her knife. Five dacoits and she had helped Nick rout them!

Then she saw him fall across Pavan's neck, the dark blue of his coat stained black over his heart, and her own heart seemed to stutter and stop. *'No!'* She spurred Rajat forward. 'Nick!'

The gelding reached its stable mate before Nick toppled to the ground and the horses seemed to know what to do, perhaps trained for this, she thought distractedly as she reached for the limp body that Rajat's shoulder was supporting. With a heave, and strength she did not know she possessed, she got Nick back in the saddle and breathed again when he moved under her hands.

'Thank you, Lord Krishna,' she gasped as she steadied him. 'He lives.' She gave him a little shake. 'Nick, can you hold on? I dare not dismount, they might come back.'

'Yes.' He dragged his eyes open with a visible effort. 'Stop the bleeding...'

Anusha tore open her saddle bag and pulled out a linen shirt, worn for two days, but the best thing she had within reach. The horses stood like rocks while she fumbled Nick's coat open. There seemed to be blood everywhere, but when she put her hand on his back it was dry. 'The bullet's still in there,' she said as she stuffed the linen under his shirt. 'Can you hold that?'

He grunted, so she turned Rajat, Pavan wheeling with him as though understanding the need to keep Nick within her reach. But he managed to stay upright in the saddle, one hand on the reins, the other pressed to his shoulder. He was doing it by sheer will-power, as far as she could see—his face was white under the tan, his eyes unfocused.

Anusha smelled the town before they reached it. The thick, cloyingly sweet smell of boiling sugar filled the air and they began to pass small sugar-mills along the side of the road with pairs of oxen yoked to a beam that turned the crushing wheels while men pushed in the canes.

'These look honest people. We must stop.'

'No.' She leaned from the saddle to catch the muttered words. 'The town…there'll be a Company agent.'

That was true. Anusha fought the instinct to get help, any help, as quickly as possible and rode on. A qualified doctor and someone of influence, that was what they needed. She began to call to people as they passed and the road became busier, lined with market stalls, an encampment of gypsy tinsmiths, more sugar-mills. They all pointed onwards.

Assuredly there was an *angrezi*, at least six of them,

came the replies. Where? At the big house or at the sugar-boiling place or perhaps at the riverside. Who could tell what the *angrezi* would do?

There was no one, *no one* in this bustling, stinking chaos, she thought in despair and then, suddenly in front of her, there was figure wearing a broad straw hat, head and shoulders above the crowd.

Anusha urged Rajat forward, shouting in English, abandoning Nick to catch the man before he vanished into some side street. 'Sahib! Sir! Help, please, for an officer of the Company who is hurt!'

The man started, frowned at her and pushed forwards, the bearers at his back hurrying with him. 'An officer? Where, boy?'

'There!' She pointed and the men ran and caught Nick as he slid, completely unconscious, into their arms.

'The bullet will have to come out, of course. As soon as possible.' The cadaverously thin doctor stood looking down at Nick, hands on hips as though sizing up a choice cut of meat on the butcher's block. His patient was laid out, stripped to the waist, on the agent's best spare bed on to which he was bleeding sluggishly.

'Not yet.' Nick opened his eyes and Anusha sat down with a thump on the nearest chair, ignored by the entire household. She had thought he was dying, dead, if it had not been for that steady soak of blood, yet he could speak. She scrubbed the back of her hand across her eyes and tried not to sniff.

'And why not, might I ask?' Doctor Smythe was already reaching for his instrument case.

'Because it is going to take some digging. I don't think I am going to be at my best when you've finished and there are things I need to organise first.'

'There is nothing you need to organise!' Anusha exploded from the corner and pushed to the bedside to glare down at Nick. 'Nothing except getting better, you stupid, stubborn man,' she added.

The doctor and the agent both turned on her. 'Now look here, boy, your master may give you licence to speak your mind,' Mr Rowley, the agent, snapped, 'but insolence I will not have—'

'Gentlemen, allow me to present you to Miss Anusha Laurens, daughter of Sir George Laurens of Calcutta and niece to his Highness the Raja of Kalatwah.' Nick's voice was slurred, but he sounded amused. 'One does not have to give Miss Laurens licence to speak her mind, she does it anyway.'

'Ma'am.' They both bowed, both looked utterly scandalised.

'Major Herriard is taking me to my father,' Anusha said quickly, scrabbling for her English. Better to explain and hope Nick would stay quiet and rest. 'It was necessary to not be found…to evade…the Maharaja of Altaphur who wishes to marry me, which is why I am as a boy, disguised. We were ambushed by dacoits outside the town.'

'Outrageous!' It was not clear whether that was directed at the dacoits, the maharaja or her travelling, dressed as a boy, with a man. Probably all three. 'Well, you are quite safe here, Miss Laurens. You will doubtless wish to change into your proper clothes and make yourself comfortable while the doctor deals with Major Herriard. My wife will organise that.'

'I have no proper clothes and I do not leave Major Herriard.' She did wish Englishmen were not all so large. Anusha set her feet apart and squared her shoulders—he was going to have to carry her out of there.

'Rowley, I need a pinnace, something that will get us downriver safely to Calcutta.' Nick cut through the argument raging over his body. Anusha shut her mouth and listened. 'And I need it crewing, equipping and provisioning. And I need our horses taken down by reliable grooms. If you can give me a round reckoning for that, I can pay for it now and remit any shortfall when I arrive.'

'Plenty of time to worry about organising that, let alone paying for it.' The doctor was laying out an appalling array of instruments on a strip of linen. Anusha swallowed before her heaving stomach got the better of her. 'You won't be fit to travel for a week or so after this. It will—'

'We go as soon as a boat can be made ready,' Nick interrupted him, propping himself up on his right elbow. 'The day after tomorrow at the latest. Altaphur has many agents and he will have sent word out faster than we could travel. If we had arrived in the town quietly I would not be so concerned—as it is, we might as well have sent trumpeters to announce ourselves.'

'Lie down,' Anusha snapped in Hindi. 'You are as white as a sheet. You are very aggravating, but I do not want you to die.' There was a hideous lump in her throat and she was terrified she was about to cry.

'In that case I will do my best not to,' Nick replied in the same language, then switched back to English. 'Rowley, will you organise the boat and the horses?' To her relief he lay down flat again.

'Certainly. You won't be up and about as soon as you think, but I'll sort it out right away, if that will keep you quiet. Now, come along, Miss Laurens.'

'No.' She was not going to leave him, not alone with that doctor who looked like a skeleton and his instruments of torture.

'But I don't want you,' Nick said. His hands were spread flat on the sheet as though he was fighting the need to fist them.

Mr Rowley took her arm and drew her aside. 'This isn't going to be pleasant, Miss Laurens,' he murmured. 'If he wants to scream or pass out or throw up, he won't while you're here. And if you faint it will simply distract the doctor. So think about the major and not about yourself. Yes?'

Anusha stared at him. 'You mean it would be...' She searched for the English word '...selfish, to stay?' He nodded. 'Very well.' She marched up to the doctor, opened her mouth, then snapped it closed. None of the things she wanted to say—*Don't hurt him, don't kill him*—would be any use. But princesses did not plead, they gave orders.

'Do it properly,' she said, fixing the doctor with her haughtiest stare. 'If he lives, my uncle the Raja of Kalatwah will reward you. If he dies—' She left it hanging, turned on her heel and walked out of the room without a backwards glance.

* * *

'You have no English clothes of any kind?' Mrs Rowley sounded appalled.

'No. And I do not wish to borrow any, thank you, ma'am.' That, Anusha believed, was the right way to address a married lady, but she was not sure. She no longer felt like a haughty princess, but an unsatisfactory child who had disappointed this woman in her strange tight bodice and big bell skirts. She was obviously the mistress of the house although she wore hardly any jewellery.

It was very strange—there were no women's quarters here at all. Mrs Rowley had led her to her own bedchamber, but that was right next to Mr Rowley's room, and in the corridor outside both male and female servants came and went. There was no bathhouse either, just a tub, but she had been grateful for the cool water and the soap and the big towels and had tried to concentrate on getting very clean and not thinking about what was happening to Nick.

'You are betrothed to Major Herriard, I presume.'

Anusha wrestled with the English. Mrs Rowley did not seem to have any Hindi beside very basic phrases for giving orders to her servants 'Betrothed?'

'You are going to marry him?'

'Oh, no. He was supposed to be escorting my caravan back to my father.' It seemed wise to add, 'Who has sent Major Herriard for me.'

'But there is no caravan!'

'No, ma'am. Because of the maharaja's attack. But no one knows of the lack, except you and Mr Rowley

and the doctor, of course, so it cannot matter, for I know
you will not speak of it.'

'Not matter! Of course it matters—you have been
ruined, my dear.' She looked rather scandalously
pleased at this pronouncement, as though she normally
expected the worst and was gratified when it happened.

Ruined? Anusha worked that out. 'Oh, no.' She
smiled at the other woman in what she hoped was a reassuring manner. 'I am still a virgin.'

Mrs Rowley pursed her lips. Perhaps there was another word she should have used. 'I should hope so! But
that, my dear, is neither here nor there. You must marry
the man—your father will insist upon it.'

Neither here nor there. Anusha liked the phrase.
'And that is neither here nor there also. I will not have
him.'

'Not have him? My dear, Major Herriard is…and
you are…'

'Yes? I am the granddaughter of a raja. So, if I
wanted him, it would be quite all right.' *And I do want
him, but not as a husband. I do not want* any *man as a
husband and he does not want me.*

The other woman's lips had vanished into a thin line.
*If she says I could not marry Nick because my parents
were not married, or because I am half-Indian, then
she will be very sorry for her insolence.*

Something must have shown on her face, for Mrs
Rowley gave a petulant shrug. 'That can all wait until
you reach Calcutta. Do not fear: I will let no one know
you are here.'

'The spies of the Maharaja of Altaphur will know

already, I have no doubt.' But the house and its grounds had a high wall around them and there were sentry boxes at each corner, she had been relieved to see. They would be safe enough in here.

'I meant any of the English society here.'

Mrs Rowley believed that what a gaggle of gossiping traders' wives thought of her was any cause for concern? Anusha almost said as much, then recalled that she was speaking to the wife of a trader and held her tongue. She needed this woman—or, rather, Nick did.

'Surely the surgeon will have finished by now?' The house was uncannily quiet. Had something gone horribly wrong and they were afraid to tell her? 'I will go and see what is happening.'

The older woman looked horrified, but then, that seemed to be her usual expression. Nick's bedchamber door was standing slightly ajar so she applied her ear to the gap.

'If you were not so stubborn and would simply pass out, Major, you would make life much easier for both of us.' The doctor sounded as though he was speaking through gritted teeth. Anusha sympathised with him.

There was a grunt of pain, then the rattle of something metallic dropping into a bowl. 'There, that's out, all in one piece. Now I will dress the wound and bleed you.'

'Over my dead body.' Nick sounded a trifle breathless, but very much alive. Anusha sagged against the doorframe.

'It *will* be your dead body if you develop a fever.'

'No.'

'No,' Anusha echoed and marched into the room. The doctor was bandaging Nick's shoulder, there was a heap of bloodstained rags on the floor, bowls of unpleasantly red water, and the instruments looked even worse now they had been used. Nick was white around the mouth, but he rolled his eyes at her and one corner of his mouth twitched into a smile.

'If he does not want to be bled, then he will not be,' she added. 'Thank you, Dr Smythe. What do we owe you for your services?'

'I will send you my accounting when the patient no longer requires those services, Miss Laurens. I have every expectation of being recalled to his bedside before the day is out to find him in a dangerously febrile state.' He twitched the sheet into place and bowed. 'Good day to you.'

'He looks as though he has sat on a poker, foolish man,' Anusha remarked in English as the door closed.

Nick snorted, then winced. 'Do not make me laugh, I beg you. Where did you get that vulgar expression?'

'I heard Papa… I once heard my father use it.' *Papa.* When was the last time she had even thought of her father like that? 'That is not important—what do you need?'

'Nothing except something to drink. Tomorrow I will give you a list of things that we will need and things to be done so you can check what Rowley is doing—I don't trust him to get on with enough urgency. This is a damnable nuisance, but I'll fall flat on my face if I try to do anything much for twenty-four hours—I don't need a sawbones to tell me that.'

'Does it hurt?' He shot her a look that spoke volumes. 'I am sorry, of course it does. Would opium help?'

'No.' He spoke with some feeling. 'I need my wits about me, not scattered in dreams. Are *you* all right, Anusha? You fought like a Rajput warrior—both against the dacoits and the doctor.'

She beamed at him and he blinked. 'Thank you! I enjoyed it, except when you were hurt.' But she did not want to think about the sheer terror of that, the seemingly endless search for help. 'They have given me a room and water to wash in and food and that woman with the face like a purse with the strings pulled tight has been insolent, but I think she means well and does not understand. She wanted me to put on clothes like hers and was offended when I refused.'

'I told you not to make me laugh,' Nick said with a gasp.

'Oh, I am sorry. I complain about that woman and all the while you are hurt and in pain.' He made no answer, but his eyes closed slowly, as though they were too heavy to keep open. His breathing deepened and she realised he was asleep, or perhaps in a faint, tried beyond endurance by the doctor's probing and finally able to let go.

Repentant, she fell on her knees beside the bed. 'I wish I could do something. Are you warm enough?' *Foolish question*, she told herself. *He cannot hear me.*

Nick was flat on his back under a single sheet pulled up to his armpits, his arms outside. Above the sheet the bandaging was stark white on his left shoulder, and down to his chest. The other shoulder was bare. Anusha laid her palm on the right side. 'You feel all right,' she murmured. 'Warm, but no fever.' His eyes moved beneath the shielding lids and he tensed under her hand. 'Now I have hurt you! I am so clumsy.'

He muttered something.

'What did you say?' She leaned closer to catch the words he had hissed between clenched teeth. Her plait slid over her shoulder on to his chest and she could feel his breath on her lips. 'Tell me what you need, Nick.'

'This,' he murmured, eyes still closed. His right hand slid up to her shoulder, all that was needed to tip her down, breast to breast. Their lips met. For a heartbeat neither of them moved, then his palm was cupping the back of her head and his lips parted.

He is kissing me. This was not like that careful touch of the lips after he had killed the snake. Nick hardly stirred, only his lips against hers spoke, not with words but with sensation, warm and firm and tasting of the spirits they must have given him to dull the pain.

She expected to be alarmed and found she was not, only excited and shy. None of the texts she had read spoke of kissing and, when she had imagined it, she thought the man would be on top. But Nick was controlling things perfectly well, Anusha thought hazily. Who would have thought that one hand and a pair of lips could tie her to the spot, unable to move, hardly able to breathe?

And why did this touch, this exchange of breath, of heat, make her whole body tingle? Her breasts, tight under her man's coat and shirt, ached as though they had suddenly become larger. There was a restless tin-

gle down the inside of her thighs and an insistent pulse
low down.

Anusha spread her hand on the naked skin of Nick's
shoulder and leaned closer into the kiss. She wanted to
see him, she realised, look at him while he made love
to her mouth. As her eyes opened so did his, deep and
green. Slowly, they focused.

There was not much room for him to recoil, but his
convulsive movement was as violent a rejection as a
slap. Anusha jumped back and fell on her bottom with
a thump. 'Ouch! Nick, what—?'

'Get out. Just get out of here, Anusha.'

She scrabbled to her feet, stumbled, her legs uncertain and her vision blurred with anger and humiliation.
'With pleasure,' she spat at him. 'I only kissed you because I was sorry for you—not because I wanted to.'

Chapter Ten

Blood loss, shock, a potent slug of spirits and virtually no sleep the night before were as good as a blow to the head for knocking the sense out of a man, Nick thought muzzily as he fought his way back to consciousness. It was morning to judge by the light and the lack of noise, so he had slept the night through.

He knew where he was and how he had got there. That was a relief. The last time he'd been wounded it had taken a day to get his memory back clearly and this time he could not afford the luxury of lying about, not with a boat to organise and Anusha—

Anusha. He sat up with a jerk and swore as the pain knifed through his shoulder and his head swam with dizziness. Anusha. Hell, had he kissed her or had he dreamt it? It had seemed all too real, both the delicious feel of her body, soft and curved, the cool of her hand on his bare skin, the untutored sensuality of her lips on his. The taste of her. And the words she had flung at him as she had backed out of the room: those where exactly what he would have expected her to say.

And yet he would not have kissed her, he could not have been that dazed, that unable to control his impulses, surely? No, it was a dream, he was almost certain. A delicious, arousing dream that left an ache of emptiness on waking.

Almost was not as reassuring as it might be. Nick threw back the sheet and swung his feet off the bed, hissing when his feet thumped on to the matting and jarred his shoulder.

Almost immediately the door opened and a servant peered round the edge. '*Sahib*! You are awake, but you must not get up.' He flapped his hands as though to shoo Nick back into the bed. 'The Doctor *sahib* will be angry. Go back to bed, Herriard *sahib*, and I will call him to you.'

'You will not.' The youth stared at him anxiously. 'I want water to wash, tea to drink—a lot of tea, with sugar,' Nick ordered in Hindi. 'Then I want my clothes.'

'But—' The servant shrugged and began to back out of the door. 'Rowley *memsahib* will have much to say about it.'

'Tell her I threatened to come downstairs in the sheet if you did not obey me,' Nick suggested. It was tempting to lie down to wait, but he fought the dizziness and made himself stay where he was.

When the door banged open it was neither his outraged hostess nor the servant with hot water. 'What are you doing from your bed already?' Anusha demanded. In English, he noted. Her plait swung lose over the shoulder of her coat and a shaft of desire lanced through him at the memory of that moment in his dream when she had leaned forwards and it had fallen on to his bare skin.

She looked furious, and flushed, and she was eyeing him in a way that was new. 'Why are you so angry?' he asked, a sinking feeling in the pit of his stomach warning him that it was not simply the fact he was sitting up.

'Because you do not listen to the doctor and so you will make yourself ill and you will be here in bed being a nuisance and not taking me down to Calcutta as you should.'

'Thank you for your concern,' he said drily.

'I am not concerned about you. You do not deserve any concern.'

'Why not? You were concerned yesterday, Anusha. What has happened to change that?'

She blushed, an angry darkening of the honey-coloured skin. 'You can ask? Mrs Rowley warned me how it would be and I thought her foolish.'

'So I *did* kiss you last night?' Nick ventured, with, he realised the moment he said it, a crashing lack of tact.

'If you can call that a kiss,' Anusha snapped, reverting to Hindi. 'It was not very interesting—perhaps that is why you forgot about it.'

'I am extremely sorry. It was a mistake.' *And so was saying that.* Anusha's nostrils flared and he found himself glad she did not have her knife about her. 'I mean, I should not have kissed you—I thought I was dreaming.'

That seemed to please her rather more. 'You mean you dream of kissing me?' she enquired with a purely feminine curiosity that would have made him smile under any other circumstances.

'No.' He had to put a stop to this right here and now. 'I mean I was not myself, I was on the edge of consciousness and I am afraid that if a man finds himself pressed up against an attractive woman, in a bed, when he hasn't his wits about him, then instinct is apt to take over.'

'So you would have kissed anyone?' He nodded. 'Mrs Rowley?'

'I said *attractive*, Anusha.'

She bit her lip, but he could tell she was on the verge of laughing. With any luck he had reduced that massive mistake to an embarrassing slip in her eyes. Which just left him mentally flagellating himself for such a betrayal of trust. 'What did Mrs Rowley say about me?'

'Only that it was shocking that we were travelling together and that men could not be trusted. But I told her we had spoken of such things and that you were a gentleman and were shocked that anyone might think you would ravish me.'

Oh hell. And I got on my high horse, too. Damned hypocrite. The moment my guard was down...

'*Major Herriard*!' Mrs Rowley stood in the doorway, elbows akimbo, the servant peering past her.

His first thought was relief that they had not been speaking English. Then Nick realised that he was wearing a bandage, a roughly draped sheet and nothing else. His chest was bare, his legs were bare from mid-thigh. He did not dare glance down to make sure the sheet was covering his groin adequately. 'I was looking for my clothes and unfortunately I did not hear Miss Laurens knock.'

'*Tsk*! Miss Laurens, you must leave at once.' Eyes averted, she bustled Anusha out leaving the servant to bring in the water ewer. His expression said quite clearly in any language, *I told you so.*

'And my clothes?'

'I will get them from the *dhobi wallah, sahib*. He says the blood has come out and the *darji* has mended the coat. Your breakfast is coming, *sahib.*'

It took altogether too long to wash and shave and dress. Nick ate one-handed, tried to control his fork with a hand that shook and cursed dacoits, bullets and his own physical weakness and lack of will-power.

The fact that he had been virtually delirious when he kissed her was no excuse, he told himself savagely. Damn it, George had trusted him with his daughter. The way he felt about George, the man who had given him everything a father should—even his life—practically made the chit his sister. He had told her to trust him himself. But the truth was, from the moment he first saw her, his common sense had gone south along with most of his blood.

He threw down his napkin. *I had better get a grip on my self-control again, because anything more than a fuddled kiss when I haven't the strength to lift myself off the pillows is going to end up at the altar.* He thought he could square it with his conscience not to confess last night's idiocy to George, but anything more and the old man would be reaching for a shotgun, with good cause.

The thought of another marriage made him shiver. Women wanted too much that he could not give and needed too much that it seemed he was unable to provide. He should never have married Miranda. He could not shake off the memory of his wife's death. The image haunted him of her fragile body, swollen with the child he had planted in her, racked with fever in the steaming heat of a Calcutta summer, too weak to fight.

He had no need of an heir, no title or estates to leave. What wealth he acquired he would leave to some charity or another, his body could moulder away in the English cemetery at South Park Street in Calcutta and the creepers and ferns would mask whatever inscription they put on it soon enough, with no one to shed dutiful tears over it.

'*Sahib*? Some more tea, *sahib*?'

'No, thank you.' He was growing thoroughly morbid now. Nick gave himself a mental shake. He had a career, ambition and the world was full of willing women who did not need a ring on their finger. His place in any cemetery would wait for many years, if he had anything to say to it. It must certainly wait until he got Anusha Laurens down river to Calcutta and the new life that awaited her. Moving like an old man, and hating it, Nick hauled himself to his feet and made for the door.

'That was easy. I do not know what the fuss was about.' Anusha sat cross-legged with her back to the mast of the little sailing boat and viewed the prospect of the river in front of them with satisfaction.

'Easy?' Nick grunted from the folding canvas chair beside her. 'You call finding a boat that doesn't leak, a crew that won't murder us in our beds, buying sufficient provisions, sorting out the horses and extracting you from Mrs Rowley's grasp, and me from the doctor's, all in two days, easy? It was down to my superior logistical skills and force of character.'

It took her a moment to translate that. They were speaking English most of the time now and she found it came back remarkably easily, for *Mata* had continued to speak it to her as much as she spoke Hindi. But many phrases were strange and needed working out.

'You are just tired, which makes your mood distempered, so Mrs Rowley said. Does your shoulder give you much pain?'

'A little.'

She did not know what distemper was, but it seemed unpleasant. Nick had been decidedly short-tempered since he rose from his sick bed. 'I have unpacked all our things in our cabins. There is not much room—why did you make them put in that wall? With the doors it takes up too much room.'

'So we have a cabin each.'

Ah, so we are back to that kiss. She could still taste him in her memory, that mixture of brandy and spice and man. Anusha ran her tongue tip over her lips as if she could recapture it.

Nick had said nothing about it since that morning and at first she thought he must simply have dismissed it from his mind. Now she knew he had not, it was flattering to think that he did not trust himself alone with her any more: it made her feel womanly and strangely powerful. On the other hand, if he did kiss her—and do the other things, the things she thought about every time she looked at that long, lean body and those big hands—then he would be even more short-tempered afterwards and if her father found out he would insist Nick married her.

And she did not want to marry a man who, if he wanted her at all, only wanted one thing. She tried to imagine life as Nick's wife. She would have to be whatever a European wife was. She would not be in a *zanana*, she knew that. She would have to wear those horrible clothes and learn to order a household like Mrs Rowley's and be *respectable* in the *angrezi* manner, which seemed even more restricting than the rules of the women's *mahal*.

Nick would go off on adventures, or march about the country making war, while she sat at home and had babies in a world that she did not belong to. He would not love her, even if she was unwise enough to fall in love with him. And it would hurt, every day, like tiny knife cuts.

No, she must take her life into her own hands, create herself in a new world where she would not let anyone close enough to hurt her.

'What is the matter?'

She twisted round and saw Nick was watching her, a frown bringing his eyebrows together. Anusha almost confessed something of her fears of Calcutta, the vista of loneliness that she envisaged lying before her. But, no, she must not forget he was on her father's side in this. He would see her safely delivered, even if he had to put her in a sack to do it. But she could afford to behave as he wished for now: he would get her safely to Calcutta and there she would gather the money and gems with which to escape. 'The river is interesting, but I miss Rajat.'

Nick seemed comfortable enough, his right arm hanging relaxed by his side, so close that if she leaned over, just a little, the back of his hand would brush her shoulder. It was tempting to move that tiny distance and see if his touch would wake those little thrills under her skin, the ache between her legs.

It was sexual desire, which was very interesting. Men seemed to feel it for virtually any woman who was not actually repulsive, but did women, once they were aware of it, feel it for any man? What if she had agreed to a marriage with one of her suitors for whom she felt nothing—would she have felt desire for him? All those intriguing things that men and women did together seemed embarrassing and puzzling if there was no desire. What did it mean that she felt desire for Nick?

'Why have you taken off the sling?' she demanded. A battle would take her mind off wondering what it would be like if he made love to her.

'Because it was a nuisance.' He flexed his fingers on his knee. 'And because I do not want to appear weakened to any onlookers.'

'You think we are still in danger?'

He nodded. 'Perhaps.'

'You do not seem to wish to shield me from anxiety. Is that how you treat all English ladies? I thought they were protected and sheltered by gentlemen.'

A shadow seemed to pass over his face, but he answered her robustly enough, 'Do you want me to lie to you? Treat you as though you had no wits and no courage? I thought you boasted you were Rajput—a warrior.'

'I am. And I do not wish you to—what is the word?—hide me in the dark.'

'Keep you in the dark. Perhaps there is nothing to worry about from Altaphur's men, but even if there is not, there are still those who steal from boats.' He picked up the musket which lay on the deck at his side and propped it up more visibly against his chair. 'Have you your knife still?'

'I have one of them, you took the other.'

'I will give it back to you. Sleep with them both to hand and do not go out of your cabin at night unless you know I am there.' The banks were slipping past at speed now as the flow of the river carried them down and she realised that Nick's gaze was on them, with only fleeting glances at her when she spoke. The jungle came down to the riverside in places, in others there were sandbanks, or rocky outcrops. There was a shout from the stern as the cook-boat, flat-bottomed and unwieldy on the end of its tow-rope, bumped into them.

'Fool of a son of a camel,' yelled the man at the tiller. 'Use your poles to keep off us!'

'We must moor at night and the men will sleep on the shore,' Nick said. 'They prefer to eat there in any case.'

'But that means anyone could attack us, and we waste time.'

'Look.' He pointed a little ahead where a rounded black shape rose out of the water. 'We will lose more than time if we hit one of those rocks.'

'What will we do with ourselves, on this boat for so

many days?' she wondered aloud, then felt the heat rise up her neck at the thought of what they could be doing.

'You wanted to travel—now is your chance to see one of the great rivers of the world. We will be joining the Ganges soon. It will make the Jumna look like a stream, so you will have constant entertainment just watching the banks.'

And it will carry me down to a new world. Travel seemed less interesting now; she wanted, yet dreaded, her destination. 'Tell me what it is like to be an English lady,' Anusha asked.

'How would I know?'

'You were married to one,' she said tartly and saw his hand clench as though she had prodded his wounded shoulder. 'Your mother was one, you live among them when you are in Calcutta. Tell me what I must do to be one of them.'

Nick hesitated and Anusha twisted round on the deck at his feet, her hand on his knee to shake it, as though to force an answer out of him. 'You do not tell me—is it that I will never be one of them?' Not that she cared for what those unknown women thought, but if she was to live in that world, make her escape into it, she had to understand.

'You will always be different,' he said slowly. 'How can it be otherwise? The whole way you have been brought up is different.'

'And I do not look like them,' she pointed out, determined to face all the problems. 'They will be pink like you and I am brown.'

'You are golden,' Nick said. 'Like honey. And your

eyes are like your father's, grey, and your hair is brown, not black. You could be European—Italian or from the south of France perhaps. But that does not matter, they will not be prejudiced against you because of your mother.' His mouth twisted into a rueful smile, 'At least, they won't once they know who your uncle is—deference to rank applies in society all over the world, I suppose.'

'But they will know my father did not marry my mother.' That would not matter at home in Kalatwah. The raja had three wives, four courtesans and numerous occasional lovers. Children were treated according to their merits in their father's eyes and how skilful their mothers were in bringing those merits to his attention. Europeans only took one wife at a time, their courtesans were hidden and not spoken of.

'That is true.' Nick seemed to be pondering the problem. At least he seemed willing to discuss this honestly with her, which was a relief. She needed to understand what her position would be. 'Your father has considerable standing and much respect. He is wealthy and of a good English family. There is no reason for you not to be accepted.'

He was silent for a while as they passed a village, the naked children splashing in the water, the women crouched at their washing, a man casting his net, thigh deep in the swirling muddy river.

'You will have teachers to show you how to dance and to perfect your English and your etiquette. Some of the married ladies will take your wardrobe in hand, I have no doubt, and fit you out with clothes and shoes, then you will attend balls and receptions and you will make friends.'

It sounds terrible.

Chapter Eleven

'What is the matter? You've curled up like a hedgehog.' Whatever that was, Nick seemed to find it amusing.

'What is a hedgehog?' Had she curled up? Anusha straightened her back and unwrapped her arms from around her raised knees. Perhaps she had. She did not like the sound of this new world with its lessons, its threats of the dreaded European clothing and its shocking behaviour. Dancing with men—her body had betrayed her agitation.

'*Sharo*,' he translated. 'I've never seen one this far to the east. It is a small animal with its back covered in spines and when it is in danger it curls up into a ball and there is nothing for its enemies but a nose full of prickles.'

'Like a porcupine—*sayal*?' They were ugly creatures. It was not danger that had her curling in on herself; she would be brave enough to escape, she was certain. No, it was the prospect of so much embarrassment first.

'They are much smaller than porcupines.' He showed with his cupped hands. 'Rather endearing, really. They snuffle, like little pigs.'

'I do not snuffle.'

'Not when you are awake, no,' he said with a grin and stood up. 'Don't look so outraged, Princess, I did say *endearing*.'

'Do not call me that,' she muttered as Nick strolled away to speak to the steersman. If he saw how it annoyed her, he would tease her more. She was not truly a princess, even if she was the daughter of one, for her father was not of the royal blood. And she was not an English *memsahib* yet either, and she was not going to pretend to be one of those for a moment longer than it took to learn what she needed to survive in the world alone.

The lush green of the banks blurred and Anusha blinked, angry with herself for the moment of weakness, and waved with determined cheeriness at some small boys leading the family buffalo down to the river for its evening bathe.

I will watch, learn, collect up all the money and jewels I can, she told herself. *Then I will find a ship and sail to England where no one knows me and I will be whatever I want.* Only she did not know what she wanted, only to belong somewhere and to be wanted for herself. She found her eyes were fixed on Nick's broad back. *So strange, to have this ache inside and yet, somehow, to be happy.*

There was silence from the compartment next to his. Either Anusha was not asleep yet, or she had taken to heart his teasing about her snuffling in her sleep. He had become used to the odd little wiffling noises she made sometimes—dreaming, he supposed—it had been unfair to call it *snuffling*.

Nick stretched out his long legs on the roughly made bunk and regarded with disfavour the evidence of what seemed to be a constant state of arousal. Will-power did not seem to work, neither did the illusory safety of a thin wooden barrier shut Anusha out of his imagination.

He eased his sweaty back against the pillows, uncomfortable in the heat. To call the spaces they were sleeping in *cabins* was a wild exaggeration—cupboards was more like it. There were no portholes and, with the hatch closed as it was at night, precious little ventilation.

Nick got up and rolled his shoulders experimentally. *Not too bad*, he thought. Luckily he had always healed well and he doubted anyone observing him would realise how bad the wound had been. He pulled on the *pajama* trousers and a *kurta* that was loose over his bandages, picked up his musket and a pillow and eased open the door. Then he wedged Anusha's door ajar and climbed the ladder to unbolt and push open the hatch onto the deck.

On the flat expanse of sand the small crew were gathered around a fire, talking quietly now their meal was finished. Soon they would be asleep, a man at each of the four mooring ropes, one at the foot of the gangplank, the others on the cook boat.

He laid the pillow by the open hatch, put the musket within reach, slid his dagger under the pillow and stretched out. Like this some air would filter down to

Anusha and he would have the relief of several more feet between them. His wound throbbed, his groin ached, but the air, at least, was cool on his hot body. Nick willed himself to sleep.

'Teach me about etiquette.' Anusha was proud of herself for getting her tongue around the word. Her first word of French. 'What must I know?'

Nick, slumped in the canvas chair, sat up and sighed. 'I find it a dead bore at the best of times: I am not a dratted governess!'

'Please. I do not wish to seem foolish.'

'Very well. When you meet someone new you should wait to be introduced. If you are of higher rank than they are, they will be presented to you, and the other way around. If they are the same rank as you, then you defer to an older person.

'Then you curtsy. After that, if they are of higher rank and you meet them, you make a little curtsy. For everyone else, a slight bow of the head, or shaking hands.'

'Show me how to curtsy,' she demanded.

'How should I know? I can't see under ladies' skirts when they are doing it!' Anusha merely waited. She was finding that if she gazed soulfully at Nick for long enough he usually did what she wanted over trivial matters. She had not tried it in any major clash of wills yet.

'Er…put your heels together, toes apart. Now bend your knees outwards, keep your back straight and sink down.' He frowned as she obeyed. This was no effort, her thigh muscles were strong. 'That looks about right—

and up again. The more important the person, the lower you curtsy.'

'That was easy. And bowing my head?'

He stood up and inclined his head. 'Good afternoon, Miss Laurens.'

She copied him. 'Good afternoon, Major Herriard. That is easy too. But shaking hands? I only do that with ladies?'

'Oh, no, anyone of rank.'

'Men? I touch hands with them?'

'Certainly. Some may then kiss your hand.' Anusha whipped both hers behind her back. 'Come, let me show you—you will be wearing gloves, of course.' Nick held out his right hand. 'Give me your right hand.'

Their fingers slid together. His big, warm hand enveloped hers as he closed the grip in a light squeeze, then released her. Surely he could *feel* her blush from its heat, let alone see it! He must be able to feel her pulse, jumping erratically, as she had felt his, strong and steady. His palms were slightly rough, with rider's calluses. Anusha hid her hands again.

'No, it is nothing, the merest pleasantry,' he assured her. 'Now, pretend we are at a reception and you have been introduced to me. Give me your hand again, palm down, like this.' She copied him, wary. Nick caught the ends of her fingers in his, bent, raised the back of her hand almost to his mouth and kissed the air a rice-grain's width above her skin, released her hand and bowed. 'Miss Laurens, you are in great beauty this evening. Now you curtsy and smile and say *You are too kind, Major Herriard.*'

'You are too bold, you mean!' She took a step back, hands gripped together. His breath had feathered the sensitive skin on the back of her hand. She had felt his lips even though they had not touched her, and her pulse was all over the place. 'That is indecent—and I am meant to endure those caresses from men I have only just met?'

'It is the custom, but you will never be alone with these men, there will always be older married women around you so there is nothing to fear. They will flirt a little, you will flirt back. It is quite acceptable.'

'Flirt? I do not know that word.' She sat down on the hatch cover, a safe distance from his chair, although quite what she was keeping safe from, she was not sure.

'Flirting is a game, a courtship game, that all the young ladies and the single men indulge in. A sort of teasing. The men say gallant things, compliment the ladies. The ladies pretend to dismiss such blatant flattery, they blush a little, shield their faces, but their eyes tell a different story. Then in turn they say things that make the men feel strong and manly and laugh a little that they are so bold, and so it goes on.'

'And that is allowed? You must teach me how to flirt.' It sounded shocking, but if that was necessary to be accepted, to fit in, then she would do it.

Nick shrugged and she caught a slight wince, hastily suppressed. He had denied having any discomfort, so she should not fuss. 'I am no good at flirting,' he said.

'Oh, but a man as gallant and brave as you cannot be afraid of talking to young ladies surely, Major Herriard.' She opened her eyes wide at him, wondering the next moment if it was a safe thing to do.

'You need no lessons, Miss Laurens.' He shook his head, one of his rare smiles making him look years younger and far less formidable. 'You are already an accomplished flirt. Look, we will be mooring in a moment. I will show you how to make dinner-table conversation while we eat.'

I would rather flirt, she thought, then caught herself. It was dangerous to play at love. Nick's heart might be armour-clad—hers, she was beginning to worry, might not be.

'That is a relief,' Nick remarked as they regained the deck after going ashore to the port officer at Allahabad to check on the situation in Kalatwah. He had received news only that morning, he had told them.

'Just got a message—it should be accurate. Altaphur's camped outside the walls, making a lot of threatening noises. The raja's sitting tight, wise man—he's not making foolish sallies outside. There are Company cavalry within a few days' march and his neighbours are gathering—none of them wants Altaphur turning on them next. My correspondent predicts that the maharaja will march away within twenty-four hours.'

Now, as the crew pushed off from the steps, Anusha stood beside him looking at the scene on the *ghat* with huge piles of marigold flowers and the garland sellers who were threading them, a barber shaving his client and a procession making its way with a shrouded corpse to the burning *ghat*, a little downstream.

'May locusts consume his crops, his wives all be barren and his guts be filled with worms,' she said in Hindi.

'Quite,' Nick replied with a grin. 'I do not blame you, but it's not exactly dinner-party conversation, Miss Laurens.'

'I know,' she sighed, reverting to English. 'I have spent three days learning how to address an earl, a bishop, the governor and their ladies. And I have learned that at the dinner table one may only talk about foolish things and that women are not expected to have a brain.'

'Unfortunately yes.'

'Even this flirting is foolish. Do the men not want to know that their wives will be skilled in bed? Do they really want ignorant wives?'

'Yes,' Nick said with some emphasis as the boat's sails were raised. The steersman took them out into the central current and they began to move downriver.

Anusha went to sit on the hatch cover that had become her favoured perch. 'How strange. We are all taught how to pleasure our husbands.'

Nick was halfway into the canvas chair and sat down with a suddenness that made him swear under his breath. '*Please*, not *pleasure,* Anusha. *Pleasure* means to please him in, er, bed.'

'But that is what I meant.' Was the little wretch teasing him, or genuinely curious?

'And how do you—no, do not tell me, I do not want to know.'

He did not want to talk about wives and the marriage bed. He did not want to remember Miranda shrinking in distaste from his caresses, forcing herself to *do her duty*, as she put it. He tried to tell himself, as he had so many times during that short marriage, that someone had told her something to frighten her or that she was naturally cold. But the conviction remained that he simply did not know how to make a respectable woman happy. He was a rake with too much experience, with tastes and habits that had shocked Miranda to the core.

He must be concealing his thoughts well enough, he realised. Anusha was blithely answering his question. 'By reading the classical texts, of course. And studying the pictures and talking to our mothers and sisters. Why? How did you imagine we might learn?'

'I was attempting *not* to imagine,' Nick said. He could picture her, lying in silks on heaps of cushions, idly turning the pages of some illustrated text. Those long limbs would stir restlessly in the heat with her imaginings, those full lips would curve into a sensual smile as she propped her chin on her hand and...

'I am sorry to mention such a subject,' she said penitently. 'I was forgetting that it must be many days since you lay with a woman.'

'Anusha—'

She slanted a glance in his direction. 'Do English ladies not discuss sexual matters?'

'No! At least, unmarried women do not discuss them. Unmarried girls are not supposed to know anything about such things.'

'So their husbands are supposed to teach them?'

'Yes.' He tugged off his neckcloth and opened the neck of his shirt. It was hot, that was all.

'That might be rather nice if the woman is in love

with the man,' she mused. 'But if not it must be a dreadful shock.'

'I couldn't say,' Nick said, trying to keep the edge from his voice. She looked at him, lips parted. Something in his face must have given her pause, for she lowered her lids and stayed mercifully quiet. *I couldn't say because my wife obviously did not love me. I thought I could make her love me, teach her to love. But then, you see, I doubt I am very lovable. Though I am skilled enough in bed if I am matched with a woman of experience...*

Stop it. He caught at his bitter, unravelling thoughts. *Hurt pride is all it is. Hurt pride and a valuable lesson.* He made his voice firm and matter of fact. 'Anusha, I beg you, when we get to Calcutta, do not say anything about illustrated texts, or pleasuring men or *bed*.'

'Very well, Nick,' she said.

Anusha turned to look out over the water and he caught a glimpse of her eyes, thoughtful and with all the teasing gone. She guessed he had been thinking about Miranda. Nick felt a sudden urge to tell her everything, share the pain and the anger and the sense of failure, to break through the self-sufficient loneliness. *Self-indulgent weakness.* He stared at the sun-dazzle on the water until he was certain the blurring in his eyes came from that alone and the impulse was beaten back where it belonged.

Anusha woke in darkness. It felt very late and the air was finally cooling. A little breeze brushed over the bed, which was strange because she always closed her door properly at night. But now she came to think about it, she was never as hot and uncomfortable as she might have expected in a closed cabin. The door, she realised, was ajar. Had someone opened it every night? Silent as the breeze, she slid out of bed and went to look. The door had been wedged open, but Nick's door was closed.

As she stood there in her shift, puzzling over it, there was a faint sound from the deck, a grunt, as though someone had stubbed a toe and was suppressing the exclamation of pain. Anusha reached for the dagger that lay on her pile of clothes and climbed the ladder to the open hatch.

The moon was full, lighting the wide sandbank where the blanket-wrapped forms of the crew surrounded the banked embers of their fire. The silver light washed across the deck and the man who sat cross-legged, his back to the mast. Nick.

Anusha froze, her eyes just above the rim of the hatch. There was a pillow and a blanket on the deck, a musket by the side. She knew him well enough now to guess what this meant—Nick was sleeping on deck so he could leave the hatch and her door open to let the cool night air below decks for her, while he slept on the hard boards to guard her.

But why was he not resting now? As her eyes adjusted to the light she saw him clearly. He was barefoot, bare-chested, wearing only light *pajama* trousers and he was unwinding the bandage from around his torso.

I had forgotten his wound, Anusha realised with a stab of guilt. *How could I have done that?* But he had seemed so unaffected by it that after the first day she had ceased to worry and then, unforgivably, had managed to disregard it. He was a man, a warrior—of course he would not mention it until he fell flat on his stubborn, proud face.

Nick finished unwinding the bandage, but he was still twisted round, doing something to the dressing on his shoulder. In the stillness she heard his hiss of pain and was up on the deck and running to his side before she could think about it.

As he got to his feet she laid her hand on his uninjured shoulder. 'Nick, your wound—I am so sorry, but you should have said it needed redressing. Let me see.' She tried to press him back down to sit on the hatch. He resisted.

'I can manage, go back to bed, Anusha.' The moonlight turned his hair to silver, his bare chest was so close she could see the individual hairs, the way the brown aureoles of his nipples had tightened in the cool air.

She pushed aside his hand and lifted the trailing bandage. 'This has stuck to the wound.'

'I had noticed,' he said wryly.

'Then it needs to be soaked off and the wound redressed. Come down and I will do it. You need to be lying down and in my cabin there are all those lamps you gave me. I cannot see clearly enough up here.'

'I can see far too clearly.' Nick sounded grim. 'What the blazes are you wearing?'

'My shift—you have seen it before when you woke me the night we left Kalatwah.' She pushed the end of the bandage back into his hand, abrupt because she was moved by his stoicism and felt guilty about her neglect of his hurt. 'Why are you up here on this hard deck and not sleeping? How can you look after me properly if you make yourself ill?'

'Do you know, I had not considered that,' Nick said. 'Go back to bed.'

'Not without you.' His eyebrows soared. 'Foolishness,' she scolded. She would not let him see how that unspoken thought affected her. 'Is that all men ever think about?' It eased her conscience to put him in the wrong. 'I want to dress your shoulder and I want to know why you are up here.'

Nick allowed her to tug him towards the hatch. 'It was too hot below to sleep. I opened the hatch, and your door, but then it needed guarding. I can manage.'

'No, you cannot or you would have changed the dressing before now.'

He picked up the musket and went down the ladder. 'I suppose I will get no peace unless I let you torture me.'

Anusha did nor dignify that with a reply. She filled a copper urn from the water barrel tied to the foot of the mast and followed him down. 'No, go to my cabin, the lights are better and I need my things.'

Chapter Twelve

The fact that the infuriating woman was right was no consolation. He should have redressed his shoulder at least three days ago, it was going to be a devil of a job doing it himself and Anusha's cabin had the broader bed and the better lamps.

It also smelled of the jasmine oil she used on her hair, the myriad of feminine potions and lotions that she seemed to have acquired in Kalpi and, most distractingly, of herself.

It would be simplest to take the line of least resistance, do what she wanted and then escape.

'Lie down,' Anusha said, wriggling past him with a jug in one hand and a basin in the other. The pressure of a rounded backside against his thigh was more than enough incentive to obey. Nick lay down, swamping the hollow her body had made in the thin mattress, his head on a firm, Anusha-scented pillow.

'Lie still.' She sat on the edge of the bed, her hip against his, snipped through the loose length of bandage with a pair of tiny scissors, then leaned close to peer at the part that had dried on to the wound. Nick closed his eyes and gritted his teeth. 'I haven't done anything to hurt you yet,' Anusha protested.

No, but that shift is virtually transparent with the lamp behind you, your right breast is squashed against my chest and I am fantasising about simply rolling over and crushing you into this mattress. 'Lying down must have jarred it,' he lied with an heroic effort of self-control. Why he was bothering to pretend when she only had to glance below his waist to see what the problem was, he did not know. He was rock hard. For all her theoretical knowledge she would be terrified.

Anusha got up and began to set things out on the shelf. 'It is a good thing I packed my medical box.'

Nick opened a cautious eye. 'Do you know what you are doing with it?'

'Of course.' She dropped a small sponge in to the basin and picked up a sinister sharp object. 'It is part of our lessons in the women's *mahal,* to know how to care for our man if he is sick or wounded.'

He realised that she was speaking Hindi again, as though what she was doing was taking her mind back to Kalatwah. *Our man.* She said it with complete unconcern. She was not flirting, it had been an unconscious slip. Nick felt his groin tighten again and locked eyes with Anusha. The thin, loose trousers were no shield for his all-too-obvious thoughts.

'Now, I'll just put these towels here and sponge the dressing free,' she said, settling beside him again.

She was good at this, he realised after a minute. She did not dab, overcautious and hurting him more as a result. She was firm but gentle, her hands moving on his body with an assurance that only served to fuel his hopeless fantasies.

'There,' she said with a final wriggle of the probe to lift the dressing free. 'That is better now.'

'Yes, thank you.' And it was—the heat and tightness around the wound were immediately relieved.

'But it needs cleaning,' she added, reaching up to the shelf.

'Oh, no—'

'Oh, yes. This might sting a little,' she said, tipping the contents of a small phial directly on to the half-healed wound.

'Blood and sand!' Nick reared up off the bed and was promptly pressed back down again.

'I am sorry.' She did not sound remotely regretful as she used a piece of soft cloth to sponge the liquid into the raw area. 'Now I will kiss it better. That is what *Mata* always used to say.'

'Does it work?' He could hear the desperation in his own voice, even if she could not. There was only so much will-power a man could exert.

'Tell me,' she suggested and bent to drop a kiss on the skin just beside the wound.

'It does not help at all,' Nick said with complete truth, unfisting his hands from the sheet before he tore it.

'A pity.' He could not see her face, but she sounded regretful. 'Now I will bandage it again. Can you sit up?'

Nick sat and she swayed upright with him, her fingers light on his shoulder. 'I have clean dressings and the old bandage is all right to use again if I cut off the ends.'

'Good,' he managed as she redressed the wound and began to wind the bandage around his chest and over his shoulder. Which was fine, provided he could ignore how close she had to sit or how her arms went around his rib cage and how her fingers brushed across his skin, which he had never considered particularly sensitive and was now acting like one large, throbbing erogenous zone.

'Anusha.'

'Yes?' She frowned in concentration as she tied the end securely.

'Thank you.' He could do this. He could behave like a gentleman, thank her and get out of the cabin safely. Nick produced what he hoped was a friendly, grateful smile. 'I will just go and—'

'Please, wait.' Anusha bit her lip, her lashes lowered so he could not see her eyes. *This is so difficult...* 'There is something I must say to you, something I should have said before now. When you came for me to Kalatwah, I hated you because you are the agent of my father and because I had never met a man like you.'

'You have not met many men,' Nick said. He sounded uneasy.

'No, that is true.' She glanced up and looked him directly in the eye. 'I did not trust you. I learned quickly that I was wrong when I worried about trusting you with my body. But I did not trust you with my future,' Anusha added doggedly.

'Your future? I do not understand.'

'I need to be free, to be independent, to discover who I am. That could not happen at Kalatwah, I was beginning to realise it. But it can happen in Calcutta if I can be accepted into society there—and you have begun to teach me, and you have given me confidence.' And it was true. She had not realised how frightened she had been, deep down, at what awaited her. 'Otherwise I would be shut up in my father's house and not able to go out and be free if I did not know how things were to be done.'

'But your father will find you teachers and older women to guide you,' Nick explained.

'Yes, but they will be thinking about finding me a husband.'

'And that would not be a good idea?'

'No, of course not. Why should I want a husband if I can be free? I have turned down suitor after suitor at Kalatwah because I do not want to be tied.' *And because somewhere, out in the wide world, there might be love, like* Mata *found. Only this time a love that lasts.*

'My father is a rich man, so I am rich, am I not?'

'He will give you a dowry, yes,' Nick agreed cautiously.

'So you see? I did not know how to behave and whether I would have any money, so I was planning to sell my jewels and run away from you before we got to Calcutta. But now you have been kind and explained things and looked after me so I do not need to run away.'

Nick stared at her. 'Jewels?'

'It is all right, I have them hidden.' He looked worried, but he had no need to be—she had kept them well concealed.

'Excellent,' he said, but he did not sound very relieved. 'Your father…'

'He only wants me back because of these foolish politics, because I am a nuisance to the wretched Company if I stay in Kalatwah. He does not want *me*, I do not want him.'

Nick's lips compressed, but he did not lecture her for speaking disrespectfully. It was as though he was thinking about something else entirely.

Anusha lifted a hand to his shoulder, craving the comfort of touch. Under her palm his skin was hot, smooth. He did not try to dislodge her hand. 'Nick, it will be as *Mata* used to say, will it not? She said English women did as they pleased and no one forced their daughters to get married. That is right, is it not?'

She felt the deep breath he took, as if bracing himself for something. Then he smiled. 'Of course. You will be a wealthy young lady with all the freedom you could wish for.'

'Yes? *I will be free. I can choose.* 'You prom—'

Nick caught her against his chest and kissed her. The suddenness was shocking, liberating. She melted against him, her arms around his neck, her breasts so tight against his bare skin that she could feel his nipples hardening through the thin cotton shift she wore.

Under the demands of his mouth her lips parted without hesitation, her tongue meeting his to explore and stroke. He tasted of tea and spice and something dangerous and male.

His hands slid down from her shoulders, down past her waist to the curve of her hips as she sat on the bed, and he lifted her so she sat across his thighs. Anusha gasped against his lips as she felt the hard ridge of his desire. *He wants me that much. He needs me. I need him. This is meant, this is right...*

Nick turned her to cup the weight of her breast. She had always thought them too small, but she filled his palm as he teased the tight bud until she was gasping into his mouth. This was arousal, she realised, she could feel her own moist heat, smell the heady musk of their mutual desire.

Nick lifted his head and set his hands to her waist as if to lift her away. Anusha opened her eyes and looked into his face. He had released something in her: a passion, a feminine understanding that had not been there before. He had told her she did not have to marry. This adventure had given her the courage to be free, to make her own world. And she knew what she wanted: this strong man who shielded his own hurt as well as he shielded her. She could not have him for long, she understood that, but...

'Nick, please—lie with me.'

'*What?*' Nick recoiled. It felt as though he had slapped her. *He doesn't want me. That was just a few moments' dalliance for him.* 'Anusha, I am sorry, I should never have touched you.' She saw his struggle for the kind words, the right tone to save her pride. 'You see why ladies must be chaperoned? You cannot trust men.'

He was allowing her to pretend she had not understood what she was asking, giving her a way to salvage her pride. She would not take it. 'I can trust you. I am not saving myself for a husband, so why should I not make love to a man if I want him?'

'Because it would be dishonourable of me to take your virginity. I should not even have kissed you, or touched you like that.' His eyes had become dark, the colour she had learned to associate with pain, mental or physical.

'It would be dishonourable if I did not want it,' she countered.

'I could get you with child.' He said it as if snatching desperately at an excuse.

'No, it is the wrong time of the moon,' she said with calm practicality. 'And besides, I have the means to stop it happening.' She nodded towards the pack of medicines. She had alum in there. It worked for stopping bleeding, and sweating, but it also helped prevent conception, although she did not know how.

'Your father—'

'Am I his slave?'

'No, but I am his man.' She opened her mouth to protest, but he pushed on. 'You say you trust me—he trusts me also. Would you have me betray both of you?'

'No,' she said after a moment. 'No, I would not ask you to break your trust. *Maf kijiye.*'

'Do not be sorry, Anusha,' Nick answered her in Hindi. 'You do me much honour, but it is a gift I cannot take.'

So, he salves my pride by pretending he is sorry. My protector. She managed to smile as he took his shirt and slid from the bed. She could pretend, too. Perhaps he was right, not for the reasons the gave, but because there was something fragile and tentative between them she could not put a name to, and that intimacy, with guilt on his side and something like desperation on hers, would have shattered it.

'Tomorrow we will reach Calcutta,' Nick said. They were on the Hooghly River now, he had explained, one of the arms of the River Ganges, the one that flowed to the sea through the great river port of Calcutta.

It was not exciting any longer, this journey through muddy plains, jungle, the occasional low rise with a village or a cluster of temples. Green trees, brown river, brown mud, hot blue sky and Nick being kind and proper and pretending that she had not said those things to him in her cabin, that they had not been locked together, mouth to mouth, breast to breast and that she had not felt the heat, the reality, of his desire.

Every night she ached for him. And every night she told herself to be thankful that he had shown *angrezi* honour and resisted her.

'It will be late, I think, but we will be safe back.' Anusha could hear the relief in Nick's voice. It was no wonder—they had been together for three weeks now and he had not wanted to be alone with her any more than she had at the start of this. Nick would want to hand her over to her father and go back to his own life, his own home and, no doubt, another woman for his pleasure.

Had she betrayed that she felt more than simply desire for him? She still did not understand what it was that she felt: liking, admiration—both those, of course.

But there was something wounded inside him that she wanted to soothe, to heal. It was something to do with his marriage, she was certain. He must have loved his wife desperately, whatever he said, because otherwise, why was he so alone in his spirit?

Anusha leaned on the rail as they swept by a large village with fishing boats drawn up on the muddy beach, then a bend in the river took them and they were back between low bluffs covered in vegetation. It was peaceful—the current was no stronger than usual, there were no rocks. All the warning she had was a shout and then she was tumbling across the deck, her ears full of an ominous cracking of wood as the cook-boat swept down on them, struck them hard on the stern and slammed them into a sandbank.

'The tiller has broken!' the steersman shouted.

'*Dhat tere ki!*' Nick swore. 'If they've holed the thing…'

But the damage was only to the rudder.

Half an hour later the crew stood around the slabs of splintered wood on the sand and watched Nick warily.

'Can it be mended?'

'No, *sahib*. But we can have another made at the village we passed. They had many boats, they will have carpenters.'

'Go, then,' Nick said. 'And make haste.'

'We must pole the cook-boat upriver,' the captain explained. Nick's restraint seemed to unnerve him. 'It will take all of us against the current, and then it will be dark.'

'Then hurry,' Nick said. 'Anchor this boat securely, leave us food and be back early in the morning.'

Within half an hour they had gone, leaving the pinnace moored fore and aft on a large, flat sandbank in midstream.

'There is no need to worry,' Nick said.

'I am not. No animals from the bank can reach us, the men will be back tomorrow.' It felt safe to be with Nick, even when danger threatened. Somehow, although he instinctively threw himself between her and any attack, he had given her the confidence that she could fight, too.

'All true. I will light a fire on the sandbank. Do you want to cook for a change?'

'No,' Anusha said firmly. 'I have never had to cook—there were always servants to do that. Why can you cook so well?'

'All soldiers can, although the results are not always very edible. Let us see what they have left us.'

Night fell and the jungle was dark and full of noises. Overhead the dark-blue velvet of the sky was powdered with stars and on the sandbank the fire blazed high as Nick fed it with the driftwood she had gathered while he cooked.

Anusha leaned on the rail and watched him as he sat cross-legged, the three muskets stacked as a tripod beside him. 'Go to bed,' he called without looking back over his shoulder as though he could feel her eyes on him.

If the men came back at dawn with the rudder, then this was the last night they would spend together. Her last night as a princess of the court of Kalatwah. Tomorrow she would be *Miss Laurens*, trying to recall all Nick's lessons in vocabulary and etiquette. Over the fish that he had cooked he had dismissed her thanks with a shrug—it was his duty, he had said. Perhaps he was worried that she would try to seduce him again. She just wanted to put her arms around him and hold him tightly, two people together with aching hearts.

Nick reached out and pulled something from a bag by his side. She could not see what it was, but after a few moments a soft beat floated on the still air. He had brought the *tabla* from the village.

Her feet moved, almost of their own accord. Tonight she was still Anusha and there was one gift she could give Nick.

Chapter Thirteen

The *tala* came without conscious thought, his fingers striking the taut drum skin in the rhythm that the men in his troop had taught him on long, quiet nights in camp. He could listen for danger despite it and the intricate pattern kept him alert and awake.

But it did not stop him thinking, and another sleepless night thinking of Anusha was a penance. Perhaps he deserved it—his conscience still nagged him about the lies he had told her, the way he had deceived her about the life she was going to. But how could he tell her the truth, that her father would be expecting to arrange a marriage for her, that her life as a married English lady in Calcutta would be almost as restricted as life in the *zanana*, that her dowry would go to her husband, not to her?

That she had believed him was clear from the way she had offered herself to him. She wanted to enjoy that new freedom and she thought there would be no danger that she might have to marry.

There was something else, he had see it in her eyes,

heard it in her voice. *She wants to fall in love, she wants romance like her mother did.* He had almost told her he knew, almost told her it was a cruel dream and a fantasy, but who was he to give lessons in loving? Anusha deserved to hope, perhaps even to find love with a man who deserved all that she could give.

If she realised the truth, Anusha would bolt at the first opportunity unless he locked her in her cabin, he was convinced of it. *What could I tell her? That marriages at her level in society would not be forced, but they would always be arranged? That her father would keep her closely chaperoned and give her only pin money?*

She had been on the verge of asking him to give his word. He'd had a split second to prevent her from making him choose between honour and duty.

Anusha had offered herself with a shy courage that had him impossibly hard and needy at the first touch. She tasted of tea and spices and rosewater, of sex and woman and innocence and, remembering, something shifted in Nick's chest as though his heart had jolted. It was what he had wanted almost from the first moment he had seen her, the fantasy that had haunted his nights.

He closed his eyes and let himself believe for a moment, believe that she was his and that she was not an innocent who wanted love and deserved cherishing, but an experienced, worldly-wise courtesan from whom he could part without pain on either side.

Tomorrow night, provided all went well with the rudder, he would have her back where she belonged and if she hated him for it, then that was the price to be paid.

He would not be around to see those grey eyes look at him full of hurt betrayal. He would just have to live with the memory of them.

Now when he tried to remember Miranda her blue eyes were overlain with long-lashed grey ones, her pale skin that had flushed so painfully in the heat was a pale ghost behind honey-gold curves.

Alert as he was, the subtle addition to his own drumming took him by surprise. Nick froze as a figure spun into sight, swirling skirts, tight trousers, the chime of bangles, bare feet slapping down on to the hard sand with the beat of the drum.

Anusha danced into the firelight, her shadow thrown long and dramatic behind her, the blue and red of her garments picking up the colours of the flames, the silver thread sparking gold with reflected light.

She was doing something no respectable woman would do, except for her husband or her female friends, performing one of the classical court dances. Her head moved in impossible, stylised sideways movements, her hands twisted and turned, conveying the meaning of the dance to those who could read its language. Her bare feet stamped and slapped in a complex counter-rhythm to his own hands as, almost mesmerised, he let the pace of the music increase.

The tension rose with the speed until Nick breathed as though he was running, or making love with vigorous, urgent strokes. His heartbeat echoed the *tabla* and he felt himself panting with the effort, but still Anusha twisted and wove her way through the *tala* until, just as he thought they would both collapse, she looked directly at him and brought her palms together with a sharp slap.

Nick lifted his hands from the drum and she stopped, poised like a temple carving, only the rise and fall of her breast, the sheen of perspiration on her forehead, the swinging folds of her *lehenga,* betraying that she was a living woman.

His hands shook as he put down the drum and broke the spell. Anusha moved, pushed back her heavy plait, sending the bangles clattering down her arm, and smiled at him. 'That is something I have never done before,' she said. 'I do not expect I ever will dance for a man again, so it is my thanks to you. The thanks you will not take in words.'

Speechless, he watched her pass him and did not turn as he heard the sound of her footsteps change when she walked up the gangplank and on to the deck. She had taken his breath away and he wondered if he would ever get it back.

'We are here.' It was not a question. Old memories were coming back, although not of landmarks exactly, for it was dark now and all she could see were the myriad of lights both on land and on the boats that seemed to swarm over the surface of the Garden Reach, the great pool of water that was Calcutta's harbour. Anusha leaned on the rail, recollection helped by the mingling smells of the city: human and animal waste, cooking fires, spices, flowers.

'I remember this, I think—all the great ships.' And they were still there, the merchantmen, anchored under the protection of Fort William. 'My father took us up on to the battlements of the fort to see the view once.'

'We will go to the fort now,' Nick said. 'I do not want to take you through the streets without an escort, and besides, Sir George may not be at the house.'

'Is it still the same one?'

'Yes.'

Dancing for Nick had unlocked something inside her, lifted her spirits with the release of movement, the joy of doing an outrageous thing because she chose to. *Freedom.* Now the old apprehension slithered back to fill her stomach with cold apprehension and the sour burn of old betrayal. What if she could not hide how she felt well enough for her father to do what she wanted?

'I had not thought it would be the same house, somehow.' Full of memories of *Mata* that no doubt the other woman would have tried to brush away.

'You will find it changed, perhaps,' Nick said in an echo of her thoughts as a small skiff bumped alongside to take them ashore.

Yes, it would be changed and perhaps that was not a bad thing. The present was hard enough to manage without the ghosts of the past lying in wait around every corner. Anusha climbed down into the skiff and stood with Nick to catch their meagre bundles as they were tossed down. The crew was already chattering and happy at the prospect of a night in the city with wages fattening their purses.

Anusha watched them as the skiff was poled towards the shore. They were poor, they worked hard, their lives were uncertain—was she foolish to envy them their laughter and their careless joy for one night?

'Courage.' Nick was looking at her. 'You are Rajput, remember?'

'I do not know what I am now,' she countered. 'But I will find out.' His mouth tightened. 'What is it? Does your shoulder still pain you?'

'No.' He shook his head and smiled. Knowing him as she did, it looked a little forced. 'My conscience poking at me, I suppose.'

They were speaking English, but she lowered her voice even so. 'Because you kissed me? Because you came to my cabin?'

'That must be it,' he agreed.

'There was no harm. You were very strong and said no.' She tucked her hand companionably into the crook of his arm and leaned against his shoulder, wanting to give comfort. 'You see? We are just friends now.'

Friends? A tremor ran through her as though he had touched her intimately instead of it being she who had offered this harmless gesture.

Her nostrils flared, absorbing the scent of the soap Nick had used and of the day's sweat. Under her hand there was the solidity of muscle and the beat of his heart under his ribs where the backs of her fingers touched. She was as aware of him as she had been when she had danced for him, aware at a far deeper level than the physical attraction that had flashed between them in her cabin, when he had kissed her. This was like that second when his gaze had found her in the village when,

veiled and in shadow, he could not have known her by
any rational means.

Shaken, Anusha looked up at the still profile, black
against the lights of the Princip *ghat*, the nearest land-
ing steps to the fort. There was nothing to read, only
strength and a strong masculinity of line and something of tension in the way his jaw was set. 'Friends,'
she prompted, needing reassurance, although against
what, she was not sure.

'Remember that,' Nick said. She thought he would
add something, but all he said was, 'Keep hold of me
when we land, it is crowded tonight.'

There was a festival for some minor deity. Crowds
were jostling on the wide, wet steps of the *ghat*, dropping chains of marigolds into the water, setting little
earthenware saucers with lighted candles on the surface
to bob away on the current. There was music and sweet-
meat sellers and children shrieking with excitement.

Anusha let Nick swing her ashore, then stood, feet
braced on the slippery granite while he paid the ferry-
man. 'Calcutta at last,' he said, slinging one bag over
his uninjured shoulder and taking the other from her.
'Now all I have to do is get you another half-mile and
my mission is accomplished.'

He sounded pleased about it and she supposed she
could not blame him, Anusha thought as she clutched
his sleeve and followed him towards the river gate of
Fort William. With the memory of Kalatwah so fresh,
she found the low walls and star-shaped fortifications
unimpressive, but there was nothing slack about the response of the guards on the gate or the efficiency with

which they were brought inside and a palanquin was fetched. Either Nick's name or her father's worked like a magic charm, it seemed.

Anusha climbed into the palanquin, let the curtain drop and held tight to the sides as the bearers lifted the long curved pole on to their shoulders. Then they were off. 'Nick!'

'I am here. Are you all right?' It sounded as though he was walking beside her.

'Yes. It was…just very dark and very closed. I have become used to riding and to the river. The open air.' Now she felt like a prisoner. But it would not be for long, she reassured herself. Their destination, Old Court House Street, was only behind the great government buildings and houses of the Esplanade, just north of the *maidan,* the wide expanse of grass that surrounded the fort. And she would never be a prisoner again, confined behind screens and guarded doors, forbidden to go out, veiled and hidden.

'*Nick.*' It was a whisper. She did not know what she wanted, but a hand pushed aside the curtain and curled over the edge of the window opening. Reassured, Anusha put her own over it and felt the panic subside as she was moved, blind, through the streets.

'We are here.' His hand was withdrawn, the palanquin stopped and hung, swaying, there was the sound of excited, raised voices, the clang of a gate opening. 'Call Laurens *sahib*, tell him the daughter of the house has returned.'

The palanquin was set down, the curtain drawn back.

Anusha emerged blinking into a courtyard surrounded by high, white-washed walls, a wide veranda and the low bulk of the house.

'That was where I saw you laid out like the dead,' she said as Nick came to her side. It was all so familiar and yet different. The yard seemed smaller, the house larger. Trees loomed unexpectedly and all the servants who were hurrying towards her were strangers.

'Anusha! Anusha, my dear child.' The man on the veranda was her father and yet not her father. The strong voice was the same, the height and the width of shoulder, but his hair was grey now, no longer dark gold as she remembered, there were lines on his face and what was once a flat belly now had a little paunch.

Ten years. Did I expect him to look the same, not to have changed while I have grown up? She took a step forward. 'Pa—' *No, Papa and his little girl have gone now.* The hands that had lifted instinctively to him folded neatly together as she bowed her head and willed her wildly-beating pulse to calm. '*Namaste,* Father.'

He came down the steps beaming, took her by the shoulders and for one moment she thought he would lift her, swing her up for his kiss as he always had when he came home to her. But he had no need to lift her now. Her father stooped and kissed her on the brow.

'You are so beautiful, my child. Just like your mother.' She stiffened as she stood passive between his hands and he added, his voice tight with emotion, 'It was a tragedy that she should have died so young— you must miss her very much.'

'Every day,' she said, meeting the grey eyes that

were so like her own. *What emotion do you feel, Father? Guilt?*

His brows, still dark although his hair had greyed, drew together at her tone. Anger, puzzlement or both? He released her and pulled Nick into a rapid embrace. 'Nicholas, my boy, thank you for bringing her back safe to me. I have been getting coded messages from Delhi, so I knew you were travelling alone. And we have been hearing news from Kalatwah—the maharaja has given up the siege and retreated. There has been no bloodshed.'

The relief was an almost physical thing and not until it hit her did she realise just how that worry had been filling the back of her mind, ever present like a large black vulture, patiently waiting for tragedy to strike.

'That is good to know,' Nick said and smiled at her. 'You can stop worrying now.'

'Worrying?' Her father turned at the top of the steps. 'There was never any need to worry, not with that fortress so impregnable and help on the way. Nick, you must have explained it to her. The danger was always from one or two men getting inside and snatching you, Anusha, and the furore that would cause.'

'He explained very clearly, but they are my family,' Anusha said with a glance at Nick. He smiled back, an ally. 'Of course I worry.'

Again, that frown. 'You must be tired, both of you. Come inside where we can talk. You'll be hungry, I have no doubt, and will want to wash and change before dinner. I have had the best room refurnished for you, Anusha. Do you remember it? The one at the back overlooking the garden. I hope you will like it.'

She heard the emotion under his question and steeled her heart against it. 'Thank you, I recall it.' Not the room he had prepared for his wife, then. That was a relief—she would have refused to sleep in it and somehow she did not have the strength this evening for active confrontation, only for resistance.

The wide hallway was swarming with servants, all male of course, except for one woman, patiently waiting at the rear, her *dupatta* pulled forwards to shield her face. 'This is Nadia, your maid. Nadia, take Miss Anusha to her room, we dine in an hour.'

'*Namaste,* Nadia,' Anusha said as the maidservant came forwards.

'Good evening, Miss Anusha,' the woman responded and Anusha realised that she was quite young. 'Laurens *sahib* says that I must speak English to you all the time. The room is this way. My English is good, yes? I have been having lessons from the maid of Lady Hoskins in how to be a proper lady's maid.' They passed a *punkah wallah* sitting with his back against the wall, endlessly moving his foot so the cord tied to his big toe pulled the wide cloth fans to and fro in the rooms on either side of the corridor.

The maid opened the door at the end of the passage and waited for her to go through. Anusha had forgotten the furniture would be like this: the high bed, draped in fine muslin netting, the chairs, upright and stiff and lower ones too, padded. There were no cushions on the matting-covered floor. She would have to sit upright on these chairs, something her mother had always refused to do.

A—what was it called?—*dressing table* covered in little boxes and bottles, hair brushes, a mirror at the back. A clothes press. The door to what must be the bathing room. It was all so plain—the only bright colours were the maid's clothing and a dark red throw across the bed.

The long windows were open, with slatted shutters secured across them to let in the breeze, but give privacy and security, for the whole house was only one storey high. Overhead the *punkah* creaked to and fro, stirring the air, and a faint hum of chatter from the hallway reached her through the grillework over the door.

'This is a nice room, I think,' Nadia said with an anxious glance at Anusha. 'The water boys will have filled the bath if it pleases you to take it now, Miss Anusha, and I will lay out your clothes.'

'I have no clothes,' Anusha said, and went to peer into the bathing room. The bath was large and already full of water.

'That must have been very difficult! But Laurens *sahib* asked Lady Hoskins and she has sent everything that you need. See.' Nadia threw open the clothes press and pulled out drawers. 'Gowns and petticoats and corsets and stockings and—'

'Enough. I will bathe and then I will put on these clothes again with clean linen beneath. Not my turban, though.' The maid opened her mouth to protest then, with one look from Anusha, shut it again.

'Yes, Miss Anusha.'

* * *

She remembered the way to the dining room as well, although everything within the familiar lay-out of the house looked different. The walls had been painted with pale, plain washes, the furniture was new, more European in style, she supposed. Certainly foreign and uncomfortable to someone used to soft cushions, billowing silks, quilted cottons.

By dint of sending Nadia on an errand Anusha had managed to retrieve the jewels from her turban and hide them in a loose panel beneath the window seat. Most of the seats had panels that could be prised out, she had discovered as a child—probably there were still her little caches of toys and treasures all over the house.

Now, her hair in its plait down her back, her severe men's clothing unrelieved by jewels, she was conscious of the sideways glances of the male servants in the hall. They must be used to unveiled women, but she supposed that her strange mixture of European and Indian looks, her male attire, must seem odd and shocking to them.

'She is tired, that is all. It has been a trying journey for me, let alone for a sheltered young woman.' Nick's voice came clear through the ventilation grille above the door of her father's study. Anusha slowed to listen.

'…reserved.' Her father's voice, a low rumble from further into the room. 'Cold.'

'It is a long time since she saw you,' Nick replied. 'And she has been in the *zanana*. You would expect some uncertainty, surely?'

He is making peace for me. What would she have done without Nick? He had spirited her away, kept her safe, restrained those powerful male instincts for her and taught her some of what she needed for this strange new life she must live before she could snatch her freedom. *My friend,* she thought as she walked on, unable to linger and eavesdrop with the servants hovering attentively.

He would stay, surely, for a few weeks before he went off on another mission? He must rest, allow his wound to heal, and she would have him to stand between her and this strange, half-familiar world. *Nick.*

Chapter Fourteen

There had to be a word for Nick and the place he occupied in her heart, Anusha thought as she curled up uncomfortably on one of the big rattan chairs in the drawing room. Friend was not enough, not for the trust she felt, nor, she feared, for that tingling sense of physical attraction that she felt when he was near. She was still wrestling with words in both Hindi and English when the men came in.

'Ah, there you are, my dear. Is your room to your liking?' Her father stopped on the threshold and stared at her. 'Why are you still dressed like that? Did your maid not show you your new clothes? Never tell me they do not fit? I was sent the measurements.'

By whom? 'I am more comfortable in these tonight, Father.' Best not to start an argument now. Tomorrow she must cope with the corsets and the stockings and all the other horrors of European dress.

'Very well.' His smile was kindly, but there was a tinge of uncertainty. *He does not know how to handle me,* Anusha thought. *He is nervous. Good!*

Her preoccupation with that little triumph distracted her and she missed what he added. '…hunting.' It seemed to be a joke, although Nick was not laughing. In fact, he looked as he had when they were in tiger country: alert and very, very wary. As it had then, that look sent a trickle of cold down her spine.

'I am sorry, Father I did not hear—'

'George, did I tell you that the situation—'

Why was Nick attempting to distract her father? The older man looked confused too. 'I only said that male attire is not suitable for husband hunting, however useful it might be for escaping across country,' he said.

'*Husband* hunting?'

'But of course. That is what we must apply ourselves to, is it not? We must find you a suitable husband.'

'I am here because Nick told me I must leave Kalatwah for the good of the state and to avoid embarrassing the East India Company.' Anusha found she was on her feet. 'I am not here to marry anyone. I do not want a husband!' She turned on Nick, whose face was blank now, although his eyes were wary. 'You told me I would not have to. You told me I would be free.'

'Nicholas?' Her father's tone was ominous. 'What is this?'

'If I had told her you intended to arrange a marriage she would have run away,' Nick said as though the words were being pried out of him at knifepoint.

'You lied to me.' She could not believe it. How could he have deceived her like his? 'I thought you were my friend, I trusted you and you *lied* to me. What honour is there in untruths, you fine English officer and gentleman? *None.'*

'It was that or tie you up in the cabin,' he retorted. 'I knew you would run if you heard the truth.'

'You promised me!'

'No. You asked me to promise, I never gave you my word.'

'No, because you—' *You kissed me instead.* It did not take the warning jerk of his head towards her father to make her swallow the words. *That was why you made love to me, to distract me. Not because you wanted me, not because you felt anything.* 'You told me I would have money, my freedom. I will not have money—is that what you are telling me also?' she demanded.

'What nonsense have you been saying, Nicholas?' her father demanded, breaking into their exchange. 'What money?'

'Anusha believes that her dowry will belong to her, that as your daughter she will be rich and independent. She wishes to travel, not to marry.'

There was a fraught silence then, 'Be damned to that!' Sir George said. 'Of course you are going to marry, my girl. Who has put such foolishness into your head? Nicholas—what fairy tales have you been telling her?'

'What she wanted to hear. My choice was to betray your trust and risk her running away or to deceive her. What would you have me do?' Nick kept his voice calm and reasonable, but Anusha could hear the anger in it and the frustration that he was too respectful of the older man to show.

'What you did, of course.' The anger seemed to drain out of her father. His shoulders slumped. 'Anusha, you have no idea what you are talking about, no idea about European marriage. There is nothing to worry about, nothing to fear.'

Suspicious, she watched the men through narrowed eyes. 'You will not force me?'

'Of course not! Did your uncle and I not give you perfect freedom to refuse any marriage offer made to you?'

'Yes.' Anusha cut a glance at Nick's face. He was his usual impassive self again, although she could still sense his reined-in tension. But her father had been angry with him, so perhaps that was the source of it. 'And so...I can travel? I do not have to have a husband?'

'Of course you cannot travel! And of course you must have a husband, but I will not force one on you that you cannot like.'

She stared at him. 'I *must* marry, yet you will not force me? I can choose and yet I am not free? Is it my English? I know it is not perfect yet, but I cannot misunderstand so much, surely?'

Her father stared back, obviously frustrated by her lack of comprehension. 'Nicholas, you explain it to her: I'm damn... I obviously cannot.' He turned on his heel and marched out.

'Yes, please, Nick. You explain it to me,' she said sweetly. 'And I will try to believe you this time as well. Or perhaps you could kiss me again until my brain is as muddled as soup and I stop asking difficult questions.'

The betraying flags of colour were on his cheekbones

again, but he took a deep breath and answered her patiently, 'There will be no kissing. Your father wants only the best for you. He will have decided upon suitable suitors for you to consider.'

'Who are these men? What are they?' The anger almost drowned the panic as she took an impetuous step forwards and took his forearm in both hands. She would shake the truth out of him if need be.

'I have no idea which poor fellow he has in mind.' Nick said with what she guessed was a misplaced attempt to mollify her with humour. 'But Sir George will want you safely married off as soon as possible. You are older than most of the single girls in Calcutta society.'

'*Married off!*' For a moment she could not work out the English idiom and she stared at him as though he had spoken Greek. 'To an *angrezi* husband he has picked out for me.'

'Of course. You are to become an English lady, that is all I know. What else would you do in Calcutta? How else would you live with him? He hardly needs a housekeeper.'

Anusha let go of his arm and took an unsteady stride away from him. 'Do? I want to do *nothing* in Calcutta except leave it! I did not ask to come here. I do not want a husband, I have turned down offer after offer.'

'I know. But this is different. We are not talking of a political marriage to a man old enough to be your father or to a princeling who could be murdered in a palace coup at any time. You will be an English lady and you may choose your husband, face to face.'

'Anyone?' she demanded, twisting to look at him

over her shoulder, knowing the answer perfectly well. Choice offered by a man was nothing but a mirage. 'Any man I wish?'

'Of course not, but any eligible man your father approves. As I said, he is sure to have some in mind for you. Not just anyone, Anusha, but men of wealth and influence who will give you a good life.'

Wealth and influence. So that was why she had been summoned back, virtually kidnapped from her uncle's court. The threat from Altaphur was real enough, but that gave her father his excuse. No doubt there was some alliance he wished to cement so he had thought of her, a pawn on his chessboard. At least it explained why he wanted her back after all this time.

Instinct had warned her that danger awaited and at least now she knew what it was: the risk of being married off to some Englishman who would treat her like her father had treated her mother. Only she would be legally tied to him, so she would be expected to stay with her husband however badly he behaved to her.

'Anusha, listen to me.' Nick caught her by the shoulders, turned her to face him. 'With the dowry Sir George will give and the influence he wields, there will be no problem in finding you a suitable husband, one you will like. A leading merchant, a promising army officer, the younger son of a noble house—that sort of gentleman.'

A promising army officer, the younger son of a noble house... She shot Nick a fulminating glance. Did he mean himself? Marriage to her would make him the son and male heir of the man he regarded as his father.

It would give him more money, more standing to help him build what was obviously a promising career. Had that been what his kisses and his kindness had been about—careful first steps in seducing a bride?

If Nick married her, he would march off as soon as he had planted a child in her and go to whatever exciting and interesting things he spent his life doing and she would be left with the corsets and the babies and the *memsahibs* with their disapproving mouths, and she would never belong and never be free.

'I see.' She felt strangely calm all of a sudden. She had been moved from the gilded, luxurious cage of the court to another cage, not so gilded, not so luxurious. And, she could see already, not so secure. 'He chooses some men, parades them in front of me, I say *no*, he finds some more… How long does this go on?'

'Until you find someone you like.' Nick watched her face with the patience she had grown accustomed to. It was the implacable patience of the hunter and, worst of all, there was pity deep in the green eyes. 'Anusha, I am sorry I had to deceive you, but you have no idea how dangerous it is out there for a gently reared lady alone—you would not have lasted a day.'

How innocent she had been, how romantic, to think that this alien warrior would be her friend or perhaps, in those half-waking dreams around dawn, more than her friend.

At the court, if she had refused a match and her uncle had insisted, she would have been shut up in her room until she submitted. Here, it seemed, there would be no physical coercion so it would be a game of cunning to escape. And she knew she was cunning—court life taught you how to be that.

'I understand.' She turned from him in case he saw the calculation in her eyes. 'And who will teach me to be an English lady that these desirable men will want to marry? Or would they marry anyone to secure my father's money and patronage?'

'They will want you for yourself, Anusha. How could they not when they come to know you?' *Yes? I know already that you will tell me any lies if it suits you.* 'And Lady Hoskins will take you under her wing. She lives three houses further along this street. She is married to Sir Joshua Hoskins, a colleague of your father, and they have a daughter who married last year and a son of seventeen.'

An experienced matron, one who would not be easy to deceive. Best to begin now to disarm suspicion. 'I see I will have to make the best of it,' she said with a shrug. It would not do to seem too ready to accept her fate.

'Come and have dinner, then. Take your mind off your troubles by wrestling with the silverware.'

'I am certain I will have no problem.' She stalked out of the door in front of Nick. 'After all, I have had the benefit of your lessons.'

Anusha was angry with him, her nose was severely out of joint and she was, however well she was hiding it, deeply uneasy in this house, uprooted from everything she knew and understood. Nick followed on her heels into the dining room, worry and sympathy warring in his breast. On their journey, however difficult and dangerous it had been, they had been in her world and she had been the raja's niece.

Now she did not know who she was, only that she was with the father she believed had rejected her, and a man who had lied to her and lured her into coming here.

A servant held her chair for her at the foot of the table and she sat, back straight, hands folded in her lap, chin up. Nick took his own place, halfway along the board between Anusha and Sir George at the head, as servants began to bring in the dishes that made up a typical Anglo-Indian dinner.

The way the table was arranged mirrored the Indian style of setting out an array of dishes all at once, but the dishes themselves were a hotchpotch of Indian curries, chutneys and rice and English roasts, soups and vegetables. 'May I help you to anything?' Nick offered. 'A slice of lamb or chicken?'

'Thank you. Chicken.' She eyed the vegetables, then extended her right hand towards the rice and snatched it back, lips pursed in embarrassment as she found the serving spoon and used that. The servant poured wine into her glass.

Nick laid two slices of chicken on her plate. 'Might I trouble you for the vegetables?'

She managed, he saw, with ferocious concentration and by watching what he and George did like a hawk. It would never do to underestimate either Anusha's intelligence, or her ability to learn and adapt. His conscience had ceased to trouble him for lying to her—it was his duty to protect her, by any means, and he had done so—but he was very conscious that he had lost her trust. Whatever it had been between them that was so warm and so elusive had congealed into wary watchfulness on his side and hostile suspicion on hers.

'You'll like Lady Hoskins, Anusha.' George had apparently decided to deal with the confrontation in the drawing room by ignoring it. 'And her daughter Anna—Mrs Roper now—is a delightful young woman. Pass the salt, would you, Nicholas?'

It was a slight stretch. Nick suppressed the wince as the movement overextended the healing wound in his shoulder, but Anusha saw his reaction.

'Is your shoulder paining you, Major Herriard?' she asked with such sweet concern that it took him a moment to realise she had called him by rank and surname.

'Shoulder?' George looked up sharply. 'What have you done?'

'It was the dacoits, Father,' Anusha said. 'The major was shot in the shoulder, just outside Kalpi.' She lowered her eyelashes so they feathered her cheeks and Nick suppressed a strong desire to pick her up and dump her back in her room. She was up to something. 'And he was nursed at the house of Mr Rowley, the agent. His wife was most disapproving of me.' The grey eyes lifted and opened wide. 'Do you think I will be—what is it called?—*ruined* when she speaks of it?'

A good attempt, Anusha, Nick thought and produced a smile as false as her look of anxious enquiry was. 'No need to worry, George. I had a word with the Rowleys and the doctor. One mention of your name and they were vowing complete discretion and eternal silence.'

'So I should hope,' George said with a grunt. 'But how bad is this wound? I'll call my doctor after dinner and have you checked over.'

'Tomorrow is soon enough.' There was going to be no escaping an examination, he knew the older man well enough for that. 'It has healed well. Miss Laurens was good enough to dress it for me.'

'Was she indeed?'

'The major was incredibly brave,' Anusha remarked. 'There were the dacoits and the king cobra, and the maharaja's men and the tigers.'

'Tigers?'

'We saw one pug mark,' Nick said with a repressive stare at Anusha who was doggedly cutting chicken with the unfamiliar cutlery. 'The men sent after us were easily headed on to the wrong trail. The dacoits were…troublesome. Fortunately we had trained cavalry horses.'

'And the king cobra?' There was a smile lurking in the concern. Nick knew George had seen his youthful self swarm up trees to escape snakes and knew all too well that they brought him out in a cold sweat.

'The major was…' Anusha's voice trailed away. 'He was… He saved my life and I thought he had been bitten.' All the *faux* sweetness had gone, and so had much of the blood from her cheeks. 'Excuse me. I am suddenly very tired. I will go to my chamber.' She put down the cutlery with a little clatter, pushed back the chair before the servant had a chance to reach it and walked swiftly from the room.

'Well,' George remarked as they sat down again. 'I

think a full, unexpurgated report is called for, hmm?
And no false modesty, Nicholas, or I'll ask Anusha for
all the details.'

Chapter Fifteen

The *punkah* had been still for over an hour. Distantly there were the noises of the city, and the house creaked as it cooled, but there were no human sounds except the watchman's sandaled feet as he had padded past a hundred heartbeats ago.

Anusha slid out of bed, miscalculated the height and gasped as her heels jarred on the floor. After a few moments, when no answering sounds reached her, she breathed again and slipped into a dark robe. Her bare feet made no sound on the matting and her door opened without a sound, thanks to the *ghee* she had used to oil the hinges earlier.

She moved along the corridor by the light of her little lamp, its flame shielded by her cupped palm, the soft sounds of her movements masked by the snores of the man sleeping across the front door. He did not stir as she turned into the passage leading to the drawing room, the one that passed her father's study.

That was where the maps would be, his strong box, news sheets with shipping advertisements. Ammunition that she could not use now, but which she needed to locate. How easy would the strong box be to open? Anusha tried the study door, found it unlocked and went in.

It was as she remembered it from her childhood. Then she would come to this room on a Saturday to sit on Papa's—*Father's*—knee and receive a shiny silver rupee that was all hers to spend in the bazaar when her *ayah* took her there.

She sat down in his big chair now, her vision blurred as the room filled with daylight and the sound of Papa's laugh when she brought back trinkets and toys and sweetmeats to show him at the end of the day.

Weakness. Just memories of a man's indulgence to a child—now she was a woman. A daughter who was a possession and a bargaining counter, but whose value was diminished by her mixed blood and her illegitimacy.

Anusha lifted down the set of red leather ledgers and there, just as she remembered, was the heavy iron safe. It was bigger than anything she had tried to open before and it would need more than hairpins.

'An urge to visit the night bazaar and so a need for spending money?' a low voice behind her enquired. She whirled around. Nick was watching her, his back against the closed door. How had he found her? And how the devil had he got inside the room, closed the door behind him, all without her hearing him?

'I want to see if there is somewhere safe for my jewels.'

'Liar,' he said softly. 'At three in the morning?'

'I could not sleep. How did you hear me?'

'I was watching for you.'

'Where?' As her breathing steadied she began to take in details. He was wearing a robe of heavy black silk, belted at the waist and in the vee of the neckline she could see skin and a curl of hair. His feet were bare, his hair loose on his shoulders.

'In my bedchamber.'

'You are sleeping here?'

'I live here. I have a suite of rooms at the rear of the house.'

'The women's quarters,' Anusha said flatly. Where she and *Mata* had lived for twelve years.

'Yes. When you left George had part of it converted for me. I can see your window and the light shines through the shutters.'

No sooner had she and *Mata* gone than Nick had invaded their territory, filled the space they had left. 'You are spying on me.' She picked up the ledgers and thrust them back on the shelf, aligning the edges perfectly to give herself time to think.

'It seemed wise to do so. Was I right?' She had forgotten how he could move like smoke, like a tiger. He was beside her when she turned, so close that she could smell the familiar tang of his skin overlain by something new, the soap he had washed with that night, she thought, dizzy with reaction to the shock of his appearance, of his closeness.

'You cannot stay awake every night.' Somehow Anusha managed to get her tongue around the words.

'No, but I can put a watchman to sleep across your door and another to sit beneath your window. Who knows how vindictive the maharajah might be? You must be protected.'

'You do not believe he will try to snatch me here,' she said scornfully.

'No. But your father might if I suggest it.'

'And you are his spy and my jailer.'

'I am your friend, Anusha. I wish you could believe it.' Nick moved closer. The flickering light sent shadows chasing across his face, turned his hair to gilt, made his eyes dark and mysterious. The air was thick in her lungs and it was hard to breathe.

'I—' She meant to curse him, but all that came out was a small gasp. To her horror she felt tears prick the back of her eyes. *I want to believe you. I want to trust you.*

'Anusha.' Nick gathered her to him, into the softness of silk, against the hard strength of his body. She buried her face into the fabric and felt skin against her cheek, the beat of his heart against her ear. Every fibre of her being told her that he was safety and protection and desire, every instinct told her he was danger and betrayal. *And desire.*

'It hurts, doesn't it? To be back here, to not understand. But you were a child then, you are a woman now. Talk to your father, try to reach each other. He loves you.'

The heavy silk absorbed the tears, but she still could not speak as the realisation of what these feelings meant swept through her. *I love you.* Wordless, shaking with the force of her discovery, she wound her arms around Nick's waist and held on to as much of him as she could grasp. He moved, the sensation of being supported and surrounded intensified, and she realised he had sat down on the edge of the desk and was holding her against his chest as she stood between his spread legs.

He made no move to caress her, or to touch her other than to flatten his big hands on her back, but gradually, as she relaxed, she became aware that he was aroused, hard against the softness of her lower belly as she rested against him.

I do *trust him,* she thought, her mind finally calm. *He did what he had to do because he loves my father and he owes him everything. And I want him and he will stand here all night comforting me because he thinks that is what I need... That is* not *what I need. I love you.*

Anusha nuzzled into the overlap of the robe, the tickle of chest hair strange and arousing over smooth skin and hard muscle beneath.

'Anusha—' He stopped with a gasp as her questing mouth found a nipple that contracted into a hard knot at the first stroke of her tongue. Her fingers closed over the ends of the sash that held his robe closed and she tugged as he shifted to hold her away from his body. The robe fell open and she rocked forwards against him, close against the splendour of his nakedness.

'Anusha,' he said again and this time it was a groan. She lifted her face to him, her lips parted in invitation, and he bent his head and took them. She could sense the conflict in him even as his mouth made love to hers, his tongue slipping between her teeth to stroke and plunge and plunder. He tasted hot and male and urgent and through the thin cotton that she wore she felt his heartbeat kick.

'No,' Nick muttered, lifting his head so the kiss was broken. But it was as though he did not have the strength of lift right away and his breath stroked her lips and his eyes were wide and brilliant. 'No,' he said more strongly.

Anusha clung to his neck, lifted one knee on to the desk and then the other so she straddled him, her night robe crumpling up to leave her exposed. Then, before he could twist free, she lowered herself so that the heated length of his erection was trapped along the soft intimate folds that were hot and moist and ached for him.

'God, Anusha, *no.*' Nick bucked his hips, but that only pressed him closer and she moved with him, rocking in a rhythm that made her sob with need. 'Sweetheart, stop. Stop, please while I still can—'

He was struggling with himself, with her, with his fear of hurting her and his need to take her. It was a fight, a battle and one she was desperate to win...*because I love him.* Anusha stopped moving, consciencestricken. Nick would never forgive himself if he took her virginity here, like this, she knew. It would break him, break the bond with her father, break his honour.

She fell against his chest and tried to keep still. 'I am sorry, Nick. I just...I just need you so much.' *If I tell him I love him he will leave. He does not want love.*

Silence, broken only by the sound of their panting breaths, the hiss of the lamp wick, a dog barking in the night.

'I need you, too,' Nick said, his voice harsh as though the confession had been extracted under torture.

He was a sensual, virile man and she knew he had not had a woman for weeks and here she was offering herself. Of course he *wanted* her—it did not mean anything else. Anusha tried to climb down. 'Wait.' He stood, lifting her with him, walked to the couch in the corner, sat down again and set her by his side.

His face was sheened with sweat and she could see the big artery in his neck pulsing, but his hands were steady as he wrapped himself in the robe again and tied the sash. 'You ache,' Nick stated as though he asked her if she was thirsty.

'Yes.' She wanted to touch his hair, smooth the gilt silk under her fingers, but she dare not touch, make it more difficult for him. In a moment, when her legs had stopped shaking, she would get up and go to her room and stop tormenting him.

'Come here then, sweetheart. Let me make it better.' He lifted her on to his lap, settled her against his shoulder and kissed her, all before she could react.

She should get up… But her legs felt even weaker and his mouth was like a drug and his arms held her and she gave herself up to the kiss. Even when his hand slid up her leg, pushed back the thin cotton of her night shift, cupped her aching core, all she could do was moan into his mouth.

And then—*aah!* How could such gentleness create such violence in her body? She arched, pressing against his hand as his fingers explored, stroked, found the point…the point… Anusha stopped thinking, stopped breathing, surrendered to sensation and heat and Nick. Then his other hand cupped her breast and his fingers closed on one nipple and pinched, so lightly, and the exquisite pleasure broke over her like a wave so that she screamed and he captured the sound in his kiss.

She was vaguely aware of being lifted, of movement, of being lowered on to something soft. 'Sleep, Anusha,' Nick murmured in her ear. His hand brushed her cheek and she smiled, her body as limp as finest silk velvet, her mind utterly at peace. *I love you.* She tried to say it, but the words were lost as she drifted down into sleep.

'So you are Anusha! Welcome to Calcutta, my dear.'

'Ma'am.' Anusha dropped a curtsy. It felt very odd, her legs were still shaky after last night—the only thing that convinced her it had not all been a dream—but apparently it was correct, for Lady Hoskins smiled and nodded in approval.

'What a charming young lady, Sir George. I am sure we will get along famously, will we not, Anusha? How is your English? Do we need an interpreter and a tutor?'

'No, ma'am.' She dragged her thoughts away from memories of Nick's naked body, of his hands, his mouth… This was nothing to do with Nick, this was all about her father's plans for her and she must be constantly on the alert. But when she saw him again, would he say anything? Could he possibly have discovered that he loved her, too? *No, do not hope.*

'I recall my English from before I was sent away, and I spoke it often with my mother.' That was deliberately tactless. She noticed her father's lips draw tight and Lady Hoskins shift as though uneasy. Anusha kept her face innocently blank. She was not going to mention talking to Nick in English, she had no wish to compromise herself, not yet at any rate. Later it might be useful. *Later I might not be able to help myself.*

'Er...excellent. And your maid is satisfactory? She has turned you out very well this morning.'

'Thank you, I am very happy with her.' Anusha knew she had been difficult enough that morning to excuse outright mutiny on the part of Nadia as the maid had patiently dressed her in chemise and corset, petticoats, more petticoats to make her skirts bell out, stocking, garters and shoes that pinched her toes. And over the top of it a gown in cotton chintz with wide skirts and a tight bodice and sleeves. How anyone was expected to move in all this she had no idea—standing still and curtsying were simple by comparison.

'A new hairstyle is the first priority.' Lady Hoskins circled her. 'That weight of hair is impossible to do anything with.'

'I do not wish to have my hair cut, ma'am.' But the older woman was already gesturing to the maid. Before she could protest further, the plait was undone and shaken loose.

'It waves, it is an interesting colour, but we must have at least a foot off it. More, perhaps.'

My hair, my beautiful hair! It reached below her hips when it was loose. She'd had fantasies of letting it hang over Nick's naked body, of sweeping it back and forth until he... But that was when he had not known how keenly she desired him—he would avoid her now, she feared.

'Very well.' Whatever it took to lull her father into believing she meant to stay, meant to be a dutiful daughter. Anusha watched him from the corner of her eye. He was taking more of an interest in Lady Hoskin's attempts to turn her into an English lady than he had in anything else about his long-lost daughter, she thought resentfully.

'Excellent. Then, Sir George, with your permission, I will send for my *coiffeuse* and my maid and together we will deal with the question of hair and go through Anusha's wardrobe. I thought dinner at our house tonight? Just a small gathering of twenty to get her into the way of things.'

Anusha found that she was gazing hopefully at her father's retreating back, as though he might turn round and rescue her. But of course he did no such thing and, of course, she did not wish him to. What she wanted was to ask where Nick was, why he had not been at breakfast.

'Now, the first thing is to lace that corset properly,' Lady Hoskins said, advancing on her as the door closed. 'Your figure is far too natural.' Anusha clenched her fists and managed to smile.

'I declare it is a positive age since you came to any parties, Major Herriard. I was saying only the other day to my sister that we must quite give you up, which is such a pity, for we are always in need of handsome men in red coats.' The elder Miss Wilkinson finished this piece of inanity with a giggle and batted her eyelashes at him over the top of her fan. It was a pretty fan and a pair of charming blue eyes and she knew it.

Nick managed a smile through gritted teeth. To think that he had spent hours sailing down the Ganges instructing Anusha in how to produce just such pointless chit-chat! At the thought of her his groin tightened and he forced his concentration back to the women in front of him—they aroused no desires at all.

'Alas, duty calls only too often, Miss Wilkinson, and drags us poor men away from the delightful company of Calcutta's ladies.'

That was apparently an acceptable response. Miss Wilkinson moved a little closer and then, to his surprise, gestured to a group of young ladies nearby. Nick found himself surrounded.

'We are all *agog* and y*ou* will know, Major Herriard,' Miss Annis Wilkinson breathed. 'Is it true that Sir George Laurens has his *natural daughter* staying with him and she is an Indian *princess*?' She made Anusha sound as exotic as a cage full of white tigers, but he supposed none of these girls would ever have met a member of the royal courts.

'Miss Laurens has been residing with her uncle, the Raja of Kalatwah. The state has recently been attacked by a neighbouring prince, so I escorted Miss Laurens home to her father.' There was no point in making a mystery of the basic facts.

'Escorted her?'

Nick injected every bit of *ennui* he could into his reply and managed without an outright lie. 'Court progresses are the slowest, most tedious thing imaginable. Bullock carts, palanquins, the *zanana* tents to shield the ladies…'

'Oh!' A frisson of delighted horror at the thought of the *zanana* ran through the group. 'And does she go everywhere escorted by an enormous eunuch?'

There was a stir near the door and the butler announced, 'Sir George Laurens, Miss Laurens.'

'You may see for yourself,' Nick said, turning to look. He had avoided the main part of the house all day, and sent a message to George that he had business at the fort. He was not at all sure that either he or Anusha could control their expressions or their reactions if they met just yet and he had no desire to explain to George why his daughter was slapping his face.

Last night had been exquisite, insane and appallingly dangerous. He had been unable to get the taste or the scent of Anusha out of his head all day. Somehow he had to talk to her, assure her that it would never happen again, that he would protect her innocence at whatever cost to himself, because today she must be angry, frightened and shocked.

He stared over the heads of the crowd. He could see George, talking to his host, but he could not see Anusha.

'But she looks quite ordinary,' one of the girls said, her voice flat with disappointment. 'Just like us.'

'I can't—' *Good God.* The slight figure next to Sir George *was* Anusha. Her hair was piled up into an elaborate arrangement with one glossy ringlet left to lie on her shoulder. Her waist looked minute rising from the bell of her skirts and she tossed the lace back from her sleeves as she lifted her fan in a movement that was pure coquette. Nick found his voice. 'Ordinary?'

Chapter Sixteen

Nick swallowed and got his face back under control.

'I expected she would have a sari and rings in her nose and she'd be dark skinned with black hair and big brown eyes. But she is just like us, only her skin looks as though she has been in the sun too much,' Miss Wilkinson observed. There was a murmur of agreement. 'I like that amber silk.'

Then Anusha moved, walking into the room beside her father, and Nick felt every man in the room under eighty draw a breath. She might look like a golden-skinned version of any young lady who was fashionably gowned and coiffed, but she moved like the trained dancer she was, with a feline grace that took him in the throat and then, inevitably, considerably lower. God, he wanted her. How the hell had he ever managed to stop himself last night?

'Excuse me,' he said. 'I must go and speak to Sir George and be introduced to Miss Laurens.'

'But you've met her,' Miss Wilkinson protested. 'You

escorted her. You must have seen her. And you live with Sir George, do you not?'

'The *zanana,* remember? And I have my own wing of the house. *And not this woman,* he added under his breath. *I have never seen* this *woman.*

He had seen so many faces of Anusha. A haughty Indian princess in a temper; a brave, tired girl in youth's clothing fighting fear and hardship; a wrong-headed young woman with a completely unrealistic dream of freedom. Then there was the passionate half-innocent who had known all the theory and none of the realities of what happened between men and women until he had let his control slip and had shown her a little, just a glimpse of what he wanted to do with her.

But he had not met *this* woman, Miss Anusha Laurens, back where she belonged on her father's arm at an East India Company dinner party.

'Miss Laurens.' He bowed and wondered what she saw when she looked at him: the soldier in his dress uniform, controlled and disciplined—or the man from last night, half-naked, in thrall to her and to his desires?

'Major Herriard.' She curtsied, her face showing nothing but polite interest. But her eyes sparkled. Temper or desire?

'You are in great beauty tonight, An…ma'am.' He'd be stammering like a callow youth in a moment. Nick took in a breath down to his boots.

'So are you, Major.' The dark lashes swept up and down as she studied his scarlet dress uniform. 'As splendid as you were at court.' She fixed him with that candid-seeming stare that he knew could hide so much and added, 'I did not expect to see you here. Have you not returned to your regiment?'

'I am on leave, Miss Laurens.'

'I thought you must have left Calcutta when you did not join us at breakfast this morning.' She sent him a very direct look from beneath immaculately plucked brows. A reproof for avoiding her?

'I had business at the fort all day.'

Anusha glanced around, her expression perfectly pleasant, a smile on her lips as her eyes flickered from side to side. He knew her well enough now to read her. She was nervous and embarrassed in this crowd of strangers, she did not know how to act with the man who had given her her first sexual experience only the night before and it was only pride and her court training that was keeping her standing there.

He began to step back, to leave her to her father and to Lady Hoskins, but she caught at his sleeve. 'What am I supposed to do now, Nick?'

For a moment, stung by conscience, he thought she meant after his lovemaking, then she whispered, 'There are so many people I do not know. And *men*.'

He gently pried open her fingers from their grip on the gold lace. 'You take my arm.' He proffered his right arm, bent at the elbow, and murmured, 'Put your fingertips on my forearm.' She did so, then looked up at him, a spark of mischief in her eyes. For a moment the trusting Anusha was back with him. 'Now we take a turn around the room and I introduce you to people.'

'Men as well? They are all staring at me and there are so many.'

'Only ten, including me and your father. So eight strange men. And they are staring because they admire you and wish to challenge me for daring to be before them with you.'

'But you will not leave me?' Her fingers tightened on his arm.

She still trusts me, still needs me. 'No,' Nick promised, dizzy with relief. 'Not with the men, but I may have to give you up to the ladies.'

'I do not mind that,' she said. 'I am used to women.'

And she was used to the women of a princely court who would be like hunting cats amongst the pretty pigeons that were the young ladies in this room.

Anusha was quiet and serious when introduced to the gentlemen. She curtsied, managed a small smile and a few words, but her hand kept lifting instinctively as if to pull a veil over her face.

'You have no veil,' he murmured. 'Use your fan.' The trouble with that was the effect of big grey eyes, wide above the painted silk, on men whose imaginations were already overheated by rumour of her origins and whose gaze had been riveted on the graceful sway of her figure.

'I am proud of you,' he said when they found themselves alone for a moment at one end of the drawing room.

'Because I am curtsying just as you taught me? I do not think I can do the flirting, not yet. It is so *difficult* being with strange men like this.'

'You managed with me.' She looked up and met his eyes and the impulse to laugh died. Nick laid his hand over hers and thought of how her slender, soft body felt against his, of how her mouth tasted, of how she had ridden and danced and fought. *And shuddered into ecstasy in my embrace.* Of how it was his duty to protect her until she was safe here and found a man to marry. And then he could return to his next assignment and forget her.

'You are different,' Anusha said with certainty.

'Am I forgiven?' It should not matter—he had done the right thing for her protection.

'For lying to me about what my father intended?'

'And for last night,' he added.

'That does not require forgiveness. No,' she interrupted when he opened his mouth to disagree. 'It was me, too.'

'We must talk about it, but not here.'

'No, not here,' she agreed. 'And for the other thing, I have forgiven you,' she said, her face serious and a little troubled. 'I understand why you deceived me, I know your first loyalty is to my father. But I have not forgotten.'

'I see. Forgiven but not trusted.' That was just, but it hurt.

'I do not trust anyone,' she said flatly. 'Not you, not my father, not Lady Hoskins who is sorry her son is not older and who has twice mentioned her brother's *most promising* sons and her very wealthy cousin who has just lost his wife.'

'Come and meet the young ladies,' Nick said with a feeling of mild desperation. He just hoped George knew what he was doing. If he tried to force Anusha into the midst of the Calcutta Marriage Mart there was no knowing what she might be driven to. 'Ladies! May I introduce you to Miss Laurens? Miss Wilkinson, Miss Clara Wilkinson, Miss Browne, Miss Parkes.'

Anusha regarded them carefully, then inclined her head a very precise one inch. 'Good evening.'

'I'll...er...leave you to become acquainted.' Nick backed off, feeling as though he had three feet and all of them left ones. It might make him a coward, but he had no intention of being within earshot if they asked Anusha about eunuchs.

'Do you know the major very well?' the skinny blonde one asked. *Parkes, that is her name.* 'He is terribly handsome, is he not?'

'I do not know any men except my uncle, the raja, and my father,' Anusha said with a sweeping disregard for the truth. 'I find it most immodest the way one is expected to mix with men not of one's family in English society. And I find all Englishmen too big, too pale and not—' she gestured with both hands, seeking for the word '—not elegant.' *Except Nick. He moves like a tiger and his hair is moonlight on gold. My love, don't leave me here and walk away.*

'Oh.' Miss Parkes seemed somewhat crushed by this observation. 'But how will you find a good husband if you do not meet men?'

'My father will find one for me. Will your father not do the same?' These girls were the best way to find out how the English really did go about matchmaking.

'Well, yes. Papa will approve him. But how do I

meet men so I can decide who I want if I do not move in society—and how can the men decide which ladies to court if we do not meet?'

'But your father will refuse any man who is not rich enough, or well born enough or who has a poor character, even if you like him. So why do you meet them all first? What if you fall for a man and he is not suitable? Much better never to meet them and to rely upon your father's judgement.' *Hypocrite,* she thought to herself. Still, it was interesting to provoke these girls into telling their true feelings.

'Yes, but…' Clara Wilkinson was frowning, '…but it will make for a much better marriage if there is mutual liking first.'

'You mean it will stop the man having mistresses? I doubt it.' The girls all went pink. Interesting—obviously one did not mention mistresses. 'At least your husbands will only have one wife apiece.' What if she married Nick and he took mistresses? It would break her heart. But he would do, of course he would. She could hardly expect him to be faithful to her. Why should he be? Not that he would marry her. The death of his wife had hurt him too much. She did not believe him when he said it had not been a love match.

'Um… That is a very elegant gown, but do you not have any jewellery?' Miss Browne asked with the desperate air of someone turning the subject.

'Oh, yes, a great deal, but it is all Indian cut and the settings are not suitable for this European gown.'

'But do you not have Lady Laurens's jewels?'

'I would not wear hers,' Anusha said flatly. 'My

mother's, of course, are Indian, too.' That produced a flurry of coughs, strategic fan-waving and pink cheeks. Apparently her irregular birth was another unmentionable.

Ears attuned to the pad of bare feet on thick carpets heard the masculine tread behind her. It was not Nick. 'Ladies, I have been studying the seating plan and have come to inform you of your good fortune in your dinner partners tonight.'

Anusha turned and found herself almost toe to toe with a young man, close enough to assess the diamond stick-pin in his neckcloth and smell the oil he used on his hair. He seemed to find her mouth fascinating, so she lifted her fan as a barrier between them. His eyes slid lower and she restrained the urge to kick the insolent youth on the ankle. But of course this was not insolence, this was permitted.

'Oh, Mr Peters, do tell.' Miss Wilkinson was positively simpering. 'Who is *your* lucky partner?'

'Why, you, ma'am, and *I* am the lucky one.' He bowed and managed to take a comprehensive look at Anusha's cleavage as he did so. She folded her fan, just missing his nose.

'I am *so* sorry. Did I hit you?'

'No, not at all, ma'am. Miss Laurens, is it not? Will none of you ladies introduce me?'

'Miss Laurens, The Honourable Henry Peters,' Miss Wilkinson said with a hint of a pout. Apparently she had her eye on the gentleman himself.

An Honourable. A slight curtsy? No, he was still ogling her. Anusha gave him a cool nod. 'Mr Peters.'

'And who is escorting Miss Laurens in to dinner?' Miss Clara Wilkinson enquired.

'Let me think.' He applied the tip of one forefinger to his chin and struck a pose of mock thoughtfulness. 'You are to partner the Reverend Harris, Miss Clara.' She wrinkled her nose. 'Miss Browne has the gallant Major Herriard and Miss Laurens, I am sorry to say, has that prosy bore Langley.'

'That is Lord Langley, the son and heir of the Earl of Dunstable,' Miss Browne explained. She was apparently more than happy with her partner. 'Over there—the medium-sized gentleman with the brown hair and the blue coat. Lucky you—he is considered quite a catch.'

Along with the paunch and a double chin and a braying laugh. But he is a lord, so I am to be dangled in front of him. She tried to recall Nick's lessons. An earl was a sort of raja.

'How are dinner partners decided?' she asked.

'By rank, of course,' Miss Parkes said. 'At least, that is the start of the setting. But family members will not be put together, or husband and wife, so it is a bit muddled up. If a couple are courting, then the hostess might take pity on them and put them together. And if there are any scandals or feuds or difficulties, then she has to keep those people apart—it is all quite complicated. Have you never eaten with gentlemen before?'

'No.' Nick did not count. She tried to remember his lessons—cutlery from the outside in—and Lady Hoskins's instructions. Talk to the gentleman on her right during the first remove, then change to the left for the next one. Do not converse across the table. Put her gloves in her lap beneath her napkin. Do not let them slide off. Only sip at the wine. Pretend not to be hungry and just nibble at the food. Follow the conversational leads of the gentlemen and laugh at their jokes even when they are not amusing... *Be a little idiot with perfect deportment, in other words.*

'Dinner is served, my lady!'

The plump young lord was making his way across the room towards her, but Nick reached her first. 'Courage,' he murmured in her ear. 'You have vanquished dacoits.'

'I wish I was eating by a campfire under the stars,' Anusha murmured back. However vulnerable she was when she was near Nick Herriard, at the moment she would have given a great deal to be alone with him leagues from this crowded, alien room.

'So do I. We need to talk.'

Lord Langley introduced himself, offered his arm and guided her into the room. Anusha shot a harried glance over the table setting in front of her.

The amount of silverware flanking her dinner plate was ridiculous! What on earth did the *angrezi* need all this for? Anusha sat down with rather a thump as Lord Langley surprised her by sliding the chair in right behind her knees. She slipped off her gloves and tried to trap them under her napkin.

Everyone else was settling into their places amidst a buzz of chatter and she glanced to her left as a tall, slim man took his place.

'Good evening. Clive Arbuthnott, at your service, ma'am.'

'Anusha Laurens.' *Was* she supposed to tell him her name? And why had he not told her his title? Now she did not know how to address him. Perhaps she was supposed to know that already. But he was on her left, so he could wait. She glanced across the table and realised that Nick was sitting opposite.

He gave her a slight nod and went back to chatting to Miss Browne, who appeared highly gratified by the attention, judging by the way she was making eyes at him. Lord Langley enquired if she did not find the weather intolerably hot for the season. For some reason this question appeared to necessitate him gazing at her mouth.

'Not at all, it seems cooler here than I imagined.' *Oh, no, that is wrong. I am supposed to agree with everything he says.* Anusha managed a vacant smile which seemed to please him.

She could hardly open her fan and shield her face behind that at the dinner table. But it seemed that the ladies found nothing amiss in the close attention the men were paying to their faces, or to the snowy slopes of bosom that were exposed by evening necklines.

The ladies were all so pale, so pink. She suspected that Lady Hoskins had chosen the deep amber of the gown she was wearing because it made her own skin seem lighter by contrast. Anusha managed a smile and told herself that she was being foolishly self-conscious. None of the gentlemen meant anything sinister by their close attention to the ladies, it was simply the custom and no one had snubbed her because of her birth or blood.

As the meal was served she managed well enough by keeping an eye on what the other ladies did and with subtle prompts from Nick who would tap his finger against the correct glass, or pause, a spoon half-lifted from the cloth, so she could observe what to use next. She sent him a fleeting smile of thanks and tried not to colour up when he smiled back.

Conversation was easy, she found. All one had to do was to listen to the gentlemen talking and occasionally agree, or make a vapid comment of one's own. They seemed quite content with that. Perhaps they did not want wives who were schooled in the classical poets, in music and in the arts, women who could converse on whatever subject they raised. It was very strange. She had thought that women of education would be valued, but it seemed only those oddly named *bluestockings* believed in female intelligence.

Nick, flanked by two admiring young ladies, appeared to be enjoying himself, Anusha thought critically. It was a fine example of flirtation in action. And none of the older matrons appeared to think anything was amiss, so the constraints on the men to behave themselves must be very great, which was a relief.

And then she thought about how Nick had shed those constraints last night, how she had so badly wanted him to lose all control, and she felt the blood colouring her cheeks. *But I love him and I do not want any of these other men—that makes all the difference.*

She ventured a question when the servants cleared the table for the second remove and she turned to her left to converse. 'I am sorry, but I do not know how to address you. Is it Mr Arbuthnott, or Lord—?'

'Sir Clive. I am a baronet.' He did not appear offended by her ignorance so she tried another question.

'And is a baronet like a knight?'

'It is an hereditary title. A knighthood is not inherited by the son.'

'So it is like a little baron?' Her father was a knight.

'It is a rank lower, yes.' Sir Clive did seem rather offended by her turn of phrase, so Anusha hastened to make amends.

'I am so ignorant about English titles, you see.' She did the eyelash-fluttering thing that these men appeared to find so attractive. It certainly worked with Sir Clive. He relaxed and settled down to explaining all about the aristocracy and, to her surprise, did it rather well. By the time she turned back to Lord Langley and dessert, she realised that she had been taking to a strange man without the slightest discomfort. Quite an attractive man, in fact.

She caught Nick's gaze as she turned—he did not look very pleased. In fact, the look he directed at Sir Clive was positively cool. *He is jealous!* The thought made her want to grin, but she caught her lower lip in her teeth just in time and managed to keep her gaze demure.

Was he remembering that night in her cabin when he had held her and had fought so hard against his own desires? Was he thinking of their kisses last night, of their naked flesh pressed intimately together, of the pleasure he had given her? He would not let that happen again, she knew. He was her father's man, and his loyalty lay there and her father wanted her for some wealthy man of influence.

Chapter Seventeen

The ladies rose at their hostess's signal, the men standing, too, and they all trooped out, maintaining an air of elegance and poise until the doors shut behind them and the entire group fell to chattering and laughing. One party, Anusha assumed, went off in search of the privy and to dab at noses made shiny by the heat of the dining room, others strolled arm in arm on the terrace, heads together and, so far as she could hear, gossiping about the men. The older matrons sat down on the rattan sofas and fanned themselves. Anusha waited to see what would happen next.

Nothing, apparently, but gossip and giggling for half an hour, by which time she was bored to distraction. Anusha strolled round the room and found a chair half-concealed behind some potted palms next to the older ladies. Their conversation had to be more interesting than that of the unmarried girls.

'...so surprised to see Major Herriard here tonight,' one of the older matrons was saying. 'When was the last time we saw him at a formal dinner?'

'Oh, months,' one of the others remarked. 'Are you still thinking of trying to attach him for dear Deborah?'

'Would that I could, Lady Ames! He appears to have forsworn matrimony. Perhaps it was a love match with that pallid little Miranda Knight, although one would hardly think him a man of sentiment.'

'Perhaps Sir George intends him for Miss Laurens.' The comment was almost a whisper. Anusha dropped her fan and scrabbled for it on the floor, ears straining.

'One might have thought so—but I understand him to have told Dorothea Hoskins that he wanted considerable wealth for her.'

'Aiming high, under the circumstances…' Anusha's fingers curled into claws. 'She would not do for any of the titled bachelors, of course—they will be going back to England in the fullness of time and a half-Indian love-child is not going to be accepted at Court!'

'But she is a handsome young woman and very well bred in her manner. And he will dower her royally, I have no doubt. Out here her husband will have all the benefits of Sir George's influence. He will want to invest in his grandchildren.'

'Ah well, that is that, then. What Sir George wants, he usually gets.'

Considerable wealth. The waking dream of that morning, that perhaps her father would allow her to marry Nick, died. Nick was a professional soldier, not a trader, not a wealthy Company official. And besides, whatever she might dream, Nick showed not the slightest desire to marry her. Bed her, certainly. But proximity, normal male desire and the fact that she had virtually hurled herself at him would account for that.

And I do not want to marry, she thought fiercely. *If he loved me…but he does not. It is weak to love a man who does not love you—remember what happened to* Mata. *Remember the pain.*

'Anusha? Why so sad?' The men had come into the room without her noticing and Nick was standing in front of her. 'Is it about last night? Anusha, we still need to—'

'No.' She shook her head and got to her feet, her smile back in place. It was easy to smile at him, even with an aching heart, as he stood there, tall and so handsome in his uniform. 'No, I was wrong. There is nothing to speak about—it was a mistake best forgotten.' She stepped forwards bringing them toe to toe and for a moment she thought he would not give way. Then Nick bowed and stepped aside and she walked out into the room.

The whole atmosphere had changed. Anusha dragged her attention back from Nick's silent presence just behind her and made herself pay attention. It was, observed as an outsider, fascinating. The married women's eyes followed their daughters, but flickered back and forth to glance at the bachelors. She tried to work out who was an eligible suitor and who was not by the carefully schooled expressions of the mothers.

And then there were the unmarried girls, pretending indifference, clinging together in little groups, feigning not to notice the men and then blushing prettily when addressed.

The men, Anusha decided, were not serious in their attentions. They were enjoying the flirtation, but were they seeking wives in their turn? The rather older ones might be, she supposed—they would be thinking about families and inheritance and titles.

Her father seated himself next to their hostess and said something to her that made her nod. They glanced at Anusha and then away, as if they had been speaking about her.

I had best do some of this flirting, she thought. *Lull Father into thinking I am being an obedient daughter. Doing my duty.*

Several couples had gone out on to the terrace. It surprised her, but none of the older women seemed concerned, so it must be acceptable behaviour. How well the men must behave to be trusted so!

'Miss Laurens?' It was Sir Clive. She smiled, saw Nick watching them and added more warmth. He must not guess how she felt about him, she realised. 'Would you care for a stroll around the room?'

Anusha took his arm as Nick had shown her and they walked up and down in front of the long, open windows.

'And how do you like Calcutta, Miss Laurens?'

'I cannot say, Sir Clive. I have only just arrived. I knew it as a child, of course.'

'The riding is very good here. The *maidan* around the fort is excellent. I ride there every day. Do you ride, Miss Laurens?'

'Certainly. I do not have my own horses here, of course.'

'And how do ladies ride in Indian dress?'

'Astride.'

'My goodness! That would cause a stir here, I must say. Let us step outside—the room is growing intolerably stuffy,' he suggested.

'Very well.' There were several couples on the torch-lit terrace and servants standing around and the air was, indeed, more pleasant out there.

A series of loud bangs and a rainbow flash of lights were greeted by cries of delight. 'Fireworks near the fort,' someone said and there was a general rush to the balustrade.

'What a pity one cannot see better from here,' Sir Clive said. 'It seems a fine display—a wedding celebration, perhaps.' There was another explosion of colour, greeted by clapping. 'I know—let us go to the upper terrace.'

Anusha loved fireworks and the steps he led her to were marked with torches, so Lady Hoskins obviously expected her guests to use that part of the garden. There would doubtless be servants up there too.

When they arrived at the upper level the burst of lights was so spectacular that she ran to admire them and it was not until they died down that she realised that they were alone in a shadowed space, looking out on to a terrace below.

'Miss Laurens…Anusha.' He was very close. Far too close.

'We should go down, there is no one else here.'

'That is good, surely?' Sir Clive put a hand either side of her so that she was trapped against the balustrade, his forearms bracketing her hips. 'We came up here to be alone, did we not?'

'I came up here to see the fireworks, I thought other people would be here too.' She was not frightened, for surely this was only flirting going rather too far, but she was becoming annoyed and a little flustered. Anusha did not enjoy the sensation. 'Please move your arms, Sir Clive.'

'Not until I get my kiss.' He moved in closer. Now she could feel his heat, smell the sandalwood he used on his hair. His breath smelled of brandy.

'I have no wish to kiss you, Sir Clive.' He was too close in now for her to raise a knee sharply, or twist free. She began to feel rather more than flustered.

'Now don't tell me you are a little tease, Anusha.' He bent his head and kissed the side of her neck. She twisted her head away and his mouth found her cheek.

'Stop it! I am not teasing you.'

His lips moved down to her neck, down to the swell of her breast. 'Oh, but you were,' he murmured. 'Those big grey eyes, those long, long lashes, that pouting mouth.' He lifted his head and his eyes were bright, narrowed. Predatory. 'I know what they taught you in that *zanana*—how to please a man and all manner of exotic tricks to do it, too, I'll wager. Now you can show me some of them.'

'We need to speak about Anusha, George.'

Nick took the older man by the arm and steered him into a deserted retiring room.

'Now? Here?' Sir George regarded him from beneath lowered brows and Nick wondered if he still had the uncanny power to detect wrongdoing that he had possessed when Nick had been a scrubby seventeen-year-old. His conscience was giving him hell and it probably showed.

'I am worried about her. You need to talk to her about her mother, George. She'll never settle to marriage with that in the forefront of her mind because she's expecting to be rejected again, let down.'

'I never intended—'

'I know. You did the only thing in an impossible situation. But she doesn't trust you and she sees marriage as a trap at worst, a burden at best.'

'So do you, unless something has changed.' The older man settled in an armchair, offered Nick a cheroot, then, when he shook his head, lit one for himself.

'We are not discussing my situation.' He wondered sometimes what a happy, loving marriage would be like, but that was just a daydream. He had seen his parents' marriage, seen George's troubles, experienced for himself the dull ache of a loveless union between two people without a thing in common. He should have done something—been kinder, more indulgent. Or perhaps firmer. He shook his head, exasperated at his own lack of understanding. No, marriage was not for him, not again.

'I know. And I know, too, that I put a lot of pressure on you to marry Miranda, and that was a mistake. I won't try to interfere with your love life again, believe me, Nicholas! But I want happiness for Anusha, security, respectability. I'll find the right man for her.'

'Then talk with her, convince her that you love her,

that you loved her mother and never stopped. Let her see that she can trust you. Otherwise I fear she might run away.'

'She would never do that, surely?' Nick realised he understood her far better than her father. George was underestimating her fierce determination. 'But I will talk to her about her mother. I… It shook me to find her so beautiful, so grown up—so cold. I don't know what I expected when I saw her again and I haven't handled it well.' He looked up, a vulnerability in his eyes that grabbed at Nick's heart. This was his strong father-figure? George couldn't be getting old! 'Thank heavens I've got you to help me look after her.'

If she screamed it would attract a lot of attention. Anusha thought longingly of the little knife that slipped into her riding boot. 'Oh…very well.' She lifted her face and Clive bent his smirking lips to hers. Anusha opened her mouth, let his touch it, then bit hard on his lower lip.

Sir Clive jumped back, swearing, one hand clamped to his mouth, the other lifted as if to hit her. 'You little bitch!' he mumbled.

'Don't you dare touch me again!' Anusha hissed at him. 'If I had a knife—'

'If Miss Laurens had a knife she would doubtless castrate you, Arbuthnott. So be grateful that I am merely going to break your jaw.' It was Nick, smiling, green eyes glinting in the torchlight.

'The little baggage led me on. And as for you, Herriard, I'd like to see you try to lay a finger on me.'

Anusha swallowed and gripped the stonework behind her as Nick's smile changed subtly into something lethal. 'I *was* going to break your jaw. For that I am going to throw you over the balustrade.' He moved fast, caught the still-spluttering baronet off-balance in a twisting grip against his hip, and tipped him over the edge. There was a crash, a chorus of feminine shrieks and the sound of swearing.

'Oh, I say!' Nick leaned over, his voice full of exaggerated concern. 'Are you all right, Arbuthnott? I told you not to stand up there to watch the fireworks.'

'Bloody hell! I've got thorns in my ar—'

'Not in front of the ladies,' a man said below. 'Come on, Arbuthnott, let's get you out of there.'

Nick turned. 'That has punctured his dignity.'

She found it was difficult to speak. 'Thank…thank you. I thought you were going to kill him.' Tears were threatening to choke her, she realised. Where had her courage gone?

'Did you want me to kill him?' Nick asked. 'Did you expect me to call him out?'

'To duel? That is what you mean?' She swallowed hard. 'No, of course not. It was just foolishness.' *What is wrong with me? And him? He still looks so angry?*

'He called you a baggage. What the blazes were you doing up here with him anyway?' So that was what was wrong with him—he was angry with her. As though it were her fault! What hypocrites men were. 'Well?' he snapped. 'What was it? Were you looking for another man to pleasure you, like a cat on heat?'

The injustice of it stung like a whiplash. Anusha tried to be angry, but all she felt was utterly miserable.

She had been frightened, confused, she had needed him and he had come. And now he thought she had encouraged that man?

'How am I expected to know there would be no one else up here? It is all shocking and strange…all these men, being expected to flirt with them…strolling about, arm in arm down there,' she stammered. 'Do I tell one of Lady Hoskins's guests to his face that I do not trust him?'

Nick spun on his heel and stalked away to the other side of the terrace, his shoulders rigid. She sank down on a low bench and felt the tears begin to slide down her face. It was too much. *I love you and I cannot have you and now you think I am just a…just a…*

He turned as abruptly as he had left her. 'I am sorry. I apologise. You are quite right and I am not angry with you. I am angry with myself.'

'It is—' She tried to say *all right*, but her voice vanished in a sob. It was not all right, it never would be. This was the reality: she loved him, she could not have him and she would have to marry some other man who would not understand her, a man she could never love.

'Hell!' He strode across the terrace and fell on his knees beside her. 'Anusha—he hurt you?' He took her hand, but she tried to shake him off.

'No,' she managed. 'You did. I am so unhappy. I can't be brave any more, Nick. I do not want to be here, I do not understand the rules, I do not want to marry some *suitable* man and now you…you hate me. And…'

'No.' His fingers tightened on her wrist. 'I don't hate

you, Anusha. It will be all right, you will become accustomed to this life and then you will meet a man you can like.'

Nick winced at the inadequacy of his own words. He was spouting platitudes and she knew it. *You hate me. God, that hurt. But not as much as she is hurting.* 'I was frightened for you and it made me angry—you must be used to that by now.'

She ignored his feeble attempt at a joke. Nick had never seen her like this, almost defeated.

'Anusha, please.' He hated this. Every instinct told him to protect her as he had tried to do ever since they left Kalatwah and all he had done was to reduce her to abject misery. How to stop her crying? He had never managed it with Miranda. 'Anusha. Oh, hell.' Nick pulled her roughly into his arms, crushing her against his jacket front, against gold braid and buttons. 'Come here and don't you dare cry.'

'I'm not.' Her voice was muffled and shaky.

'Liar.' Somehow she was locked tight against him now and his mouth was in her hair.

After a few minutes she sighed and wriggled. Nick opened his arms and she sat back, scrubbing her fingers across her eyes. 'Here.' He found a handkerchief and she blew her nose with a defiant lack of elegance that made something twist inside him. This was genuine misery, not a fit of the vapours or tears to be interesting.

'I am sorry.' She had her voice under control again, almost. 'Thank you for looking after me.'

'Better now?'

She shook her head. 'No. I do not think it will get any better. I will have to marry someone, I suppose, and try to be a proper English wife. He will not love me and he will have mistresses, I suppose.' She squared her shoulders, a little gesture that clutched even deeper at his heart. 'It is my fate, so I must not be a coward.'

'I want to help you. How can I help you, Anusha?' He would fight anything for her—tigers, rakehells, a pit full of cobras—but this blank, brave misery defeated him.

'Find me someone to marry who will not break my heart,' she said with a bitter twist of a smile.

Who? A suitable *husband would either break her until she was just another dutiful wife or goad her into rebellion and scandal. What man is going to understand her heritage, her pride, her fears as I do? As I do.* The words seemed to echo in his head. He would make a poor excuse of a husband for any of the conventional little misses dancing downstairs, but for this woman perhaps he might be better than the alternatives.

Nick sat back on his heels and tried to think with his head and not with his protective instincts. He was well born, which mattered to society, if not to her. He could afford a wife, even if he could not keep her in luxury. He would be faithful to her and that, at least, would be no hardship. And she clearly found him physically attractive enough to want his lovemaking—in that, at least, this should not be a repeat of his marriage to Miranda.

'There is one man I could think of,' he suggested, before his brain could catch up with whatever was doing the thinking for him at the moment. 'One who would do his best to look after you and understand you, give you freedom.'

She understood him immediately, he saw it in the widening of the grey eyes, still shimmering with tears. 'You?'

'You're not looking for love, I understand that,' he said. 'You needn't worry that I'd be expecting it either. And I will be away a lot, but you'll not miss me.'

'I won't?'

'And I will be faithful, so you have no need for concern about mistresses. All I ask is that you don't take any lovers,' he finished.

'I…wouldn't. Nick, you don't want to get married again, to anyone. You told me.'

'I wouldn't mind being married to you.' As he said it he realised it was true. She would be wonderful in bed, stimulating out of it. Probably reckless enough to get into any number of scrapes but, he felt deep down, honourable enough to keep her promises to him. 'I am not a rich man,' he added. 'But I can afford children if you want them. Only if you want them.'

There was an ache inside now. He could almost think it was anxiety that she might refuse. What was the matter with him? This was a practical solution to her problems that would not cost him much except some money. And George would be happy that at last she was settled, if not brilliantly. But if she said *no*, then he would try to think of something else, it was not as though his heart was involved.

'I would be such a trouble to you.'

She was wavering. The unexpected relief made him

speak roughly. 'You have been trouble since the moment I saw you, you and your damned mongoose.'

'It is Paravi's mongoose—'

'Do you never stop arguing?' He kissed her, dragging her tight against him. He wanted her, was all he could think as he plundered her mouth, felt her response, tasted the sweet, sensual tang that was uniquely Anusha. And this way he could have her and she could have what she needed.

When he let her go she did none of the things he expected. She did not smile, or slap his face or even weep. Anusha buried her face in her hands for a long moment, then lowered them and met his gaze with eyes that held the same resolution that he had seen in them when they left the palace.

'Yes,' she said, her voice steady. 'I will marry you, Nick.'

Chapter Eighteen

Is this wrong? The question spun round and round in her mind as Nick took her arm and led her to the steps. *But I love him and I will make him the best wife I can possibly be and he doesn't want anyone else. He will never guess I love him; he knows I desire him, he will think that is all it is.* She was still dizzy with the shock of the assault, her own misery, Nick's incredible proposal. *I am not thinking properly,* she realised as they entered the reception room again. 'There is my father.'

'Yes,' Nick agreed. 'I think we had better go home and confess.'

When they found him her father took one look at her, then glanced sharply at Nick, but said nothing except, 'Tired, are you, my dear? Then let us call the carriage.'

As the vehicle jolted over the rutted street Nick said abruptly, 'I have asked Anusha to be my wife and she has accepted me.'

'This is very sudden.' He did not sound displeased. 'I cannot pretend that I am not delighted, of course, but are you both certain?'

Anusha could not be sure, his face was lost in the gloom of the carriage, but Nick sounded perfectly happy when he said, 'I am very certain, sir.'

'So am I, Father.' She tried to sound pleased, but not so eager that Nick might guess at her feelings.

'There will be many disappointed young men,' her father said with a chuckle as they drew up at the front steps.

'Father—'

'Anusha, I must speak with Nicholas. You are tired, child. Go to your bed, we can talk in the morning.' He dropped a kiss on her cheek and she nodded and made herself smile.

They would want to talk about money, she supposed. It would be good for Nick, if her father dowered her well. Something else she could do for him. 'Goodnight.'

'Goodnight.' Nick took her hand, just he had on the boat, and bent over it. This time he did not kiss the air above it, but her knuckles through the thin kid gloves she wore. Her fingers tightened in his, but when he released her she looked at him, a long, steady look from those grey eyes that were so like her father's, then turned on her heel and walked away, her full skirts swishing around the corner.

'She seems a trifle shaken,' George observed as he opened the door of his study.

'I found someone bothering her, dealt with him and then we talked. She is frightened of marriage, George, marriage to one of those eligible men you've got your eye on. And I realised I could see why—they won't understand her, they'll try to force her into a mould and make her lose everything that makes her unique, makes her Anusha.

'She knows I didn't want to marry, that I made a mull of things with Miranda. I expect she's afraid I'll take a string of mistresses and neglect her, whatever I promise. But she doesn't feel she belongs here and yet she knows she can't put things back as they were.' He shrugged. It was painful laying out all these reasons in cold blood, the reasons he was the solution of a problem, not the man of her dreams. 'Anusha meant it when she said she wanted to be free. She doesn't know who she is and I think she wants to find out. I can at least protect her, understand her a little—she trusts me for that.'

'Well, she's not a fool, so she should know when she's fortunate,' her father said robustly. 'She will make you a good wife, Nicholas. She's no pale little waif like poor Miranda. She's intelligent, she's strong and she doesn't appear to be shy with you. And, though I say it myself, she's a beauty. Takes after her mother.'

'The question is, can I make her a good husband? If I couldn't make a marriage work with a meek little wife who *wanted* to be married in the first place, what hope have I got with one with spirit and wits who is making the best of a bad job?' Nick enquired. *And what does a happy marriage look like, anyway? Can I make her happy?*

'I'm not trying to wriggle out of this, I just want what's best for her. I am sorry if I have disappointed you, George. Sorry if I am not the son-in-law you wanted for her.'

'Disappointed me? Hell, no! Nicholas you'd never do that. She is just too much for us to handle, that's all. I only wanted…security for her, I suppose. Safety. Just do your best to make her happy, that's all I ask.'

'Happiness I cannot promise, but I will do my level best. You have my word on it. And I will protect her with my life, that I can swear to.'

Anusha walked into her father's study as soon as she heard him moving around in there. A sleepless night fighting with her conscience had left her in no state for an Anglo-Indian breakfast.

'Anusha.' He got to his feet and came round the desk to urge her into a chair. 'You look—'

'As though I have not slept. Yes, Father, I know. It was all very…sudden.'

He almost went back to the big chair behind the desk, then came back and sat down opposite her. 'It is the best thing for you. Have you changed your mind? Don't you *want* to marry Nicholas?'

'I do not want to be a trouble to him.'

He watched her from under dark bushy brows for a minute. 'You like him, do you not?'

She nodded. *Of course I like him! Can you not see that I love him?*

'Do you desire him?'

'Father!'

'Well, do you?' He had coloured up and he was frowning, but he persisted. 'You haven't got a mother to ask you about these things. Don't pretend to me you don't know what I am talking about, not with your up-bringing.'

Anusha pressed her lips together and stared up at the painting over the mantelpiece of the Garden Reach of the Hooghly River with the fort in the background. If she said anything it would all come tumbling out, how she desired him, loved him, wanted him and how selfish it was of her to tie him down in marriage. And Father would tell Nick and then he would be uncomfortable and pity her.

'I married too young,' her father remarked in a conversational tone. 'I married a very suitable bride, an intelligent, handsome woman I hardly knew.'

'I don't want to hear about—' *I do not want to hear you justifying yourself to me.*

'But I am going to tell you,' he said gently. 'And you will listen to the story of my stupidity and where it took me. I married Mary and she fell pregnant almost immediately. She lost the child after three months. We tried again. She lost another. And another. The doctors said she should not attempt to carry a child for at least a year to allow her body to recover. You understand what they were asking me?' She felt the blood hot in her cheeks, but nodded, her eyes still fixed on the painting.

'I was young and arrogant and I did not see why we should wait. It reflected on my virility that my wife was not with child, I thought, and besides, I was not cut out for self-denial. Within four months she was pregnant again and this time she brought it to term. It almost killed her because her body just could not cope.

The child died and the doctors told us she could never conceive again.'

Anusha heard the pain in his voice and the self-recrimination. *It serves him right,* she thought, trying to harden her heart. Then, *Oh, poor woman. Poor things—how old had they been?*

'I had an opportunity to come out to India with the Company, to make my fortune. I assumed Mary would come, too—I did not ask, just told her. And she refused. I had almost killed her, I had ensured she could never have a child and for the first time I saw what I had done to her, not just to myself.'

'Why did you not divorce her? Or she you?'

'In English law there were no grounds for divorce in our circumstances. A wife being barren and a husband being a selfish fool are not enough. So we separated. I made sure she wanted for nothing financially and she made her own life in England. But her sense of duty was strong. She wrote to me every month and I began to write back. Gradually it seemed we could be friends, even at that distance. Or perhaps because of it.'

'But you were living with my mother.'

'I will not pretend I lived like a monk, Anusha. But some years after I came to India I met your mother at your grandfather's court and we fell in love.'

'She deliberately sought you out, she told me.' Long hot afternoons, with her mother's voice, soft and reminiscent, telling the story of that long-ago love affair. 'It was very shocking.'

'Indeed. I was thirty-five, she was twenty. By some miracle the raja approved the relationship, because he could refuse her nothing and because he could see the Company would be a great power in the land. We were in love and we were so very happy when you were born.'

'And then you sent us away, you did not want us any more.' She tried to keep the hurt from her voice, but she knew that it showed.

'Mary thought I was ill and she had come to believe it was her duty to be with me. The letter telling me she was on her way reached me before there was anything I could do to stop her. She was my legal wife—I could reject her, risk her life again by sending her back for another three months of danger and misery at sea, or I could do what honour told me I must, and welcome her.

'I tried to discuss it with Sarasa, but she refused to even listen. I could see no way out of it except for you both to go back to Kalatwah where I knew you would be safe and treated with respect. I would not dishonour both women by keeping one as a mistress behind my wife's back.'

His voice caught and he stopped speaking. Anusha turned her head slowly, painfully, to look at him. There were tears running down his face although he made no sign that he realised.

Something turned over in her heart: his pain, as though it were hers, and the realisation that she had never tried to see anything but her own anger and betrayal. 'Then you still loved us, Papa?' Her face was wet, too, she found.

'With all my heart. Never doubt it, Anusha. With all my heart.' He reached out and she took his hand in hers.

'So it was not because, with Nick, you had a son and

did not want a daughter any longer?' It was shameful to reveal her fears and jealousy, but she had to know.

'No! He was the son for Mary that she could never have. For me, it took longer, for I was still mourning you and your mother, but I grew to love him like a son. Anusha— love isn't finite. I could love both of you, and I do.'

'Oh.' She held his hand and let herself feel at last. 'Oh, Papa!' And then she was in his arms and they were both weeping and nothing else mattered except that she was home again.

'Good afternoon, Miss Laurens.'

Anusha looked up from the two miniatures her father had given her. One of her mother, the other of his wife, the woman who had saved Nick's life all those years ago. She put them down carefully and watched him as he came and stood in front of her. 'Where have you been all day, Nick?'

'I thought you and your father needed time alone together. Are you all right now? Your eyes are red.' He was still in uniform, his face cleanly shaven, his hair tied back. He looked formal and remote.

'I have been crying,' she said with dignity. 'So has Papa. He is going to send a cow in calf to that village,' she added, thinking suddenly of the way that Nick had looked up from the fireside, directly at her, and something had clicked into place in her heart. *I fell in love with him then, I just did not know it.*

Nick smiled and then, to her shock, went down on one knee.

'What are you doing?'

'This is the correct manner for making a proposal. I feel a trifle idiotic, but if you will forgive that… I hardly did it properly last night. Miss Laurens, will you do me the honour of accepting my hand in marriage?' When she did not answer him, and continued to look at his clasped hands resting on his raised knee, he added, 'I wanted to make sure you had not changed your mind.'

Does he want me to? Is he hoping that I have? Anusha looked into the face so close to hers and knew that she should say *no* and knew that she simply did not have the strength.

'I will do my best to look after you, to give you as much freedom as I can, to make you happy,' Nick said as she was silent, not trusting herself to speak.

'But you wish you did not have to.'

'Make you happy? Of course I want to do that.'

Strange how she had never noticed that thin scar across his right knuckles, how the tendons stood out when his hands were tightly clasped. Perhaps he was as nervous as she was. She knew she was blushing and saw from his face that he could read her mind, a little.

'There are more ways to make someone happy than sex,' Nick said drily, 'but at least that will be a good start, if we are going to be so frank.'

She swallowed. 'What about your mistresses?'

'Plural? I have never had more than one at a time and I do not have one at the moment. Anusha, look at me.'

She managed to lift her head. He was very serious, although his eyes were smiling. Perhaps this was going to be all right after all.

'I told you last night. Anusha, for some time now

there has been no other woman but you and there never will be, I swear. I will be faithful to you, always.'

What Nick promises, he does. And he would promise that for me? To be faithful even though he does not love me? Oh, Nick. I do love you. Anusha managed to smile and was rewarded by the way he looked at her. 'I have not changed my mind. I will marry you.'

'Thank you. I am honoured.' He leaned forwards and kissed her lightly on the lips and she closed her eyes and let herself dream.

Chapter Nineteen

~~~~~~~~~~~~~

It took a month to be married, they told her. 'So short a time?' Anusha asked. 'But what of all the preparations and the feasting and the dancers?' Lady Hoskins laughed and Anusha blushed. This was a different world and she had forgotten.

The time seemed to flow past like water and as the day grew closer a panic closed around her heart like a fist. She had trapped him. She should have known when she had wept in his arms that he would always protect her, only this time it was not with his life, but his freedom, and he would grow to resent her, she was certain.

Ajit returned from Kalatwah with messages and news: everyone was safe, they missed her. The maharaja's spies had been eliminated, for the moment. He slipped back into Nick's service, a soft-footed, smiling shadow.

The horses arrived from Kalpi, tired, but unmarked by their journey. Nick took her to the *maidan* early each morning so she could ride Rajat astride in her Indian clothes, but she knew she would have to master the side-saddle soon.

Nick had been using part of the disused women's quarters as his bachelor's rooms when he was in Calcutta, although he had a house in the hills a day's ride away. Now her father had them turned into a self-contained home for the newly-weds with two bedchambers, dining room, drawing room, a study for Nick and a sitting room for Anusha and a wide veranda overlooking the gardens at the rear.

Except for these morning rides they seemed to see very little of each other. Nick was at the fort most of the day and when he was at the house he seemed remote and formal. It was expected that a bridegroom kept his distance, Lady Hoskins explained, and of course, she did not want to be a trouble to him, but she missed him.

'Do you mind?' Nick asked ten days after their betrothal as they sat on their veranda and watched the gardeners turning a small patch of tangled vegetation back into a garden. He had come back mid-morning and, unusually, seemed intent on spending time with her.

Anusha did not pretend not to understand him. 'Not having a separate house of our own in Calcutta? No, Papa would be lonely and so will I be when you are away.'

'You will miss me?' It was asked casually.

'Of course. And I will worry about you, now I know the kind of risks your missions lead you into.'

'Don't worry. I cannot imagine that any future commissions will necessitate escorting dangerous young ladies.' *He means it as a joke*, she told herself. 'How will you spend your time when I am away?'

'I shall help Papa and be his hostess. Lady Hoskins says that is the best way to learn to be a proper English lady. Then when you come home I will know how to…deport myself.'

'Comport.'

'I thought that was something for putting fruit in. And I will make the house nice and buy clothes and accustom myself to them.' Instinct told her to keep the conversation light. Like that she could almost pretend they were still on their journey. She flipped her skirts back and forth, exposing a bare foot.

'Anusha! Are you patterning your feet with henna?' Nick dropped to one knee and lifted her foot in his hand. 'Wicked woman.'

'No one can see under my stockings and shoes.' His thumb was stroking the top of her foot, following the complex twisting design. She glanced around, the gardeners had gone. It seemed a very long time since they had been alone together.

'So this is just for your husband?'

'No, of course not.' She tried to cover herself, but he bent his mouth to the bare skin and desire washed through her. 'Stop doing that!' But she twisted in the chair, tried to position her foot in the perfect place for his caresses. 'Nick!' He sucked her toes into his mouth and began to tease them with his tongue. 'Nicholas, that is very…very…'

Unable to speak, he waggled his eyebrows at her lasciviously and she collapsed into giggles. It felt so good to laugh, such a long time since she had. 'Idiot man, stop it at once or the servants will see.'

'How very European and repressed of you, my dear.' He released her foot and sat back in his chair. Anusha wriggled her wet toes and tried to look reproving.

'I am trying to learn to be good.'

'Well, don't learn it for the bedroom,' he said, his voice suddenly husky.

'No. I won't.' The silence that followed seemed to need a lot of filling. Anusha scrabbled for a safe topic. 'Lady Hoskins says that I am fortunate not to have to learn all the things that an aristocratic lady must know, like how to go on at court and how to wear the strange court dress, and being a political hostess and holding a salon in London and managing an enormous house in the country. She says that young ladies are brought up from childhood to know all that.'

'So I believe. I never saw much of it, with my father being estranged from my grandfather, but court life is a nightmare, by all accounts, and London society is a good match for the plotting in a *zanana*. Although I doubt rival heirs are ever garrotted by eunuchs.' He studied her face, suddenly serious. 'You can put that in the balance of positive things about this marriage— you will have nothing more to worry about than Calcutta society.'

'I do not need to find things to be glad about,' she said carefully. 'But I knew that I would never marry an aristocrat anyway. Lady Hoskins explained that, too.'

'Why not? There are a good sprinkling of lordlings

around—younger sons, heirs-in-waiting, men doing a more-than-usually-adventurous version of the Grand Tour.'

'Because I would not be received at Court, of course.' Surely he knew that better than she did? 'My parents were not married and my mother was Indian. You only have to look at me.' She extended one arm, the lace around her sleeve falling back to reveal the honey-coloured skin. 'And Papa is in trade. It is a good thing— I would not want to have to balance an ostrich on my head.' Whatever that was.

'Just some of its plumes,' Nick said absently. He was frowning. 'Is that woman telling you that you are not good enough?'

'For the English Court? Of course.' It did not worry her—after all, she would never go to England, she accepted that now. 'I thought they would snub me here because of *Mata*, but they do not, so that is all right.'

Nick still looked troubled. 'Are you sure? If anyone says anything about your birth or your looks—'

He would fight them for me. I do love him. It made her want to cry, a little, so Anusha reached over and rubbed at the crease between his brows and scolded instead, 'Stop frowning. You do not look handsome when you frown. No one is unkind to me.'

'Good.' He leaned forwards and smoothed her skirts back over her bare feet and she gave an involuntary murmur of disappointment.

'Stop tempting me, you wicked woman. I am resolved to resist ravishing you until our wedding day.'

'Oh.' She tried to sound disappointed, and one part

of her was, the part that ached and yearned and tingled when he touched her. But it was also…charming that he should respect her and should obey the conventions in order to do this properly for her. Unless it meant that he was not as eager for that part of their marriage as she was. But if he was not, then what did they have? Only his sense of duty?

'That does not mean that I do not intend kissing you until your toes curl. Kissing you all over,' Nick added, so softly that for a moment she thought she had mis-heard him. Anusha sat up sharply, but he was lying back in the wide rattan chair, eyes closed, apparently about to drift off to sleep.

Was he playing games with her? He must be. Or it was her own longings that she was hearing? Anusha got up and crept bare-footed into the house and the shut-tered gloom of the drawing room. There was no fur-niture here yet, only a pile of rugs, haphazard on the floor at her feet, their vivid colours spilling patterns like all the riches of the garden. The sight stopped her in her tracks, memory clogging her throat so she had to swallow hard against it.

'What is wrong?' Nick came in, silent behind her, and caught her by the shoulders to pull her back against his chest.

'Those carpets. There were rugs heaped like that in my rooms that day I was packing and you were the other side of the screens and we quarrelled. Or I tried to quarrel and you walked out on me. Very unfair.' Anusha took a deep breath and kept her voice light and amused. 'That was the last time I was in that room before everything changed.'

'Poor love,' he murmured, holding her close.

'What…what did you call me?' She could have bitten her tongue the moment she asked.

'Mmm? Oh. Poor love.' She could feel him listening to his own words properly for the first time. 'Just an expression,' he said lightly and so carefully that she winced. 'Do not worry, Anusha. I am not becoming starry-eyed and sentimental. I know you don't want that.'

'No, of course not. But I do want those kisses you promised me,' she said, fixing a smile on her lips so he would hear it in her voice as she turned and laid her cheek against his chest.

'Kisses? Ah, yes, I promised to kiss you all over. I'll just lock the doors.' She watched him as he padded across the room to secure the inner door, then slip the catch on the pair of doors on to the veranda. Nick was wearing loose *pajama* trousers and a hip-length *kurta* in subdued patterns of brown and green that made the colour of his eyes seem more intense. His feet, brown and strong, were bare like hers.

The sight of him, his sheer physicality and grace, affected her as it always did, with simple, trembling desire. He must have seen it in her face for he coloured, just a little. That was another thing that she loved about Nick, the fact that he seemed surprised that she found him so desirable, that she wanted to look at him. He was so handsome and so masculine and yet he never seemed aware of it.

'What?' He lifted an eyebrow.

'It is so unfair that European men can lounge about in Indian clothes and yet I am trussed up like a fowl in these things.' She waved a hand at her chintz skirts and tight bodice.

'There is no reason why you cannot relax in your Indian clothes in private,' Nick said. 'You will just have to scramble into your corsets if someone comes to call.' His fingers were working on the long row of buttons down her back, his mouth kissing each inch of skin as it was exposed.

'No one scrambles into a corset!' Anusha protested, trying to stand still as he slipped her bodice free and undid the ties of her skirts. They pooled around her feet, followed by her petticoats, leaving her in her corset, chemise and very little else.

Her breath came out with a *whoosh* as he freed the laces: partly the loosening of the constriction, partly tension that was building too fast. 'Poor darling,' he said, rubbing her ribs lightly with the palms of his hands. *Darling, not love.* 'I'll kiss it better.'

He held her between his hands while he caressed each red crease on her skin with his lips, trailing down each side of her rib cage in turn until he reached her navel, then twirling inside it with the point of his tongue. 'Nick!' She wriggled, but his hands were firm on her hips as he knelt and kissed across her belly to the right, then down to her groin, his lips brushing the tangled curls. '*Nick.*'

She knew about this, of course. But the reality, the intimacy, was shocking. He trailed back up, across, down the other side, and her hands twitched with the effort not to take his head, press him close to where she ached and pulsed.

Nick came forwards on his knees, pushing her before him until her legs hit the pile of rugs and she toppled backwards, sprawled open to him on the soft silken platform.

His hands pushed at her thighs until she parted them, stiff with nerves for a moment. Then, when his tongue flicked out and found her, she collapsed back and abandoned herself to whatever he chose to do to her.

He chose to drive her to the edge of madness with slow, slow licks and kisses, each probing deeper and deeper into her quivering intimate heat until she was sobbing, pleading, for release. Then, as her hands grasped at the pile of the carpets and her back arched up, he parted her gently with his fingers, bent and stroked just one tiny spot with his tongue, again and again and she shuddered and cried out, reaching for him.

Nick lay with Anusha in his arms, and watched while she drifted back into reality as his frustrated body began to calm down. She was beautiful in the throes of passion: uninhibited, trusting, utterly sensual. Eighteen more days seemed an eternity to wait to make her his. But he *would* wait because she trusted him and because he wanted to do this properly for her. In this, at least, his second marriage would not be like his first.

Anusha desired him. Now she must abandon her dreams, and, he hoped, most of her fears, and marry him with only that unpredictable thread of mutual passion to bind her to him.

He had been right not to protest that he loved her, try to romance her. Anusha would have seen right through lies and he knew she did not want emotional involvement. He had heard the alarm in her voice when he had casually called her *love* just now. She needed to be herself, not emotionally tied to a man she did not love, he understood that.

It was a relief, of course. He could not cope with the clinging, needy, love of a woman. He had hurt Miranda by not being what she wanted in that way and he did not want to hurt this woman. At least he would *try* never to be cruel. His mother's sobs echoed down the years to the man who was once a small boy standing outside her bedchamber in the dark night listening, helpless. *Why can't you love me, Francis? All I want is for you to love me...*

'Nick?' The real woman in his arms stirred and smiled up at him, her eyes a little unfocused. Then Anusha's gaze sharpened and she lifted her hand to touch his cheek. 'What is it? What is wrong?'

'Nothing. Just an old memory from long ago.'

There was a knock at the inner door. 'Nicholas *sahib*?' The door handle rattled. 'Laurens *sahib* asks if you can come to his study to speak to him.'

'Tell him ten minutes, Ajit,' Nick called back. He stooped and kissed Anusha on the mouth, taking his time, gently exploring, and she curled her arms around his neck and responded with an ardour that had him as hard as iron again in seconds. 'I must go. Let me help you dress first.'

He watched as she walked to her clothes, not at all shy of his eyes on her nakedness. Why could she bring the heat to his cheeks whenever she looked at him with those gorgeous eyes heavy with desire or calculating feminine assessment? She was the one who should be bashful.

Then, as he stood over her helping with that confounded corset, he saw the colour in her cheeks and the way her eyes shifted a little, shy under his scrutiny, and something inside him twisted, almost painfully. 'There,' he said briskly. 'That's the last button.'

'Will you be here for dinner?'

'No, it is mess night at the fort. I'll be rolling back in the early hours, drunk as a lord.'

'Do lords get more drunk than anyone else? Why is that?' She was on her knees finding hair pins.

'Just an expression.'

'Even so, I am glad you are not a lord!'

He was still chuckling when he tapped on George's door and let himself into the study. The amusement vanished at the look on the other man's face. 'What's wrong?'

'A ship from England has just docked. There is post for you.' He reached across the desk and dropped half-a-dozen letters in front of Nick. 'It brought the newssheets, too. I glanced through the Deaths column first—a morbid habit. Nick, your uncle has died.'

'Which uncle?' His mother had three brothers, he

seemed to recall, not that he could put a face to any of them.

'Grenville. Viscount Clere.'

It took a moment. His first thought was that his father would not care: there had never been any love lost between the two brothers. Then he realised. 'My father is heir to the marquisate. My God, losing Grenville and having to see my father in his shoes—it'll kill the old man.'

'By all accounts your grandfather is holding up remarkably well. The newssheets cover a month after the funeral and he was certainly alive and apparently in good health. What his state of mind is, one can only guess.' George nodded towards the letters. 'Those might be some guide, I would hazard.'

'These?' Nick lifted the topmost, its stained and dirty canvas cover bulging over the shape of a seal beneath. 'Why?'

'Are your wits wandering, Nicholas? You are now second in line to the marquisate of Eldonstone. Those will be from the lawyers and your grandfather. Possibly your father.'

To go back to England? To the grandfather who had washed his hands of him, the father who hated him, the stifling life of the English aristocracy, a mountain of responsibilities he did not want in a world that was alien to him now. He had made a new life for himself here, one he loved.

'No.' He found he was on his feet. Nick gave the stack of letters a push that scattered them across the

desk top. 'No. Be damned to that. I can't…I cannot deal
with this now. I have an engagement—mess dinner.'

He strode out, leaving the door swinging open. Behind him he heard George's chair scrape back. In the
hall, as he headed for his bedchamber, he saw Anusha,
her eyes wide and questioning as he strode past her
without a word. How the hell could Fate do this to him?

Chapter Twenty

'Papa?' Anusha slipped into the study through the open door. 'What is the matter with Nick?'

'Eavesdropping?' He smiled, but his eyes were sombre.

'I heard his voice in here, then I saw him in the hall. I have never seen him look like that, as though Kali were on his heels.' Danger only made Nick more focused, more alive, but whatever this was had deadened something in him. She felt more fear than she had since he had taken her from the palace. 'Tell me what is wrong.'

'Most people would say there is nothing wrong at all,' he father said with a grimace. 'He'll tell you himself when he is over the shock, but his father's elder brother has died, which mean that Nicholas, God willing, will be the Marquis of Eldonstone one day.'

'That is good for him, is it not?' Even as she asked it Anusha felt the ground beneath her feet shift as realisation struck. A marquis was an aristocrat, a high-up one. Nick should be marrying a lady born and bred and trained for being a marquis's wife. Her stomach swooped as she clutched the edge of the desk. *Not me.* Not the illegitimate, half-Indian daughter of a trader, however rich and powerful her father was here.

'It is—if what he wants is wealth and vast estates, about six houses, and all the political power and influence he chooses to exert from a place at the top of English society.'

'And if he does not want it?' Perhaps Nick could give it up. He did not love his father, he did not seem to be pining for England. Hope fluttered fragile wings.

'There is no remedy for that. He cannot renounce the title, only death can free him,' her father said drily. 'If he does not take up his inheritance then all that he will become responsible for will be neglected, dealt with at arm's length by agents. I do not think that Nicholas could do that. There will be hundreds of people involved.'

The floor seemed to shift again. 'Then he needs a wife who is born of the aristocracy, does he not? One who knows what to do to help him, one who will be accepted.'

'He is marrying you.' Her father said it with a gentleness that only made the pain worse. *Pity. He understands what this means, he understands that once Nick has given his word he keeps it. He will insist on marrying me.*

'*Ha*,' Anusha agreed. It was as though suddenly she could only think in Hindi. And with the change of tongue came the realisation of what she must do.

The women of her family had walked down singing to the pyres, rather than lose their honour to conquering armies. She had inherited that sense of honour, too. In the agony of a broken heart she would sacrifice everything that she now treasured and hoped for—the reconciliation with her father, her love for Nick—rather than stand in the way of his duty and his honour.

'Anusha?'

She struggled to find the English words. 'I am sorry, I keep…I am keeping you from your work, Papa. I will see you at dinner time.' Four hours before dinner to plan and prepare, perhaps an hour or so afterwards. Nick would be coming home late, as drunk as a lord. She bit her lip to stop the sob of desperate laughter that threatened to escape. How right he had been in his prediction. Hysteria would not help, now she must be cold as ice. When he sobered up and started to think straight she must be long gone or she would have no hope of escape.

'Nicholas *sahib*. Lean on me.' Ajit stood by the step down from the carriage.

'I'm not that drunk, Ajit.'

'Yes, you are, *sahib*.'

Nick clutched the doorframe, missed the step and was neatly fielded by Ajit's wiry strength. 'So I am. Drunk as a lord.' He'd said that to Anusha, hadn't he? It had seemed funny then. It probably still was, but he seemed to have forgotten how to laugh. Still, this felt good—nothing was real, everything floated, he was feeling no pain whatsoever, except whatever was digging its talons into his heart.

'You are going to bed now, *sahib*.' It wasn't a question. Ajit pushed and pulled him up the steps and into the hall past the startled watchman. 'Quietly, *sahib.* Laurens *sahib* and the *memsahib* will be asleep. They do not want to hear your singing.'

'Al'right.' The corridor was bending oddly and the floor was swaying like a rope bridge over an up-country ravine, but Nick struggled on until a final shove from Ajit landed him neatly on his bed, head to the end, buckled shoes on the pillow. 'Go'way. Tha' you.'

'Shoes, *sahib.'* Ajit pulled them off, then started on his neckcloth.

'Go'way,' Nick repeated. 'Go'bed.' The darkness swirled dangerously when he closed his eyes, but he fell into it gratefully.

'Nicholas *sahib*! Wake up!'

Earthquake? Nick dragged his eyes open and squinted at Ajit's face. No, the room was still, the man was shaking him. 'What's the matter? And what the hell is the time?' It was still dark and his head felt like a bag of hot, wet sand.

'Half past three by the clock, *sahib*. Someone has stolen Rajat.'

'When?' Nick pushed himself upright and struggled against dizziness and nausea. He'd been back an hour and the blood in his veins was fighting a losing battle against the brandy.

'The groom saw when he stabled the carriage horses. The stall is empty, the saddle and bridle gone.'

'But—' Something was wrong with that. Nick tried to work it out. 'Rajat would kill anyone who tried to take him, so would Pavan.'

'I know.' Ajit clutched his turban. 'I think and think—perhaps he was drugged?'

'Or taken by someone who he was used to.' What little blood was circulating seemed to drain to his feet. 'Oh, no, she wouldn't.'

'The *memsahib*? But why?'

'I don't know, can't think. Find out if she is safe in bed.'

Nick got his feet on the floor and somehow made it to the washstand. The water was lukewarm, but he plunged his head into it and towelled himself dry. He was still in dress uniform and he struggled out of the tight jacket, the high stock and the fitted breeches and started to drag on civilian riding clothes and his boots.

'The *memsahib* is asleep,' Ajit reported from the doorway.

'Are you sure?'

'I opened the door a little and looked in. I could see the shape in the bed under the covers.'

The brandy was acting like a blow to the head, but his instincts for trouble had not deserted him and the hairs on the back of his neck prickled. He walked doggedly to Anusha's bedchamber, went straight in and pulled back the mosquito netting. Without its shrouding effect the bolster down the middle was obvious. 'Get her woman here *now.*'

Half an hour later, amidst a flurry of servants, Nick stood forcing down scalding black coffee while George paced up and down, the skirts of his silk robe flaring out with each agitated turn. 'What the devil is she doing? Her woman says she has taken several changes of linen, and the clothes she wore when she arrived have gone—this isn't a moonlit ride on the *maidan*! I know Anusha is upset, but—'

'What is she upset about?' Nick poured more coffee.

'She knows about the inheritance.'

So that explained it. 'She's run away,' Nick said flatly through the splitting headache that was making his eyes cross. 'She thinks she isn't good enough for an *aristocrat*.'

'It would not be easy for her,' George said. 'Or for you, perhaps.'

'I know that. But anyone who tries to tell me she isn't acceptable and refuses to receive her is going to be exceedingly sorry—and that includes the whole damned court of St James. She's been brought up to be a princess, her bloodline goes back into the mists of time, she's got more courage than most of the men I know. Hell, George, what am I going to do if I can't find her?'

'You will find her.' The older man gripped him by the upper arms and gave him a shake. 'You will. Now think—where would she go?'

Through the pain in his head and the fear in his gut and the ache in his heart the answer came to him. 'She's gone back to Kalatwah, the only place where she thinks she'll be accepted.'

'But how? If she's taken the horse she can't be going to try to find a boat.'

'Have you been in your study? Come on.' Nick strode out, George on his heels. 'Look at those map rolls— they've been disturbed. And the ledgers in front of your safe have been moved—she can pick locks. Check the money, I'll find which maps she's got. I have a horrible feeling that Anusha is intending to ride all the way back. If she's planning that, then she'll most likely find a group of travellers heading that way. My guess is that she'll start by going to Barrackpore.'

There was a groan from the other side of the room. George turned from the open safe and dumped a pile of gems on the desk. 'She's taken money and she has left her jewels in return.'

'Don't worry. I will get her back.' Nick realised he was the one offering reassurance now. His headache was ebbing as he sobered, but it was replaced with a knot of fear for Anusha and something else, an emotion he could not quite define, but which gave him hope and at the same time terrified him. 'Ajit and I will try the gates around the city—if nothing else, she's riding Rajat and he's distinctive.'

He strode to the door, calling for Ajit as he went. He would move heaven and earth to find her. Anusha was his, whether she realised it or not.

Sunrise. Anusha shifted in the saddle and looked back over her shoulder for the twentieth time, or so it seemed. The road behind the cavalcade of Bengali traders to which she had attached herself was clear. But of course it would be and she was fearful for no reason. Nick would have come home drunk, as he had threatened, no one would notice anything amiss until Nadia came with her morning tea and then there would be confusion and questions and it would take an age before they worked out that she had not slipped out for a morning ride, but had fled.

'You are sorry to be leaving Calcutta, my young friend?' One of the merchants who had given permission for her to join the party brought his horse alongside. 'You leave your sweetheart behind perhaps, eh?'

'Yes,' she agreed, keeping her voice gruff. The tail of her turban was pulled across her nose and mouth, as if to protect her from the dust of the road and the tight long-tailed jacket flattened her breasts and covered the curves of buttocks and thighs. If she did not get too friendly with anyone she had a reasonable chance of staying undetected, she hoped.

'That is a fine horse,' the man continued, apparently settling down for a long chat. 'It would not be for sale, I suppose?'

'No, I am sorry, but it belongs to my master who sends me on this errand.' *Hoofbeats behind.* Anusha twisted round as a troop of cavalry swept past, leaving the traders cursing in their wake and her heart thudding so hard that for a moment she thought she would be sick.

The dust cloud swirled in the early light and then settled, along with her pulse. 'You must have left in haste to have no provisions for the journey,' the trader went on. 'If your master has not given you enough money for a pack mule, you can put your supplies in my wagon if you wish.' He waved aside her thanks. 'We help each other on the road, or where would we all be? At the mercy of dacoits, that is where! Barrackpore is a good place to get supplies and we will be there for the noon meal.'

He talked on, quite content, it seemed, to have no response from her beyond a nod, or a grunt of agreement. Anusha felt her head begin to droop and pulled herself upright. There would be time to sleep tonight and at least the weariness might keep her unconscious long enough to give some respite from this heartache.

Why did I have to fall in love with him? I should have known it was impossible. There was the nagging worry that her presence in the palace might be a problem for her uncle, although her father had said that Altaphur was thoroughly chastened for the moment and skulking behind his frontiers. Might he still try to kidnap her if he knew she was back? If necessary, she would marry some prince of her uncle's choosing, Anusha vowed. Then she could not be a pawn to threaten Kalatwah or cause her father and the Company a problem.

If she could not have Nick, it really did not matter who she was with. It was strange that a breaking heart was physically painful. She had never believed that before…

'Wake up, young friend!' A hand on her shoulder roused her. 'You are swaying in the saddle. And here come more riders in a hurry—what is there in the air today that everyone must rush and cover innocent travellers in dust?'

Disorientated, she reacted slowly and the riders were in amongst them before she could gather her wits.

'*Sahib*, there is Rajat!' *Ajit*.

She wrenched the reins, turned towards the fields and the tangle of jungle beyond, but Rajat was reluctant, neighing for his stable mate, as Pavan, his rider tall in the saddle, swept through the ox carts and horses towards her.

'Anusha!'

Hemmed in by a camel behind, she turned at bay. *How has he found me so fast? What can I do now?*

'Leave this young man alone! He travels with our protection,' the burly Bengali trader shouted and forced his horse, with courage she could appreciate despite her anguish, between Pavan and Anusha's mount.

'If you think this is a young man, my friend, you have need of spectacles,' Nick said without looking at the man. 'Anusha, why did you leave?'

'You are a woman and this is your sweetheart?' the Bengali demanded, looking from one to the other, amazement on his round, honest face.

'Yes,' she said. Nick was looking implacable—she did not trust him not to use force if her protector persisted and the poor man did not deserve that. 'Please do not agitate yourself. We had a…disagreement. I will go aside with him and discuss it.'

'Do you want us to wait?' The other traders had begun to gather around them, hands were resting on knife hilts.

'No. I thank you for your help.' It was hopeless: Nick would never allow her to leave. She would just have to convince him with words that they could not marry. 'Goodbye, my friends. Travel safely and with profit.' She turned Rajit's head and fell in between Nick and Ajit, who was mounted, she saw, on her father's favourite hunter.

'You should have let me go,' she said. Nick looked

dreadful: his chin was stubbled, his eyes were bloodshot and his brow was furrowed as though he had a crashing headache. *I thought I would never see you again.*

'I will ride ahead, *sahib,*' Ajit said and spurred towards the road.

'Go back to Calcutta,' Nick called. 'Tell Laurens *sahib* that she is safe.'

Ajit raised a hand in acknowledgment and cantered off.

'Why the devil did you do it?' Nick turned in the saddle and searched her face. 'Your father is beside himself with worry.'

'I am sorry. You came because of him, then?' *Not for me.*

'I came for both of us! You were going to marry me, I thought you were reconciled to that. I thought you were happy.'

'I was. But I cannot marry a lord.'

'I am not—'

'You will be. You will be a marquis and I am no wife for you. You know that; we talked about what a wife of a lord must be, and a marquis is a very important lord, almost a prince.'

'Anusha, I do not want to be a marquis.' He sounded so violently miserable that she wanted to take him in her arms and kiss him.

'Papa said you could not do anything about it. That you would be one and that he knew you would do your duty, and I know he is right, for you would not do anything dishonourable.'

'Anusha… Damn it, I can't talk to you on horseback like this. Look, let us sit down there.'

There was a small shrine set on the edge of the fields, its stone platform so like the one where they had spent that first night that Anusha caught her breath. Silent, she let him lead the way, then slid down from the saddle and sat on the edge of the platform, her knees drawn up, arms tight around them as if somehow she could contain the misery.

Nick stood in front of her, hands clasped behind his back. Perhaps he did not trust himself not to touch her. 'I know I cannot avoid it. If I outlive my father, then it is my destiny to inherit.'

She nodded. Destiny—fate—she believed in that. It was her fate to love this man. And to lose him.

'But I cannot do it without you, Anusha. No—' he held up a hand to stop her protest '—I know what I said. I know how hard it will be for you, that I have no right to ask it of you, but I will fight anyone who tries to insult you, override anyone who tries to bar you from any privilege due to a marchioness. *I cannot do it without you.*'

Chapter Twenty-One

'But I know nothing! Why do you need me?' *He needs me?* Anusha hardly dared breathe.

'Because I love you,' he said, his eyes intense on her face. 'Because I do not think I can live without you.' She gasped, dizzy with disbelief and hope, as Nick pressed on, like a man fighting against odds to express himself.

'No, let me explain. I did not realise, I had no idea what love for a woman felt like. Who have I ever loved in my life except for Mary and George, my surrogate parents? It was not until we were searching, questioning everyone along the northern gates and I was so... so *afraid*, that I realised what it was, why I felt as if half of my being had been torn away.' His voice, usually so strong, so certain, shook with the emotion that gripped him.

'I know you do not love me, Anusha. I realise that you agreed to marry me because it was the only way out of your problems.' He turned on his heel and took a step away from her, looking out over the field as though he could not bear to see her rejection on her face, as though he left her free to tell him that she did not want him.

When, speechless, she did not answer, he went on doggedly, baring his heart and soul to her to be torn apart. 'But we have friendship and desire, surely? That is a start. We do not have to go to England now. My father is alive and well, by all accounts, and he will not want me back any more than I want to go. It may be years before we must return. Time for you to become accustomed, perhaps to grow to love me a little.'

Anusha slid down from the wall and crossed the dusty earth until she was standing by his side. 'You *love* me?'

'Yes.' He was still looking into the distance. 'I am sorry, I do not want to make you feel you have to stay, to marry me, because of how I feel. I won't ask more of you than you feel able to give. It is just that I—'

'I love you, Nicholas.' Unable to bear his pain any longer, Anusha took his hand and he looked down at her, green eyes blazing. *It must be true*, she thought, almost dizzy with joy. *It is not a dream. I can feel him, here, skin to skin, pulse to pulse.* 'I love you too, so much that it felt as though I was cutting out my heart when I left you. I thought that to leave you was the only honourable thing to do, because you had never *wanted* to marry me in the first place. *Oh!*'

He pulled her to him so fast that she lost her footing, was lifted and kissed until she was dizzy and then hugged so close that she could hardly breathe. 'Nick!'

'My love?' He set her on her feet again, but did not let go of her. 'Was I squashing you?'

'Yes, but I do not mind. Nick, tell me truthfully—will marrying me make things more difficult for you when you inherit this title?'

'Honestly? I do not know,' he said, tracing his index finger down her nose, along the line of her lips, as though he had never really seen them before. 'Will there be bigots and snobs who are too stupid to see your quality and your intelligence? Perhaps, but I will not let them rule my life and by the time it comes to it, you will be able to out-marchioness any lady you might meet.'

'Is that what I will be, a marchioness?' It was an unwieldy word on her tongue, almost as bad as the reality of the role would be.

'Indeed. And everyone, except members of the royal family, dukes and duchesses and marquises and other marchionesses, must bow or curtsy to you. That does not eliminate many people, so you will become very top-lofty, my lady.'

'Top-lofty? That is better than totty-headed, I think.' Anusha pulled his head down for another kiss and pretended not to notice a group of camel herders staring, wide-eyed, at the sight of a *sahib* kissing a youth by the roadside. 'Mmm. I thought I would never be able to do that again, never feel your arms around me, never taste you on my tongue.'

Nick appeared bereft of speech, something so unusual that she felt herself begin to gabble out of sheer happy nerves. 'You must have an heir now, as soon as possible.'

That made him smile and he turned his arm around her shoulders and began to walk back to the horses. 'Are you proposing that we go home and begin dealing with the matter at once?'

'Perhaps.' She cut him a glancing look and saw his lips twitch. 'Yes?'

'No, wicked woman. We wait until we are married, which is only seventeen days now, so you will have to behave.'

'So will you. Nick, do you remember that first night together at the shrine? Is it not a good omen that we find that we love each other at another shrine?'

'A very good omen. I think we should leave an offering. I have an oil flask in my saddle bags. Have you your knife? There is a flowering bush over there.'

Together they poured the sweet oil over the Shiva *lingam* and placed a spray of flowers at its base. 'I found a branch with fruit and flowers,' Anusha said, leaning against Nick, her head on his shoulder, their fingers entwined. Were there tears in his eyes? There were in hers. 'For the future.'

'This is your house?' Seventeen days later Anusha stared, delighted, at the sprawling white bungalow with its low sweeping roofs and the wide, shaded verandas all around it.

'It is *our* country house, Mrs Herriard. I thought you might not mind travelling all day after the wedding if there was peace and quiet and privacy at the end of it.'

'It is beautiful.' Grooms ran out of the compound to take the horses as she slid down from the saddle of the chestnut mare that was Nick's wedding gift.

'I wanted to find some height, and a view, and this

was the best spot I could find within a day's ride of Calcutta. I come here when I can.' He pointed. 'See, there is the Hooghly over there, but the hills make it healthier and less humid, even in the summer.

'Come, let me show you your new home.' He bent and, before she could protest, swept her up in his arms and strode up the front steps. 'This is an English wedding custom: the bridegroom carries his bride over the threshold.'

'I like it.' Anusha buried her face against his neck, then wriggled to get free when she found herself being carried straight past a row of servants, all bowing a welcome over their joined hands. '*Namaste!*' she called as her new husband simply kept walking whilst offering the same greeting. 'Nick, put me down!'

'Of course.' He shouldered open a door and set her on her feet in a room that seemed to take up the entire width of the back of the house.

White muslin curtains blew in a breeze that was cooled by the dampened mats hung in front of each opening. A marble pool had been set into the floor in front of the wide double windows and, as well as a big European bed, there was a wooden-framed Indian one swinging from chains attached to the ceiling beams.

'A proper bed,' Anusha exclaimed.

'I was hoping it would be a most *improper* one,' Nick said. 'Shall we bathe?'

'In the pool? Oh, yes.' She remembered all the lessons of the *zanana*. 'I shall undress you, husband.'

Nick had sat down on the edge of the bed to pull off his boots. He raised one eyebrow, but stood and opened his arms. 'If you wish. And then I will return the favour.'

'Oh, no, I must disrobe for you.' He was in Indian dress and she began by untucking the end of his turban and coiling it neatly into her hands.

'There are rules?' He shrugged out of his coat as she finished with the buttons and she folded it across a chair. Like him she was wearing tight trousers and a long jacket and had ridden astride, but today their clothes were cut from luxurious silks and brocades to mark the wedding journey.

'Of course.' Anusha pulled Nick's shirt from the waistband of his trousers and over his head so his hair fell across his face and he had to shake it back.

Has he any idea how magnificent he looks? Anusha ran her hands over the flat planes of his chest, teased the tight knots of his nipples with the pressure of her palms, then drew her fingers down the hard muscles and over the flat stomach to the drawstrings of his trousers. Under her hands she felt his skin tighten and smiled.

'What is it?' She could smell the faint musk of aroused male, the tang of sweat from their journey, the spice of his skin.

'Do you remember, in the bathhouse?'

'I recall a rather incompetent attendant with cold hands and very little technique.' He sounded amused, but his breath caught when she pushed the trousers over his hips and let her hands run down his flanks. His erection sprang free and Anusha closed her eyes as she caressed it with both hands in one long stroke before pressing him back.

'My lord should lie down.' For a moment she thought he would simply seize her, but Nick took a deep breath and did as she bade him. Reclining on the swinging bed in arrogant unconcern for his aroused nudity, he took her breath away.

'I am sorry I was so clumsy in the bathhouse,' Anusha apologised. 'I had come out of curiosity and then I touched you and I was undone.'

'I think I was undone the moment I laid eyes on you,' Nick murmured.

'Truly?' She took off her turban and freed her hair, swinging her head so it fell free over her shoulders. 'I should not be wearing these clothes,' she added, suddenly aware that this was not how she should appear before her new husband.

'I could not agree more,' Nick said with a wicked chuckle that had her blushing and laughing as she shed her few garments. It was impossible to do so with the erotic expertise she knew she should display, but he did not appear displeased with what he saw. But then, Nick had seen her naked before, she thought, suddenly feeling more confident.

'My lord will bathe now?'

'My lord and his lady will bathe.' Nick got up, swept her into his arms—he appeared to enjoy doing that, Anusha thought with a smile—and walked down the steps into the pool. It was deep enough to cover him to the chest when he sat down, laughing at her struggles as the cool water washed over her hot skin.

His laughter died away as he looked into her eyes and she gazed back, drowning in the green depths and the love she saw there. Her love, her English gentleman, her *noble* man. It was her last coherent thought before he took her mouth and his hands began to move, sure and subtle, weaving magic out of water and oils as he caressed her and bathed her.

'I should be washing you,' Anusha protested when she had the strength and was floating, languorous and yet tingling with arousal.

'I am at your disposal.' Nick laid his arms along the marble surround and slid down until his head rested on the edge and his hair drifted around him, gold silk on the surface of the water.

Anusha oiled and stroked, her hands caressing over skin roughened with hair, puckered by old scars, smooth as polished stone. She massaged his long legs, then, greatly daring, took a deep breath and went under the water to take him in her mouth.

Nick shuddered, arched and she used her tongue and her lips while her breath lasted and finally surfaced, seeing stars and little else through a curtain of wet hair.

'Oh, my love.' Nick moved fast. She was wrapped in towels and somehow he had flung some on the swinging bed, for she landed on thick cotton, as Nick fell full length beside her, setting the whole thing swaying.

'There are many subtle things we can do on this bed,' he said as he pushed the wet hair carefully from her face. Anusha nodded, hoping she could interpret the illustrated texts well enough to satisfy him whilst her legs were trembling and her heart was beating like a *tabla*.

'But I do not think,' Nick said between kisses as he bent his head to her breast, 'that I am going to attempt any of them today. I intend to be a straightforward Englishman and simply worship you.'

And he did so, with his mouth and his hands and his words, until she was mindless with pleasure and desperate with spiralling tension. Soothed and provoked, kissed and teased, she moaned his name and arched under him, begging for him in Hindi and English and soft, incoherent murmurs.

Anusha had no inhibition or fear left in her by the time Nick settled himself over her. She cradled him in her thighs, curled her legs around him and opened her body and her heart to him as he thrust, slow and strong, and made her his.

'Nick,' she said and opened her eyes on to his as he looked down at her, every strong line in his face refined by tension, his eyes full of love and desire.

'I am here,' he said, as if she could doubt it, and began to move, gentle at first and then with a rhythm that swept her with him, up and up until everything exploded and they were one and indistinguishable and she did not know where her body ended and his began, nor her mind either.

'Anusha,' Nick murmured and rolled over with her still tight in his arms. The bed swung wildly and she clutched at him and laughed, her wicked laugh that never failed to make him smile.

'I am here.'

'Are you happy?' It was a brave question to ask of a new bride who had just lain with her husband for the first time, he thought with a wry smile. What if she said *no*?

'I think perhaps it is not permitted to be this happy,' she said and came up on her elbows to smile at him. 'Are future marchionesses allowed to be so?'

'I have no idea,' he confessed. 'But we will make new rules and do as we will and I predict that we will laugh more than any other lord and lady in the whole of England.'

She curled down beside him and her hands began to explore. She was brave, a little tentative, and he realised she was putting her theoretical learning to the test.

'I also predict,' he said, trying not to gasp, 'that you will be the only aristocratic lady in England with an understanding of the Indian classical erotic texts. I am not sure what I have done to deserve it, but please, my love, do not stop!'

Anusha rested her arms on his chest and kissed along his collarbone. 'Oh, I do love you, Nicholas!'

'For ever.' He drew her up for his kiss and the two words that were a question and an answer and a vow all at the same time. 'For ever.'

* * * * *

Author's Note

In the early years of the East India Company's rule in India their officers and men were encouraged to marry local women or to take Indian mistresses, for that was seen as an important way to gain understanding and acceptance. Many officers had liaisons with ladies from the princely families and there was little prejudice—many British men became Hindu or Muslim, studied the languages and culture of the sub-continent and raised families in Anglo-Indian households.

It was only from around the 1820s, when English wives and missionaries began to settle, that attitudes changed for the worse and such liaisons were frowned upon. Company officials were expected to live lives as close to the English norm as possible and doors to advancement slammed in the faces of Anglo-Indian children.

I was first enchanted by the world of the eighteenth-century Anglo-Indians when I saw paintings of them in the National Portrait Gallery's exhibition *The Indian Portrait 1560-1860.* William Dalrymple's book *The*

White Mughals tells the story of one such liaison, in this case between the Resident at the court of Hyderabad and the high-born daughter of the Nizam's Prime Minister. But that love story ended in tragedy and I was determined that my lovers would find their happy ending.

An amazing two weeks touring Rajasthan, staying in royal palaces, gave me settings and more fantastic memories than I could ever use. The states of Kalatwah and Altaphur are, of course completely fictitious.

Begums, Thugs and White Mughals, the Journals of Fanny Parkes, gave me essential information for the trip down the Jumna and the Ganges from the pen of an intrepid Company wife. From a very different point of view, but full of fascinating detail of such things as sugar production and the difficulties of travel, Bishop Reginald Heber's *A Narrative of a Journey Through the Upper Provinces of India* gave me a great deal of information.

COMING NEXT MONTH from Harlequin® Historical
AVAILABLE JANUARY 22, 2013

THE TEXAS RANGER'S DAUGHTER
Jenna Kernan

Outlaws don't become Rangers...or even suitable husbands for proper young women like Ranger's daughter Laurie Bender. Big, bad Boon should know this—he once rode with the most notorious outlaw in Texas! To redeem himself, and to be in with a shot at a coveted Ranger's star, he must now rescue this feisty little lady from his former gang.
(Western)

NEVER TRUST A RAKE
Annie Burrows

Rumor has it that the Earl of Deben, the most notorious rake in London and in need of an heir, has set aside his penchant for married mistresses and turned his skilled hand to seducing innocents! But if he expects Henrietta Gibson to respond to the click of his fingers—he has another think coming. For she knows perfectly well why she should avoid gentlemen of his bad repute!
(Regency)

DICING WITH THE DANGEROUS LORD
Gentlemen of Disrepute
Margaret McPhee

Venetia Fox is London's most sought-after actress, darling of the demimonde and every nobleman's desire. But she's about to face her toughest role yet—seducing a confession from the devilishly handsome and very dangerous Lord Linwood to bring her father's murderer to justice!
(Regency)

HAUNTED BY THE EARL'S TOUCH
Ann Lethbridge

Arriving at Beresford Abbey, orphan Mary Wilder has her hopes of finding a place to belong dashed when she meets Bane Beresford, the enigmatic earl. He is as remote as the ghosts that supposedly haunt the abbey, but his touch awakens within her a fervent and forbidden longing....
(Regency)

You can find more information on upcoming Harlequin® titles, free excerpts and more at www.Harlequin.com.

HHCNM0113

REQUEST YOUR FREE BOOKS!

HARLEQUIN® HISTORICAL:
Where love is timeless

2 FREE NOVELS PLUS 2 FREE GIFTS!

YES! Please send me 2 FREE Harlequin® Historical novels and my 2 FREE gifts (gifts are worth about $10). After receiving them, if I don't wish to receive any more books, I can return the shipping statement marked "cancel." If I don't cancel, I will receive 6 brand-new novels every month and be billed just $5.19 per book in the U.S. or $5.74 per book in Canada. That's a savings of at least 17% off the cover price! It's quite a bargain! Shipping and handling is just 50¢ per book in the U.S. and 75¢ per book in Canada.* I understand that accepting the 2 free books and gifts places me under no obligation to buy anything. I can always return a shipment and cancel at any time. Even if I never buy another book, the two free books and gifts are mine to keep forever.

246/349 HDN FVQK

Name _____ (PLEASE PRINT) _____

Address _____ Apt. #

City _____ State/Prov. _____ Zip/Postal Code

Signature (if under 18, a parent or guardian must sign)

Mail to the **Harlequin® Reader Service:**
IN U.S.A.: P.O. Box 1867, Buffalo, NY 14240-1867
IN CANADA: P.O. Box 609, Fort Erie, Ontario L2A 5X3
Want to try two free books from another line?
Call 1-800-873-8635 or visit www.ReaderService.com.

* Terms and prices subject to change without notice. Prices do not include applicable taxes. Sales tax applicable in N.Y. Canadian residents will be charged applicable taxes. Offer not valid in Quebec. This offer is limited to one order per household. Not valid for current subscribers to Harlequin Historical books. All orders subject to credit approval. Credit or debit balances in a customer's account(s) may be offset by any other outstanding balance owed by or to the customer. Please allow 4 to 6 weeks for delivery. Offer available while quantities last.

Your Privacy—The Harlequin® Reader Service is committed to protecting your privacy. Our Privacy Policy is available online at www.ReaderService.com or upon request from the Harlequin Reader Service.

We make a portion of our mailing list available to reputable third parties that offer products we believe may interest you. If you prefer that we not exchange your name with third parties, or if you wish to clarify or modify your communication preferences, please visit us at www.ReaderService.com/consumerschoice or write to us at Harlequin Reader Service Preference Service, P.O. Box 9062, Buffalo, NY 14269. Include your complete name and address.

Rumor has it that the Earl of Deben, the most notorious rake in London, is in need of an heir and has set aside his penchant for married mistresses and turned his skilled hand to seducing innocents!

Read on for an exclusive sneak peek at
NEVER TRUST A RAKE
by Annie Burrows

"You are the most arrogant man I have ever met!"

"No. Just truthful. If I were to kiss you, I would take great care to ensure you would never be able to look at a man's lips in quite the same way again. When you next spoke to a man, any man, you would not be able to help wondering if his lips could wreak the magic that mine did. Your eyes would linger on them speculatively. And he would know that you were summing him up. Know that you were wondering what it would be like to kiss him. And then he would want, above all things, to show you."

Magic? He was declaring that his lips would work some kind of magic upon her? And yet, it appeared, the magic was already beginning to work. Because as he spoke, she found it impossible to tear her eyes from his mouth.

And he did have a reputation for being so very good at carnal things that any lady who'd been fortunate enough to attract his attention wanted it again. And suddenly it was not just his mouth she was thinking about, but his whole body, naked, in a rumpled bed where he was rendering some faceless female delirious with desire.

He smiled, a lazy, sensuous smile that did funny things to her insides. And made her heart race. Or had it been racing like this for some minutes already?

"Exactly so," he purred softly. "You are wondering what my lips will feel like. So naturally, I wish to oblige you."

HHEXP29724

"How can you tell what I'm thinking?" Her voice came out in a horrified squeak. Goodness, if he knew she'd just been picturing him naked, she would never be able to look him in the face again.

"It is the way you are looking at my mouth, Miss Gibson. With curiosity. And longing. And best of all, with invitation."

"I…I wasn't…"

"Oh, but you were. Last chance, Miss Gibson. Stop me now, or I will kiss you. And I promise you, if I do that, you will never be the same again."

Will one kiss change Henrietta Gibson's whole world?
Find out in Annie Burrows's
NEVER TRUST A RAKE.
Available January 22 from Harlequin® Historical.

HARLEQUIN® HISTORICAL:
Where love is timeless

SHE'S EVERY NOBLEMAN'S FANTASY… BUT ONE MAN IS ABOUT TO BEAT HER AT HER OWN SEDUCTIVE GAME.

Venetia Fox is London's most sought-after actress and she's about to face her toughest role yet—seducing a confession from the devilishly handsome and very dangerous Lord Linwood to bring her father's murderer to justice!

Linwood can see through Venetia's ardent attempts to persuade him to open up. His past is murky, but he's no criminal. And her interest in him has Linwood intrigued enough to play along….

DICING WITH THE DANGEROUS LORD
BY MARGARET MCPHEE

Gentlemen of Disrepute

Rebellious rule-breakers, ready to wed!

The game begins January 22
from Harlequin® Historical.

HARLEQUIN® *Romance*

*Discover an emotional new story of love
and family from*

PATRICIA THAYER

Single mom Gina Williams is usually wary
around men. But she gets the feeling that
beneath ex-soldier Grady Fletcher's rugged and
guarded exterior lies a kind, trustworthy man.

So when Gina's little boy goes missing, there is
only one person she'd turn to for help—a man
whose survival instinct is as strong as his heart.

HER ROCKY MOUNTAIN PROTECTOR

Available February 5, 2013, wherever books are sold.

Rediscover the Harlequin series section starting December 18!

NEW LOOK
·······
ON SALE DECEMBER 18

Lying in Bed

LONGER BOOK, NEW LOOK
·······
ON SALE DECEMBER 18

The Other Side of Us

LONGER BOOK, NEW LOOK
·······
ON SALE DECEMBER 18

NOCTURNE
HEATHER GRAHAM
KEEPER OF THE NIGHT

LONGER BOOK, NEW LOOK
·······
ON SALE DECEMBER 18

ROMANTIC suspense
COWBOY WITH A CAUSE
Carla Cassidy

KISS
THE ONE THAT GOT AWAY
KELLY HUNTER

NEW SERIES HARLEQUIN KISS™!
················
ON SALE JANUARY 22